Praise for
Something Blue and Other Colorful Deaths

"As a writer, L.L. Soares knows how to grip us and scare us, but he also knows how to move us. These stories never let go of their sense of compassion. Soares in damned good! I wish I'd started reading him a lot sooner, but I intend to read everything he writes from now on." —Ray Garton, author of *Live Girls* and *Sex and Violence in Hollywood*

"L. L. Soares writes about the monstrous: monstrous intrusions into our reality, transformations of the self and the world around us, and the kind of body horror that results when one's flesh is suddenly changed into the *other*, something loathsome and unwelcome. Soares terrifies by asking the reader: what happens when you discover that the world around you isn't what you thought it was, when you realize that it's not comfortable and familiar at all, but something alien and awful? And perhaps you are too." —Andrew Byers, *The Bookworm's Lair/Hellnotes*

"When I started *Something Blue and Other Colorful Deaths*, those first tales jabbed me like an emotional icepick to the heart. As I read further, the author lowered his aim. Those stories were like repeated stabs to the gut. These diverse tales could only be pulled off by a master horror author, and L.L. Soares leaves the reader with no doubt he is in that category. Heartbreaking, gut-wrenching, and terrifying." —Tony Tremblay, author of *The Moore House* and *Do Not Weep for Me*

"At times deeply strange, at times brutal, always compelling, *Something Blue* is a first rate collection of horrors rooted deeply in humanity, and all the more disturbing and terrifying for it." —Matthew M. Bartlett, author of *Gateways to Abomination* and *Where Night Cowers*

SOMETHING BLUE

and other colorful deaths

stories by

L.L. SOARES

TREPIDATIO
PUBLISHING

ISBN: 978-1-68510-080-3 (sc)
ISBN: 978-1-68510-081-0 (ebook)
Library of Congress Control Number: 2022951318

First printing edition: March 31, 2023
Published by Trepidatio Publishing in the United States of America.
Edited by Sean Leonard
Proofreading and Cover/Interior Layout by Scarlett R. Algee
Cover Art and Design by Mikio Murakami

Trepidatio Publishing, an imprint of JournalStone Publishing
3205 Sassafras Trail
Carbondale, Illinois 62901

Trepidatio books may be ordered through booksellers or by contacting:
JournalStone | www.journalstone.com

For Peter N. Dudar
Friend, brother, and one helluva writer

Contents

Introduction

I'VE KNOWN L.L. SOARES for a long time, long enough to consider him a valued friend even though we've never met in person. That sort of thing has become quite common these days thanks to the internet and instantaneous communication, but I'm old enough to remember a time when the only communication options were telephone calls and pen pals, which may be why I feel a bit uncomfortable claiming to value the friendship of someone I've never met. It somehow rings disingenuous to my aging ears, like something a TV talk show host would say. But it's true, and now it's common enough for everyone reading this to understand, I think.

His friends know him as Lauran. He's a fellow monster kid and possesses a clear and passionate love of the genre in literature, film, television, and anywhere else it might pop up. This love shows brilliantly in his work, love for the genre, and for his characters as well.

Yes, I consider Lauran a friend even though we've never met, but I'm also a fan of his work, and in the following paragraphs, I hope to introduce you to both.

* * *

There is something I think most horror writers are familiar with, something all have experienced at one time or another. Sooner or later, a horror writer hears these words, or something like them, from a reader upon meeting for the first time: "But you seem so normal. And you're so...so *nice*." The words are always spoken with anything from mild surprise to outright shock, as if they'd imagined the writer to be a slobbering, twitching, hunchbacked freak, or a scary, enraged serial-killer type with a serious Norman Bates vibe. So many people seem to think that horror writers really live in the pages of the dark fiction they write. But if that were the case, those writers would be in prisons, or on the run from angry villagers, or dwelling in great Gothic haunted houses, or living in caves or under bridges, or simply confined to an institution, and probably would get very little writing done.

The fact is that most horror writers are pretty normal people. In my experience, they tend to be friendly, quiet, more often than not on the shy side. Writers spend a lot of time alone, working; the job fits well with shyness, or social awkwardness. That's usually the strangest thing you'll find about horror writers when you meet them. But in general, they aren't much different than everybody else.

Lauran is an extremely nice guy, fun to talk to, not at all the kind of caricature some people expect when they meet their favorite horror writers, so I'm sure he's heard that vaguely plaintive claim—*But you seem so normal. And you're so...so nice.*—more than once.

I have noticed that he is unfailingly kind. In all the years I've known him, I've never known him to say a negative word about anyone. Every time he contacts me about writing something like a blurb or this introduction, he is virtually apologetic for doing so, as if he might be disturbing me, when the truth is that it's always a pleasure to hear from him. He is one of the kinder people in a genre made up of people who are predominantly good, but not always kind (like most humans). But I've never known Lauran to be anything but.

I had the pleasure of ushering in the new year of 2023 by reading the stories in *Something Blue and Other Colorful Deaths*—it was the last book I was reading at the end of 2022 and the first at the beginning of 2023.and it occurred to me that the kindness I have always noticed in Lauran is abundant in his fiction. Sure, it's horror fiction, and it's the kind capable of haunting your dreams and turning them into nightmares. These stories stir images in the mind that are hard to banish and can conjure feelings of fear and dread while capturing us with situations and emotions that are as vividly real as anything in our own experience. They work not only on our fears, but also our emotions. I was brought to tears once and made misty-eyed a couple of other times. As a writer, Lauran definitely knows how to grip us and scare us, but he also knows how to move us. These stories never let go of their sense of compassion—and what is kindness after all but compassion for our fellow human beings?

It comes through in the stories you're about to read. Quite clearly, I think. The people he chooses to write about—broken, lost people, characters who are deeply flawed, paralyzed by guilt, traumatized or traumatizing—are obviously people for whom he feels compassion, even if he may not approve of certain things they do.

Some of these stories are set in or around Blue Clay, Massachusetts, the fictional city in which Soares's novel *Buried in Blue Clay* took place (a novel I strongly recommend, by the way). It's Lauran's own version of King's Castle Rock or Charles Grant's Oxrun Station. There's a beach in Blue Clay that Soares returns to repeatedly in his fiction. That beach is a beautiful, haunting place, surreal and dreamlike, that has stayed with me since I first read about it and I was delighted to return to it in this collection. It's an otherworldly place, that beach, made up of a glimmering expanse of sheer blue clay. But there are things living beneath that beautiful blue surface, things that writhe and stretch and reach upward toward the creatures who, in their own way, writhe and stretch and reach on the other side of that blue surface. Those would be Soares's all-too-familiar characters—the broken, emotionally shattered characters for whom he has such compassion—who sometimes hear the call of the things that lurk inside that beach's soft and pliable cerulean clay. In addition to that haunted stretch of beach, you will encounter two aging sisters for whom Christmas never ends, a man being crushed by the monster of his own guilt and self-hatred, snake people, Glinda the Good Witch, crocodiles, ravenous blue insect creatures, and more.

I should stop there before I spoil anything for you. I don't want to interfere with your visit to Blue Clay in any way. It's a place that will linger in your memory after you leave, in no small part because of the kindness and compassion of the man who created it, a writer who never loses sight of the dark side while remaining true to the human heart.

—Ray Garton

SOMETHING BLUE

and other colorful deaths

Something Blue

IN THE TALL GRASS, something blue and translucent was huddled in a ball, barely moving. Half-submerged in the earth.

Waiting.

* * *

Jude found Shirley hiding under the porch. She had been crying again. It was a sunny day and the grass was very green. It wouldn't do to ask why she was crying. She never answered the question, and it was obvious enough without prying further. Jude crawled in beside her. It was dark under there, with stripes of light coming in between the boards.

Jude hummed to himself and looked up through the slits in the wood.

"How long are you going to hide?" he asked her.

"Longer," she said. "I just got here."

Jude nodded, not sure if she could see him, between her sobs, and knowing that it didn't matter. He knew she felt his nod, even if she couldn't see it.

Shirley used to tell him that she wanted to dance. Like the grown-ups on TV. Fred Astaire and Ginger Rogers, that kind of stuff. She used to talk about it all the time. But she hadn't mentioned it in a while.

"Shirley!" her father called out from above them. His voice was always so harsh, almost painful to hear. Jude didn't know how he stayed under there, with Shirley's father above his head, shouting like that. His first impulse was to run away.

It didn't take long before the man went back inside. He didn't even try to find her. Maybe he just liked to hear himself shout.

"Does it hurt?" Jude asked her, digging in the dirt with his hands. Not even realizing what he was doing.

"It's not so bad now," she said.

"My sister's coming today," he told her. "I haven't seen her in a few years, so it's a big deal."

"How's she getting here?" Shirley asked. "She driving?"

"She's coming by train," Jude said. "Around four this afternoon. My dad's going to go pick her up."

"It must be nice, having her come home again."

"I never did know her all that well," Jude said. "By the time I got old enough to care, she was gone. Traveling around the country. I hear she even spent some time overseas. Do you know she's more than ten years older than us?"

"Almost like another mother, rather than a sister."

"I know," Jude said. "I thought so too."

Shirley had stopped crying by then. She wiped her eyes one last time and grabbed Jude's hand. She squeezed it for a moment and then moved toward the opening that led out from under the porch.

"Do we have to go so soon?" Jude asked. "My eyes were getting used to it."

"Can't stay under there all day," Shirley told him. She grabbed his hand again and pulled him out into the sunlight. "It's too nice to hide under the porch."

"What do you want to do?" Jude asked. "I have a good three hours before Ellen comes home."

"Let's go for a walk," Shirley said.

* * *

Jude got back home just in time to see his father's car pull up into the driveway. There was a woman on the seat next to him. She had short, brown hair and a far-away look in her eyes.

"Give me a hand with her luggage," Jude's father said as he got out and went to the trunk. The brown-haired woman got out on her side and stared over at the house. Jude looked at her, but she didn't even seem to notice him. She was prettier than the photographs she had sent them, the ones in frames on the living room table.

"Come on," Jude's father said, standing over the open trunk and pulling things out. "I haven't got all day. I've got to go to work soon."

"Yeah, sure," Jude said.

"I wish to fuck you could drive and you could have gotten your sister," Jude's father said, handing him a bag. It wasn't as big as the suitcase, but it was pretty heavy.

Jude walked toward the house. His sister, Ellen, was still standing over by the car, looking around like she was a tourist in some new city she had never seen before. *Had it really been that long?*

Jude wished his father would introduce them or something, because he really did feel like they were strangers. And he was too shy to start a conversation himself. He looked at her briefly as he walked past, and thought about what Shirley had said about Ellen being old enough to be more like a mother than a sister. He hadn't really known his mother either, and he would probably have felt as strange around her, if she had suddenly appeared out of nowhere.

"Can you hurry it up, Jude," his father said, coming up behind him. "I told you I was in a rush, didn't I?" *It seemed like he was always in a rush.*

"Yeah, yeah," Jude said, and put the bag he was carrying down on the front porch. He dug in his pocket for his keys and opened the door. He could hear his father behind him, wheezing as he carried the suitcase. Jude wondered how heavy it was.

They went inside. Jude dropped the bag on the floor.

"In the spare room," Jude's father said, moving past him. "Come on now."

Jude lifted the bag again and followed his father into the room that had, until recently, been little more than a storage space for everything they didn't want. His father had had him move it all into the garage they didn't use.

Jude put the bag down again and noticed that his sister was nowhere in sight. He wondered if she was still on the front lawn, lost in her thoughts, when she appeared in the doorway, looking into the room.

"So this is it, huh?"

"It will have to do for now," their father said. "Last I looked, this wasn't a luxury hotel."

"You haven't changed at all," Ellen said to her father. "But, Jude, I would never have recognized you. You sure have grown up."

So she did notice me, he thought, looking right into her eyes for the first time. "Hi, Ellen."

"The last time I saw you, you were as high as my knee," Ellen said.

"That's because the women in our family have a tendency to leave on us," Jude's father said. "Don't get too used to her, Jude. She'll be leaving us again soon enough, I'll bet."

"Oh, Daddy, let's not ruin the visit before it's even begun."

"Yeah, sure. I've got to get my ass to work. I'll see you both tomorrow. At least it'll be Saturday. But don't you dare wake me up early. Keep it quiet around here."

Jude's father worked the late shift, and Jude knew to make as little noise as possible when his father was sleeping. He left the house as often as he could. Not that he always had somewhere to go.

"Don't worry, Daddy," Ellen said. "We'll be as quiet as mice."

"Make sure you are."

Their father went back out to the car, closing the door behind him. Jude heard him mutter under his breath, "Girl must live in a goddamn barn."

"I better let you get unpacked," Jude said, and moved toward the door.

Ellen just stood there. "Thanks for helping Dad bring my things in."

"Yeah."

She didn't seem to notice he wanted to leave. "It's just so strange to see you now. You're so tall. How old are you now, fourteen?"

"Thirteen," Jude said. "I won't be fourteen for about six months."

"You're so tall for your age. You must be the tallest kid in your class."

"Yeah, I guess so."

"You play basketball?"

"I tried for the team, but I was all thumbs. I'm not really into sports. I tried out more for Dad than anything else. But I guess I disappointed him."

"No way you can please that man," Ellen said. "Better not to even try."

"I guess you two don't get along too well," Jude said.

"I don't know. We get along okay, I think. He can be pretty gruff, but there's a big heart under all that gristle. He's written me some really sweet letters over the years, believe it or not. And he pretty much insisted I come here and stay for a bit when I told him about the tough times I was having."

"Tough times?"

"Didn't he tell you?" Ellen asked. "I was pregnant, but I lost the baby. I lost my boyfriend too. Kind of a double whammy."

"I remember Dad saying you were going to have a baby," Jude said. "I didn't know the other stuff."

"Daddy isn't the most informative man in the world sometimes," Ellen said. "Hell, *ever*."

"Well, I guess I should give you some privacy, to unpack and all," Jude said. He tried to leave, but Ellen was still blocking his way. This time she took the hint and stepped aside.

"We have a lot of time to catch up on things," Ellen said. "I want you to feel free to talk to me anytime. And you can tell me anything. I'm a real good listener."

Jude nodded and squeezed past her. She went into her room and started moving bags around and unzipping zippers.

* * *

"What's that?" Shirley asked.

They had been walking through the tall grass, hand in hand, when she had spotted something moving. Something blue.

"What?" Jude asked, looking at where she was facing, trying to see what she saw. Something displaced the grass up ahead of them.

Shirley moved cautiously in that direction.

He looked at her and thought about how they had been kissing not an hour before. They had been friends for a while, but he was liking the new direction their relationship was going. He wanted to go back to that now, and had no idea why they were here, chasing after a mouse, or probably a snake, in the tall grass.

"Let's go somewhere else," Jude said. "I don't want to be here, Shirl."

"I never saw anything like it before," she said. "I never saw any animal that kind of color before."

"Let's get out of here," he said, and watched her poking through the grass.

She parted the grass and something big leapt up at her. But it was trapped in the earth and could only reach so far. She jumped back, unable to get a clear view of the thing, seeing only a flash of blue in front of her.

"What is it?" Jude asked her, grabbing her from behind so she didn't fall.

Shirley looked down and saw this bright blue glow that enveloped her vision, bathing everything she saw. And then she was staring into water, bright turquoise water down around her feet, replacing the field they had been in. She could feel Jude holding her from behind and was grateful, because she was afraid she might drown.

"Water?" she said.

"What are you talking about?" Jude asked. He stared at the thing in the grass in front of them. It looked like an insect, but it was bigger than him. It had a thick, segmented body, with some thin, bony appendages that could have been limbs. It struggled to free the rest of its body, but could not. Its face stared up at him over Shirley's shoulder, and the face was the most terrible thing about it. Despite mandibles that snapped at them, there was something strangely human about the face. Maybe it was the eyes. Instead of being insect eyes, they were close to human. Staring up at Jude with a sadness like he had never seen before.

"Oh my God," he said softly. "Shirl, we need to get out of here."

"No," she said. "The water is too deep. We'll drown if we move."

"What are you talking about? There's no water here."

"Can't you see it, Jude? It's almost up to our knees now, and rising. The most amazing blue water I've ever seen."

The thing with the sad eyes snapped its mandibles at him again and struggled to free itself from its earthen trap. But its struggles were futile. Its body made clicking sounds with every movement.

"We're going to drown here," Shirley said again. She felt so tense in his grip, and she was talking like someone sick with a fever.

"It's a field of grass," he told her. "There's no way you can drown here."

"Wait," she said, moving in his grip. "I see a clearing. I see a way out of here."

"Good," Jude said, wanting to get far away from the thing with sad eyes as quickly as he could, but he was more concerned about her. About the strange tone of her voice.

"Look," he told her. "Just relax and let me guide you. I'll get you out of here."

But she pulled away from him and jumped forward, clearly thinking she was going in the right direction. He tried to pull her back, but she moved so fast, and then the thing in the earth leapt up again, and Shirley was close enough for it to wrap itself around her and wrestle her to the ground. She let out a scream as its body embraced her, as its mandibles buried themselves in her neck.

"Shirl!" he shouted, moving forward, but the thing lashed out at him with its limbs. They sounded like whips, the way they made the air hiss, and he backed away. He knew it was already too late. Her blood was spraying the grass; some even got on his sneakers. She had screamed just once, and then began sobbing loudly as the creature drained the life from her.

Jude looked for a weapon, a rock, anything that he could use to try to get the thing to let go of her, but there was only grass for as far as he could see. He tried to move forward again, but the whip-like limbs slashed at him, and the end of one of them connected before he could pull away, ripping through his shirt sleeve, opening a thin but painful cut in his hand. He had never faced anything so strong before, that moved so fast.

"Let her go!" he shouted, unable to look at the insect thing, and staring at Shirley where she lay. She had stopped moving now, stopped making any sound at all, and he knew it was too late to save her.

So he turned around and ran.

* * *

Jude had stopped crying by the time he got to Shirley's house. He stopped outside the front door and wiped his eyes. Then he took a deep breath and rang the doorbell.

On the third ring, Shirley's father came to the door. He had been drinking and his eyes looked glazed over, but his anger was still there. It was always there. Jude's father was angry a lot too, but he never took it any further than shouting. Shirley's father didn't have such limits, which is why she hid under porches.

"What the fuck do you want?" her father asked him, clearly annoyed at having been disturbed. "And where's Shirley?"

"Mr. Lowell, we were out in the woods, and she fell. You better come with me, sir. She really hurt her leg bad."

"Goddamn girl," he said, coming outside and pulling out his keys to lock the door. "It's bad enough she's clumsy around here all the time, now she's got to be falling down in the woods too. How far out is it?"

"Not far. I can show you the way."

"Do I need my car?"

"No, not really. It's really not very far."

"Well, let's get this over with then."

It took Jude a little while to find the exact spot where Shirley had been. The grass was high, and he wouldn't have found her at all if he didn't spot a flash of blue movement. It was squirming under the grass. In his mind, he could picture it devouring what was left of Shirley.

"Where the fuck is she, anyway? Is this some stupid joke?"

"No, she's right here, Mr. Lowell."

He came over and looked down at the grass. "Where?"

"Over there," Jude said and pointed.

"I don't see her," he said, getting closer. But there was something moving then, and as Shirley's father got closer still, he saw it. It was shaking and squirming next to the mangled body of his daughter. But he didn't see the creature for what it was; he didn't even see Shirley lying there. What he saw instead was a beautiful blue woman, naked and holding an injured leg, trying to get up.

"You're not Shirley," he said, pushing the grass aside. "And you're so blue."

The woman smiled at him, relieved to finally have someone to help her. She did not speak as she looked down at her leg and then back at him. He understood what she wanted.

He knelt down beside her and looked at the leg. It was twisted in some strange direction that didn't make sense.

"It looks bad," he said. For some reason the fact she was blue did not bother him. He saw nothing unusual about it. In fact, it made her even more beautiful.

She tossed back her long, blue hair and smiled at him again. At the same time, a single tear ran down her left cheek. Her eyes were so sad.

Then her face changed slightly. Kurt Lowell stared into the eyes of his estranged wife, Anne. It had been so long since he saw her. He should have been angry, but instead he grabbed her arm and moved his face closer, eager to kiss those lips after all these years. She was wearing some spicy perfume that he found intoxicating. It made it hard to think clearly.

The blue thing wrapped its long, hard limbs around Shirley's father, and pulled him tight in a violent embrace. At first, he saw only his wife, painted blue, hugging him close, her mouth hungrily seeking out his, and he didn't resist, even though her grip seemed way too strong. He didn't panic until he felt his ribs start to crack, then the woman's face sprouted ant-like mandibles, which closed over his temples, crushing his skull like a walnut.

He made some noises, none of them too loud, and Jude stayed a safe distance away. Close enough to watch, but nowhere near where the thing could reach him.

When Shirley's father had first seen the blue woman, Jude had seen it too, for only an instant, and then he saw it for what it was. Shirley's father hadn't been so lucky.

He watched the creature feed on him, and then ran out of the field, back to his house. This time he wasn't crying.

If Shirley had to die, at least he had found a way to pay back her daddy for all the beatings he had given her.

* * *

"You've been so quiet," Ellen said, coming into his room. "Ever since you got back home, you've been sitting in here, not saying a word."

She flicked on the light.

"And why are you sitting in the dark, anyway?"

"I'm sorry," Jude said, looking at this strange woman from his past. "I guess I'm just kind of depressed, that's all."

"Girl troubles?"

He thought for a minute. He could see the thing in the grass ripping up Shirley's throat with its mandibles.

"It's been a bad day, that's all."

"I've had a thousand bad days," Ellen said, sitting down on the bed next to him. "I told you you could confide in me, didn't I? I'm your big sister, and I want to help you. I'll listen to whatever you want to talk about."

"It's nothing you can help with," Jude said.

"What happened to your hand?" she asked, seeing the bandage he had wrapped around it.

"Nothing. I just fell down in the woods and cut it, that's all. It's nothing serious."

"Are you sure?" Ellen asked. "You don't want me to look at it?"

"No," he said. It still stung and he didn't want anybody touching it.

"Okay, okay," Ellen said. "So what's her name?"

"Who?"

"Your girlfriend, silly."

"Shirley. Shirley Lowell. She lives just down the street in that yellow house with the green shutters."

"That house? I remember seeing it on the way here. Ugly damn thing."

"Her father's too lazy to paint it something else."

"Is her father the problem?"

"Kind of," Jude said. He really didn't want to be having this conversation. He was feeling depressed, and thinking of lies was making things harder.

"It's funny, I almost thought you were too young to have a girlfriend. But I guess I had boyfriends at your age too. I just think it's funny it seems so long ago to me now. Is she pretty?"

"Yeah," Jude said. "She's pretty."

"So what's the problem with her father?"

"I don't know. He's just mean, that's all. Shirley doesn't have a mother either, you know, like us."

"We have a mother, Jude. She just took off on us. She probably didn't want a family."

"Shirl's mom, she left because of her dad. Because he used to beat her. That's what Shirl says, anyway. But Shirl's always been sad that her mother didn't take her with her. That she left her behind with *him*."

"That's funny," Ellen said. "Her mother left because her dad was mean. And our dad is mean because his wife left him."

"We have a lot in common, you see. That's how we became friends in the first place."

"Friends *first*," Ellen said. "That's nice. So what are you trying to tell me, that her father beats her too?"

Jude didn't want to talk about this anymore. He didn't want to keep thinking about Shirley, dying out in the grass, over and over in his head.

"Naw, I don't think he does. He's just mean, I guess. He doesn't seem to like me much."

"And he doesn't want you hanging around with his daughter, is that it?"

She was sitting very close to him on the bed. Too close. It made him uncomfortable, but he couldn't bring himself to move away from her. Instead, he just tried to ignore it.

"Yeah, something like that."

"I guess that's a tough break," Ellen said. "Now that I notice it, you look like you've been crying."

"No, nothing like that."

"You can always sneak around, make plans to see her where her father won't know. There are ways around it, you know."

"I know."

"Don't take it so hard," Ellen said, touching his leg. "You're so young. It can't be as bad as all that."

"Yeah, you're right."

"This seems bad now, but when you get to be my age you'll see how silly it all is. If you're meant to be together, you'll find a way."

"Ellen," he said, wanting so badly not to talk about Shirley anymore. "Did you know our mom really well, before she left?"

"I was about the age you are now when it happened," Ellen said. "So, yeah, I remember her clearly."

"What was she like?"

"She was pretty, but she used to drink a lot. I remember smelling liquor on her breath. She used to do embarrassing things. When I was really small, I remember thinking she was the best mom in the world. I loved her a whole lot. But at the end, she was always shouting all the time and carrying on. I guess I'm glad she left."

"Really?"

She thought about that. "No, I'm not glad. I thought I was, but it didn't last long and I started missing her really bad. I'll tell you; I'm so shocked she never came back to us. That we never saw her again. I was always so sure she'd come back one day. When I first left, I was convinced I'd go and find her somehow, and bring her back, but I didn't really look all that hard. I didn't really *want* to find her."

"I don't remember her all that well," Jude said. "I mean, I miss her and all, and wish she'd come back. But I can't picture her in my mind.

The *real* her. Not clearly. I guess that's what photographs are for. But Dad hid the ones of her. Hid them all away."

"She was really pretty, Jude. Like some kind of angel."

"Do you think she's got another family somewhere? A family she likes more than us?"

"I don't even want to think about that, Jude. Really, let's not go there."

"Okay."

"What time does Daddy get back from the late shift, anyhow?"

"I'm usually asleep by then. Around one or two in the morning, I think."

"And he sleeps most of the day."

"Yeah, I don't see him much during the week."

"How has he treated you over the years, Jude?"

"He's been okay. He can get kind of cranky sometimes, but he tries to be fair."

"So you don't hate him at all?"

"No, he's okay. Sometimes he's hard to be around, but I think I understand him well enough."

"He's a good man, Jude. He's tried really hard to be a good father to you."

"I know. I could tell he was really happy you were coming home. I'd never seen him in such a good mood, all week long."

"You wouldn't know it from the way he acted when he picked me up. Hardly said a word to me the whole way up, and then he complained at you when we got here."

"That's just his way."

"I know," Ellen said.

"Ellen, can I ask you something personal?"

"Sure, Jude. You know you can."

"What happened to your baby?"

"I just had a miscarriage. It happens. Supposedly it's nature's way of getting rid of a baby that might have something wrong with it. At least that's what they told me. I don't know how much I believe that. It hurt awfully bad, being so sure I was going to have a baby, and then losing it like that."

"I'm sorry, Ellen."

"Thanks."

"Where's the father?"

"He's long gone. Like Mom. I think he only stuck around because of the baby. Once that fell through, I don't think he felt he had any ties to keep him there. It all happened very sudden like. He left like a thief in the night, as they used to say."

"I'm really sorry."

"Well, it's all old news now. I was feeling pretty low, and Daddy told me to come home and try to forget it all for a while. I frankly couldn't think of something better. So, for once, I decided to take him up on his offer."

"Why haven't I seen you in so long? I mean, sure, we'd talk on the phone once a year or something, but I never knew what to say to you. I really didn't feel like I knew you all that well. Why didn't you ever come for a visit, at least?"

"I don't know, Jude. It was real hard coming back here, even now. There's a lot of pain for me here. It's not as bad as it was, but it's there. I think Momma leaving us hurt me more than I realized.

"I got caught up in a lot of things while I was away. A lot of different guys. Different places. I know that's not really an excuse, but it's the best I can give you right now. I don't really know the answer myself."

Jude nodded. "That's good enough, I guess."

"It's getting late. I bet Daddy doesn't like you being up when he gets home."

"He doesn't care, as long as it's not a school night. But I am pretty tired. Maybe I will get some sleep."

"Me too," Ellen said. "It was a long trip out here, and it's finally catching up with me."

She got up off the bed. He found it easier to breathe. "Have a good night's rest," she told him.

"You too," Jude said. "And Ellen?"

"Yeah?"

"Thanks for listening to me. About Shirley, I mean."

"Anytime, kiddo. Thanks for listening to me too."

She left the room, closing his door behind her.

Jude stretched out on his bed, still in his clothes, and closed his eyes. He had wanted to tell Ellen what happened, but something kept him from verbalizing it. And now he wanted to sleep so badly, to block his mind of what he had seen today. But he was also afraid that blue thing would haunt his dreams. And maybe he would see Shirley, dying all over again. He didn't want to risk reliving it in his mind, but he didn't have much choice in the matter.

Even though he was sure he wouldn't fall asleep, he nodded off anyway.

* * *

Jude had a vivid dream just before he woke up. It was about Ellen and she was naked, and when he woke up, he felt really strange, almost like he had wet the bed.

The house was quiet. His father was asleep, his bedroom door closed. As he walked past the door, Jude could hear his father snoring. He made sure to be very quiet as he showered and got dressed. The cut on his hand still hurt, a reminder of what had happened the day before, that it had been real. He put a fresh bandage on it.

He noticed the door to Ellen's room was wide open. He was compelled to go over and look inside. Her bed was all made, and she was not in the house at all, as far as he could tell.

He went outside and resisted the urge to go over to Shirley's house. There was no reason for him to go back there. There wasn't anybody home anymore.

Jude got his bike out and rode around the neighborhood for a while. He passed the field with the tall grass a few times. It was a huge vacant lot that had been neglected for as far back as he could remember. He wondered who even owned it. Whoever it was, probably had forgotten it even existed.

One time when he rode past, he saw someone walking through the grass, coming out of the lot. It was Ellen, and seeing her near there made his heart beat faster. He was afraid for her. After losing Shirley, he didn't want to lose someone else he cared about.

She saw him standing at the edge of the lot, on his bike, and called out to him.

He didn't move.

"What are you doing here, Jude?"

"Just riding around."

"I figured you'd be with your friends."

"I don't have that many friends," he told her. "There aren't a lot of kids around here."

"Except for Shirley."

"Yeah, but she went away somewhere today. She's not home."

"You know, I'm your friend," Ellen said. "I mean, I'm your sister and all. But I'm your friend too, right?"

"Yeah, sure."

"Are you hungry?"

"I guess so."

"I was going to go home and get a bite to eat," she told him. "Want to come along?"

He really didn't have anything better to do, now that Shirley was gone. And he was sick of riding his bike. "Sure."

He rode slowly alongside her as she walked.

"Where did you go all morning?" Jude asked. "When I woke up, you'd already left."

"I just went exploring. It's been a long time since I've been here. Besides, I needed the exercise. So I walked into town and back. Things haven't changed as much as I thought they would have."

"You know, you shouldn't walk through that tall grass," he told her.

"Why not? It's a good shortcut."

"There's a lot of snakes and stuff in there," he told her. "You know, the venomous kind. I've seen them."

"Really?"

"Yeah, it's not safe. I just wanted to warn you."

"Okay," Ellen said. "Thanks."

He noticed her hands were dirty. There was a trace of blood.

"What happened to your hands?" he asked her.

"I slipped on some mud and fell," she told him. "I guess it *is* dangerous in there."

* * *

They ate ham and cheese sandwiches. Their father was still asleep. Jude knew from experience to never bother him, or make too much noise, when his bedroom door was closed. Ellen didn't need any telling. She moved around the house as quietly as she could.

"What time does he usually get up, anyway?" she asked, softly.

"It varies," Jude said. "When he first gets home he doesn't go right to bed. He has a few beers and watches TV. So he tends to sleep pretty late into the day."

"Do you see him very much in the course of a normal day?"

"Not really."

"When was the last time you had a babysitter?"

"Not for a while," Jude said. "He trusts me on my own."

"You *are* really mature for your age, Jude, that much is true."

"Thanks."

"Why don't you go outside for a while. Get out of this stuffy house."

"Okay."

He went to his room first, killing time looking through books and comics. When he came out, he noticed the door to the garage was open. Nobody ever went out there. He went and looked. Ellen was looking through the old workbench for something. He was going to ask if he could help, but he felt like he was spying on her. So he left.

* * *

Jude went back to Shirley's house. As he stood on the front porch, he found it hard to believe she was dead. That the house was empty. He had to convince himself.

He went around the back and found the window to Shirley's room. He tried to lift it. It wasn't locked. So he opened it and slipped inside.

He explored the house a bit. He'd been in there before, but never alone, unsupervised. Now he could look wherever he pleased. He saved Shirley's room for last, looking through her closets, through her drawers. Touching personal girl items he had no right disrupting.

When he was convinced Shirley and her father were gone, that they were never coming back, he slipped out the window again, and closed it after him. Then he ran out to where his bike waited in the driveway, and rode away as fast as he could.

* * *

As the afternoon progressed, Jude rode around and around the neighborhood. As far as he dared to go and back. He passed the vacant lot again and noticed someone out in the high grass. He stopped his bike and got off, staring out in that direction.

Curiosity compelled him to go see who it was. Inside, he hoped it was Shirley, that somehow she was okay and needed someone to show her the way home. Even though he had seen her bloody body, crushed like a doll before him.

He moved slowly, softly, through the grass, not wanting to attract attention to himself.

When he got close enough, he saw that a woman was on her hands and knees, digging in the earth with some kind of tool. He watched her dig for a while, staying hidden, trying not to breathe too loudly.

She stopped and stood up. Jude saw that it was Ellen. She had grass and dirt stains on her jeans. She wiped her forehead.

"Ellen," he said.

She turned around, looking panicked for a moment.

"What are you doing out here?" he asked her, moving forward, into the clearing. "I told you it was dangerous out here, didn't I?"

"No, it's okay," she told him. "I haven't seen any snakes."

"There's worse things than snakes," he said, trying to see what she had been doing, but the tall grass obscured her handiwork.

"I'm fine. Just trying to keep busy. You know how long the days can be around here."

She got back down on her knees again. He wanted so badly to grab her arm and pull her out of this place.

Something moved next to her. Something blue. It pushed the grass aside and wrapped itself around her so quickly, he didn't have time to react.

"Ellen!"

"I'm okay," she said, standing up. The thing embraced her. He could see it moving in its strange, segmented way, enveloping her body in its own, and in those thin, brittle-looking legs.

And then, suddenly, things changed. Ellen stood before him, radiant and beautiful, with gigantic blue wings that blocked out the sun and the sky, such a deep blue that they seemed to be *made* of the sky. Such a sharp, soul-piercing blue that he could feel tears welling up in his eyes just looking at the color.

"There's nothing to worry about," Ellen said, standing there, fluttering her enormous wings before him. Holding out her arms. "Come here."

He knew what he had seen. But the wings made it hard to remember. He wanted so badly to *touch* them. He felt so small and alone and he wanted to be comforted by those arms that reached out to him.

The arms were blue now too. As radiant as the wings.

He looked into Ellen's face and saw his mother's face too. He had not seen her since he was a tiny child, but he was sure it was her, and suddenly she was so real to him, so clear. It wasn't hard to remember her at all now. It was like she had never left.

"Come on," Ellen and his mother said in a strange double-voice. "We won't bite you."

Jude couldn't resist anymore. He knew it was dangerous, but he just didn't care. He ran toward them, the two women who had left him when he was young, come back to him. They were a family again.

He felt the arms hug him close, and then the wings lowered above him, covering them like some enormous blue cloak.

The mandibles grabbed him hard around the head, and beneath them a mouth said, in the double-voice of Ellen and his mother, "You got us food, but we don't need you anymore. We've got someone new."

And then the long, hard insect legs wrapped tightly around him, holding him in place, and the mandibles squeezed him into oblivion.

* * *

Ellen waited until the blue thing was finished eating, then she removed her clothes as it instructed her. It was no longer trapped in the earth, thanks to her help. She had done the thing that the boy hadn't. She had set it free.

When it was done, it wrapped itself around her again, holding her as close as it could, luxuriating in her warmth, filling her bodily orifices with parts of itself. Holding her tight, but not tight enough to harm her.

She went out of the tall grass then. And anyone who saw her saw a radiant, beautiful young woman, wearing the most dazzling blue dress they had ever seen.

Ellen walked in the direction of her father's house.

He should be up by now.

Little Black Dress

"YOU'RE NOT GOING TO wear *that*, are you?"

"Why not?" Julie asked, looking down at the box on the table. It was a faded white box with the words *Naughty Witch* printed on the top. A cellophane window gave a peek at the contents inside. Mostly fish netting. Part of a rather skimpy Halloween costume put out by some generic costume company.

"I don't know," Amy said, looking over her shoulder. "It looks like something a stripper would wear."

Ever since she'd been a teenager, Julie had seen this costume, or one of the many variations of it, in the seasonal Halloween aisle of pharmacies or in the occasional costume store. It was always in the "adult" costume section. Sometimes it would be in a cardboard box, like this one. Other times it would be in a plastic bag with a photograph showing some model dressed in the "naughty" costume.

In almost all cases, it consisted of fishnet stockings, a minidress, a cape, and a black, pointed hat.

Ever since she'd been a teenager, Julie had wanted to wear the costume. When she was sixteen, she finally got the nerve to buy it. She even tried it on in her room. But she never wore it in public. She put it in the back of her closet, but was so afraid that her mother would find it that she ended up discarding it in the dumpster in back of the convenience store near her home, wrapped in a paper bag.

"So what?" Julie said. It had taken a lot of nerve to buy it again. Especially since this time she was determined to finally go through with it. To wear it to the party. "It *is* Halloween, after all. What's the harm in it?"

"I guess it just doesn't seem like the kind of thing you'd wear," Amy said. "You know, you're pretty strait-laced."

And she was. Where some girls wouldn't have thought twice about wearing something so provocative, Julie agonized over it. But the costume signified so much to her. It symbolized the bad girl she'd always wanted to be, but never had the courage to attempt.

She had spent her whole life doing the right things, trying to please everyone.

But her life was passing her by. She was a studious twenty-year-old, striving for good grades. Still afraid of boys. Awkward in just about any relationship. More some girl who belonged in the 1950s than the year 2001.

What the hell was *wrong* with her?

Fear was part of it. She knew what her mother would say if she saw her in such an outfit. "You are asking to get raped, wearing something like that." It was her mother's voice that made her want to throw the box away again. But it was also that voice that made her want to put it on, in defiance. To go out into the world as someone else, someone braver and freer and, maybe, someone even a little dangerous.

"I'm going to try it on," Julie said, taking the box in the direction of her room.

Amy took a sip from her beer and watched her go.

Inside her room, Julie removed her clothes slowly. When she was naked, she stood by the bed, looking down at the box. It looked old. It had probably been in the back room of the drugstore for years. Each year it had been trotted out and put on the shelf. Each year it had been left behind, unbought. Collecting dust. Waiting for her to come in and buy it.

She slipped the stockings on first. She'd never worn fishnets before, and they felt more comfortable than she thought they would. She had imagined they would feel like bondage clothes. She took her time pulling them on, then putting on the garter belt to attach them to. She'd never worn one of those either. It seemed ancient to her, archaic. But also kind of liberating. Sexy.

The dress felt like some kind of vinyl when she took it out of the box. It was short and tight. At first, it seemed too tight and she was afraid she wouldn't be able to get it on, but she kept trying and, eventually, squirmed into it. The dress was short, it ended at her upper thighs, barely covering her crotch. Once she had it on though, it seemed to expand with her body. It felt almost comfortable.

The cape was black and sheer. She draped it around her shoulders, and could barely feel it at all.

She added some high-heeled black shoes that she seldom wore. They complimented the costume perfectly.

The hat was last. A flat circle of more black vinyl. She shook it and the pointed top popped up. She put it on her head and looked in the mirror.

It made her laugh, to see herself like that. A naughty witch, after all these years of secretly yearning.

She had even dyed her mousy brown hair black a few days before, in preparation. She thought it suited her much better.

Looking in the mirror, she realized that, despite her penchant for dressing rather conservatively, she had a cute figure. She'd spent her whole life hiding it. She'd always thought she was a little chubby, and was never really happy with herself. But now, something about the way she looked in the costume made her feel better about herself.

There was a knock at the door. "Julie, how's it going in there?"

She continued to look at herself in the mirror. To pose.

"Okay," she said.

"Come on out, so I can see it."

"Okay," Julie said again and went to the door.

She opened it and stepped out into the living room. Her roommate and best friend stood there, looking her over.

"Not bad," Amy said. "Not as cheesy as I thought it would be. In fact, it's pretty sexy."

"I know," Julie said.

* * *

While they were walking to the party—it was only three blocks away from the house they rented off-campus, after all—a man pulled up beside them in his car and asked if they needed a ride.

"No, thanks," Amy told him. "We're okay."

"Are you sure?" the guy asked. Julie could hear the desperation in his voice, and it scared her. She could hear her mother's warning again, and it made her feel self-conscious about what she was wearing. Maybe it did attract the wrong kind of attention. But it was Halloween. Wasn't she allowed to indulge even then? Wasn't the world safe enough to at least give her that little freedom?

She could feel the guy's eyes on her, but didn't look in his direction. She simply pretended he wasn't there.

Amy, however, looked sternly at the guy. "We're sure. Leave us alone, okay?"

"Yeah, yeah," the guy said, clearly annoyed at their disinterest, but not enough to take it any further. He stepped on the gas pedal and drove away.

Maybe there wasn't anything to be afraid of, Julie thought. Amy was with her, after all.

"There it is," Amy said as they turned the corner. She pointed across the street to a brightly lit house. It looked like the party was already in full swing. The front lawn was full of people, in and out of costume.

* * *

She had brought a broom with her. It wasn't much of a broom, an anorexic-looking thing they used around the house. They'd gotten it cheap at the supermarket. That was the operative word for most of the things they got for the house—cheap.

Amy was dressed as some kind of cross between a Goth and a biker chick. Black leather jacket. Exaggerated make-up. It wasn't all that much different from the kind of thing she would wear to any other party. She just wasn't much in a creative mood, Julie guessed.

"Well, look who's here," Andy Feldman said, seeing them enter the house. "Hi, girls. Help yourself to the refreshments."

Andy had let Julie know he was interested in her, but she had been too shy to pursue it. Well, at least so far. He wasn't really her type, but he was a nice enough guy. And it was flattering that he showed her so much attention.

He clearly was surprised by how she'd dressed this evening. It was out of character for her. But she could tell it was pleasant surprise. She could feel other eyes on her too. The attention made her self-conscious, but also pleased her.

"You look amazing," he told her softly, as he handed her a cold bottle of beer. "I've never seen anyone look as good in a costume like that. It's like it was made for you."

"Thanks," she said, blushing. She felt so embarrassed about blushing that the redness lasted even longer.

"Amazing what a different image will do for you, huh?" Amy whispered to her. Then, "I'm going to find Paul. See you soon." And she drifted out into the crowd.

Julie turned to Andy, who was smiling at her. "Drink up," he told her.

The bottle was already open. She brought it to her bright red lips and drank.

* * *

About an hour later, Julie found herself in one of the upstairs bedrooms. She was fucking Andy. It all came about so spontaneously; she hadn't really had much time to consider it before it happened.

She was on top. She hadn't even taken the costume off. The minidress, which had seemed tighter before, was much more flexible now, riding up her hips. She hadn't worn any underwear, but she had no idea anyone would find out. At least not so soon.

She was very conscious of how the costume felt. The stockings, the dress, the garters, all seemed to enhance the sensations. The only things she had taken off were the shoes. They were somewhere in the shadows that obscured the floor.

She hadn't had much to drink, and this wasn't the first time she'd had sex, of course. There had been some clumsy experiences with a couple guys since high school. But this was different. She was aroused this time more than ever before. No doubt her being in charge had something to do with it.

Andy seemed very happy to let her call the shots. It wasn't like the past. He wasn't another awkward boy, as scared as she was. And she definitely wasn't scared now. There was no reason to be. She wanted it as much as he did, and if she remembered correctly (it had all happened so fast), she had been the one to initiate it.

The orgasm took her quite by surprise. Another person had never given her one before, and it was stronger than past ones she'd experienced alone.

She had enjoyed it as much as she imagined men enjoyed sex. Being in charge, having her needs met. *Taking what she wanted.*

She found she was breathing as hard and labored as Andy was. She even cried out, something she'd never done before. Getting caught up in the moment.

When they were done, she stretched out on top of him.

"Shit, that was good," she said softly in his ear.

* * *

When they went back downstairs, she continued to be a source of attention. It was a strange feeling because she'd never experienced it before. Was she really different tonight? Or was it just the costume? Maybe she had been drinking more than she thought, or someone could have spiked her drink.

She was talking to an attractive grad student she had just met, wondering what it would be like to bring him upstairs, and marveling at this new sense of self-confidence that she had been able to tap into, when Amy grabbed her arm. It was so sudden, it frightened Julie until she saw who it was. Amy was crying, and saying something about Paul.

Reluctantly, Julie excused herself from the conversation she'd been having and pulled Amy over to one side of the room. "Tell me what's wrong."

Much of what Amy said made little sense to her, but she knew that she had had a fight with Paul. They always fought. And they always got back together. It was something they did. But Julie knew the situation wouldn't fix itself tonight.

"We're leaving," Julie told her, taking charge of the situation. Which was another oddity. Usually it was Amy who decided what they did. Julie usually preferred it that way.

* * *

The cool night air made Julie aware of the fishnet stockings. They certainly weren't much protection against the cold. She also noticed that she had left the broom back at the party. Funny how that occurred to her out of the blue. It didn't matter much, though. She could go back and get it some other time.

Amy was still crying. She'd had way too much to drink, but at least now she was walking it off. Well, sort of walking. Walking mixed with stumbling.

"It's okay," Julie said, trying to console her. "Everything's going to be okay."

Julie thought back on the night as they walked. She felt clear-headed, and she remembered everything that happened. And she didn't regret any of it. It was like she was a different person. A not altogether unpleasant person. In fact, Julie liked the new her very much.

Between her own thoughts, and guiding Amy, who was crying and who occasionally stumbled, Julie did not hear the car drive up slowly beside them, keeping pace with them. She noticed it by accident, in her peripheral vision. She knew immediately it was the same car as before. The creepy guy who had bothered them. Now that Amy was drunk and crying, maybe he thought they were easier pickings.

"Need some help?" the driver asked.

Julie realized she had not looked at him before. When Amy had been yelling at him to go away, she'd concentrated first on the car, then on Amy as she shouted. But she had never looked directly at the man behind the wheel.

She looked at him now.

No longer timid or fearful, she stared right into his face. He was a middle-aged man. The kind you'd instantly associate with having a wife and children. With a few more years added, he might even be old enough to be her father. But an otherwise unremarkable face. Except for the eyes. They were sharp objects, those eyes. They pierced her with a mixture of anger and lust, hatred and desperation that was so raw it hurt her to see it. She had never seen anyone look like that before. So intense with bad emotions. What was remarkable was that he was able to hold all that bile inside himself. And not explode.

It was clear he wanted her, wanted *them both* most probably. But also that he hated them for that. For making him *want*.

She remembered before, when he first talked to them, before she'd seen his face, Julie's first impression had been that he had been a *creepy guy*. Now that she saw him face to face, she could tell that he was worse than that.

She stared right into those eyes and did not flinch. His intensity didn't dim, but he was silent for a moment. She could see him swallow.

"I asked if you needed any help," the man said again, clearly annoyed that he had to repeat himself.

"Go away," Julie said softly.

"Don't you want my help?" the man said, glaring back at her. Neither one of them looked away.

Amy had fallen. She was down on her knees, oblivious to the danger. Crying and saying something incomprehensible between the sobs.

"No," Julie said. "We're fine. We don't need any help."

"It sure doesn't look that way to me."

The car had been moving slowly beside them as they walked. Now it stopped. It could have been stopped since the man started talking. But Julie did not notice until now.

"Look, we don't need any help, okay? Leave us alone."

The words were calm. She marveled at her sense of control. While it did not make him go away, her assertiveness gave him pause for thought. He hesitated before he made his next move.

He got out of the car.

Julie looked back. The party house was on another block, out of view. There weren't even any stragglers to be seen. The street they were on now had a few houses, but they were far between. And all of them were dark. It was too late for any trick or treaters to be out.

I could scream, Julie thought. *Someone is bound to hear me.*

But he was so close now. What if he lashed out at her if she screamed? What if he did something to Amy?

Before she could pull away, he leapt forward and grabbed her arm.

"Come with me, goddammit," he said. He bent down to grab Amy's arm as well.

Julie froze. It was as if time stood still. He was moving, but she was a statue, planted in the tarmac, watching.

What would the Naughty Witch do? she thought, suddenly aware of the costume. It was a silly thing to think. In other circumstances, it would have been laughable. But, becoming aware of the costume she wore, she could feel it tight against her skin again.

I wish you were dead, she thought, standing perfectly still and staring into his eyes. He had grabbed her arm, but had not moved her. She was in the same spot she had been before.

There came the urge, the need to say it out loud. To *verbalize* it. Like a spell.

"Leave me the fuck alone," she said softly. "I wish you were dead."

In her mind's eye, she saw his heart being crushed in her hand.

The hate-filled eyes widened, and lost some of their intensity. The expression on his face was first contempt, then confusion. Fear. Something was happening inside him, something he clearly did not understand. His grip on her arm, at first almost like iron, loosened. His hand dropped away.

He stood there, wobbling in front of her. A tear in the corner of his eye.

And then the eyes widened more. The spark of life leaving them. The staring, piercing eyes getting glassy.

He dropped to his knees.

All sense of menace left him. Julie looked down at his shrunken form before her on the street. She bent down to help Amy to her feet, all the while keeping her eyes on him.

He toppled over onto his side, and began to curl into a semi-fetal position. She saw a trickle of blood escape from his lips. She could see him spasm slightly before her.

Then he stopped moving. She knew he was dead.

And, somehow, her words had done it.

Suddenly, blood gushed forth from his open mouth, forming a pool around his lifeless form. Julie stepped away, careful not to let any of the stuff touch her shoes. She held Amy firmly and rushed her forward. Narrowly avoiding another puddle, this one of vomit. Amy hadn't been simply sobbing down there, on her knees, after all. No wonder she had been so distracted.

They had another block and a half to go. Julie did not look back at the car, or what had become of its driver.

As they reached the front steps of the house they rented, Amy was crying again. Julie noticed that the sun was coming up. The party had lasted so much longer than she thought.

Second Chances

WELCOME TO BLUE CLAY, MASSACHUSETTS, POP. 101,580, read the sign as he entered the city limits. It had been a long time since he'd been back here, and the legend filled him with a sense of dread that felt an awful lot like drowning. The sour burn he felt when he swallowed almost made him clutch his throat with his free hand, as the other one gripped the steering wheel a little too tightly.

Some things never changed.

Greg took the first exit after the sign and it took him another fifteen minutes to reach the Walecock estate. The old mansion looked worse for wear. Some of the windows were jagged with cracks, and the place was in desperate need of painting. Greg wondered how good a job the caretakers were doing, if there *were* any caretakers these days.

The gate was open at least, and he drove down the dirt road, past the mansion, to the stretch of private beach that gave the city its name. Strangely, not many people knew about this point of origin anymore, except for the old timers. And they rarely ventured here.

Back in the old days, there would be someone at the gate, in the old guardhouse, and they'd ask for a token sum to get inside. It had been two dollars, the last time he'd come here. Such a long time ago. But there was no one collecting money now. Greg continued driving along the length of the estate. He could hear the dirt and gravel crunching beneath his tires.

When he reached the beach, it still had the power to take his breath away.

Instead of sand, it was dark blue clay. Depending on the time of year, it could be as hard as stone or as pliant as putty. Which was why, when it was really hot, few people came here. It would get on your skin, on your clothes, everywhere, and you'd need a good scrubbing.

But it was still amazing to look at.

Greg sat in his car, looking over the blue beach. Waves licked the shoreline.

He put his feet up on the seat and removed his shoes and socks. Then he opened the car door and swung his legs outside. He walked along the grass until he reached the beach. The clay was soft beneath his soles and there was a slight sinking feeling.

The ocean roared ahead of him. He could see some kids down to his left, coming in his direction. But otherwise, the beach was deserted.

Blue Clay was a strange city. To think, the city proper was a short drive away. And yet this place seemed lost in time, a pocket untouched by the outside world. This was his first stop upon arriving in the city because it was the only place he could still feel like himself. Still feel *human*. Once he left this strange outpost, he'd be caught up in the inner turmoil again, lost in his own bad memories. But this place was still solemn and calming. It was the only aspect of this city he had ever missed.

But he knew he couldn't stay long. There was too much to do.

Staring at the expanse of blue clay, he had no idea what would cause such a phenomenon, but he was sure it wasn't normal. Perhaps a geologist could give him a plausible explanation, but here, walking toward the surf, feeling the pliant clay beneath his feet, it had an air of the exotic. Like he was on some island beach far away from everything.

What the hell am I doing here? he wondered, as he walked along the water's edge. And he thought of Becky again. He took out his wallet and slid out the picture the Friedlands had sent him. A serious-looking girl, eleven years old, staring intently into the camera. Only the faintest trace of a smile, and it wasn't reflected in those eyes.

My little girl, Greg thought.

He put the picture away and looked in the direction of the kids again. He regretted that he wasn't alone here. They were getting closer now. The strange thing was they weren't making any noise, but walked in an almost rigid single-file line. Staring straight ahead.

The closer they got, the more they seemed to look right through him. Like he wasn't even there.

It was then, looking down at his feet, that he saw the bright orange starfish.

He bent down to touch it, and it moved more quickly than he'd expected, its arms moving rapidly as it dragged itself back into the water. There was something unnatural about the quickness of its movements.

"What you got there, mister?" one of the kids asked. It was a girl. She probably went to the local college, from the looks of her. She was wearing a red bikini, and had a pretty good figure. It was funny; he hadn't even noticed the color before now, even watching them from the distance as they approached.

It was like they had been somnambulists, wandering along the beach, devoid of the true spark of life, devoid even of color. And then, all of a sudden, they were up close and full of life. Statues come alive! There was something unnerving about their sudden animation.

"It's just a starfish," he said, lost in his own thoughts. "It got away."

"I see it," one of the boys said. "I think I can get it."

Greg wanted to tell them to leave it alone, but instead he just headed back toward his car. The moment had been lost. If he was alone on the beach, maybe he could have recaptured what it used to be like, so many years ago. But the kids made him realize that it was too late.

He could hear them thrashing about in the water, moving and making noise like real kids now. He'd preferred them strange and silent, walking along the beach. He could pretend they were something different then. Something unusual. But now, they were just like anyone else their age. Brash and stupid and contemptuous of real solitude.

Greg opened the door of his car and slid behind the steering wheel. The soles of his feet were caked with clay. He rubbed them a bit, getting most of it off, then slipped his socks back on, then his shoes. He could feel the thin layer of clay that still clung to him, and it felt good. Protective, in a way.

He stared through the windshield. It looked like the kids were playing tug-of-war with something. The starfish. They were pulling it apart. He almost thought he saw red mixed in with the bright orange of it. Then he looked away, before he could be sure. *Did starfish have red blood?* He had no idea, and right now he didn't want to know.

He turned to look out the back window as he backed the car away from the beach, then he turned the car around onto the dirt road that took him away.

* * *

It only took him about twenty minutes to get downtown. The city proper. It was a weary-looking place. Mostly deserted. Some of the stores he remembered from his childhood were vacant now, with soaped-up windows and real estate company signs announcing reasonable rents. On the way here, he had passed the ugly gray factory buildings, once the backbone of industry in Blue Clay, now abandoned hulks, grave markings of another time.

One of the abandoned factories had graffiti painted across its main wall. *Redemption Is Overrated*, in big white letters.

It was getting dark, but he continued driving, giving himself a tour of the places he used to frequent when he was younger. Nothing really looked like he remembered. It was as if this were a former war zone, altered by some hideous trauma that nobody really remembered.

He knew that the real reason he was driving around like this was to waste time. He dreaded where he had to go, and found himself thinking of reasons not to go through with it. Reasons to just get back on the highway and never look back.

But every time he considered that, his thoughts would go back to that picture in his wallet. And he knew he wasn't going anywhere. Not without her.

The last time he'd seen Becky, she had been little more than a year old. He doubted she would remember him at all, not in any real memory sense. Maybe on some instinctual level she would recognize him. It was all he could hope for.

And how would he explain his long absence? Ten years was a long time to disappear. What had her mother told her? Her grandparents? Had they told her the truth? That her father had become convinced that this city was driving him mad, and he had to go far away to save his soul?

He had only been here an hour, and already he felt the familiar nameless fears that used to haunt him. He had practically been an alcoholic those last years before he left. He'd tried to stay anaesthetized as much as possible. If he hadn't, he probably would have left sooner. But the booze tricked him into thinking he could handle it. When he really wasn't handling anything at all.

He knew that Marlene had been trying to track him down over the years. She even found him once or twice, but he always managed to slip away again. Always on the move. Never staying in one place long enough to take root. There had been some angry phone calls. Demands for child support. Somehow, he had always been able to stay one step ahead and then she'd lose track of him for another year.

One time she had put Becky on the phone as soon as she had heard his voice say *hello*, hoping the little girl's voice would get to him. He remembered hearing that voice, soft and bewildered, asking who was on the other end. He could hear Marlene in the background saying, "It's your daddy," but he never said a word. He even stopped breathing, so that there was no proof he even existed. And then he gently hung the phone up without a sound.

He knew he had done the right thing in leaving. He'd done what he'd felt he had to. But the thought of having left Becky behind always filled him with oceans of pain.

She wouldn't recognize him. There was no way she could. And would she really want to go with him? To live with him, a complete stranger, after all these years? No matter how many times he played the scenario over and over in his mind, it always ended with her shouting and crying, refusing to leave her grandparents, refusing to go anywhere with him.

He wasn't a father. He was some courier, come to get a long forgotten package.

* * *

Greg looked at his watch. The dial glowed in the dark. It was after nine o'clock. He'd been driving around for hours and lost track of time.

It was too late to go to the Friedlands' place tonight, he convinced himself. Then again, he hadn't been specific which day he would arrive this week. He didn't even have to call them to let them know he was in town if he didn't want to.

He didn't want to.

There was one more landmark he had to pass before he thought about a place to sleep for the night. He got back on the highway and took the last exit before Blue Clay came to an end. He drove along the quiet country roads.

The house waited for him at the end of a long curve. It wasn't the same house he grew up in. That one had burned down long ago, and they'd built a new one since. He remembered once, when he'd been a kid, a drunk driver had taken the curve too sharply and ended up in their living room. His father had beaten him the next day, angry at the world but only able to express that anger through his son. Through the belt and the hand. But there were a lot of days like that. Too many to remember them all.

And he remembered his mother, stone-faced and sunken-eyed. She often hid behind a book. She'd given up trying to fight his father eons ago. Always watching, but never once saying, *Stop!*

Greg still dreamt of flames most nights.

Now it was a different house. A different family. It felt good that something new had replaced it, and the house that still haunted his dreams was no longer there.

It was hard enough just driving past. But then he was going into the next curve, and that took him away again.

Greg got back on the highway and drove back to the center of the city. There was a hotel there with a strange name. *The Sidelong Glance.*

* * *

Greg spent the next few hours in the hotel bar. The bartender gave him a tab, and Greg kept asking for refills.

"You're not driving at all, are you?" the man asked him.

"Naw, I'm just staying here, and then I'm going up to bed."

It was much too late to call the Friedlands now. And besides, if he called, his speech would be slurred and they'd realize that maybe he hadn't changed as much as he'd insisted he had. And then they wouldn't let him have Becky.

And he couldn't jeopardize that. Not now. Not after coming all this way.

"I'll have another one," he said to the bartender when the man came back to his end of the bar. "Make it a double."

The man hesitated, looking like he was going to start giving a lecture, but instead he just nodded his head gently and took the empty glass away.

* * *

Greg dreamt he was on the blue beach again, digging with his hands. The clay stuck to his palms, and he had to shake his hands now and then in order to keep digging. But the clay was coming away easily. He was so sure that something important was under the beach. At first, he thought he was digging for Becky. She was under the clay and would suffocate if he didn't get her out. But then things changed, and he knew it wasn't her under the clay at all.

Instead, there was a source of great white light. He could barely make out its shape. Slowly, his eyes began to adjust. It was bigger than him, with a glowing, fleshy body, wriggling there in the hole he'd dug, struggling to pull itself out of the clay, and failing.

He knelt there, feeling the urge to reach in and put his arms around the thing. To lift it up and out of the pit.

And then he woke, breathing hard, and there were tears running down his cheeks.

* * *

"Hello, Mrs. Friedland," Greg said on the hotel pay phone. He'd thought of using his cell phone upstairs in the room, but he didn't feel right calling up there, on the bed. Comfortable. There shouldn't be anything comfortable about this.

"Gregory, is that you?" Her voice made him think of paper rustling in a breeze, but it really didn't sound that way. "Are you in Blue Clay yet?"

"Yeah," he said, and winced as his hangover started acting up again. "It's been a long time since I've been back here."

"Too long," she said. "I'm so glad we were able to convince you to come back."

He thought of the private detective they'd sent to find him. The man told him that Marlene had died, and in their grief the Friedlands had wanted so badly to reunite Becky with her father. He'd liked the Friedlands back when he'd been married to Marlene, back when he had last lived in this city. They were good people.

He regretted if his actions had ever hurt them.

"I'm sorry about how things worked out," he said. "It's all so complicated."

"This is a good first step, Gregory," Mrs. Friedland said to him. "You're like the Prodigal Son come home. It was only a matter of time. I knew you'd come back to us eventually. I'm just sorry poor Marlene wasn't here to see it."

Greg remembered about a year ago when Marlene had called and said she'd found someone else. A man who was good and who cared about her and Becky. Marlene had asked him for a divorce so they could get married. Greg had promised to help her out, and moved on to another state later that week. Not long afterwards, she'd died of cancer. He hadn't heard the news until now.

"I loved Marlene," Greg told her. "I really did. I know it didn't always look that way."

"This is your chance to heal the past, Gregory," Mrs. Friedland said. "The fact that you've made it this far shows the sincerity in your heart."

"I'm really looking forward to seeing Becky again."

"And she's excited to see you as well. Ever since we told her her father was coming home, she's been so full of life. This is a very good thing you're doing, Gregory."

He remembered the last time he'd heard Becky's voice on the telephone. Calling, "Daddy? Daddy?" over and over again. He hadn't had the nerve to reply. He remembered holding his breath. He was doing it now.

"Are you close by?"

"I'm staying at The Sidelong Glance," he told her. "I got in late last night and figured it was better to wait until morning."

"Well, you remember how to get here, don't you?"

"I'll be there soon," he said. "Very soon."

"Oh, do you want to talk to her? She's standing right here, the biggest smile on her face."

Talk to her? So soon? Greg felt his muscles tighten up.

"Sure," he said. "Put her on."

There was a moment of sounds, of the phone being passed to someone. And then the voice. Different now. Not the voice of a six-year-old, but still a child's voice.

"Daddy?"

He stopped breathing for a few seconds, and remembered the last time. He forced himself to speak. "Becky? Is that you?"

"I can't believe it," she said. Her voice sounded mature for her age. Serious.

"It's been a very long time," Greg said. "And I'm sorry about that. Really sorry. But I'm going to make it up to you."

"Are you coming here now?" she asked. "Are you really coming here?"

"I'm in Blue Clay right now," he told her. "Maybe fifteen minutes away. It won't take me long to get there."

There was a soft sound. He could have sworn she was crying.

Mrs. Friedland took the phone back. "The poor child. She's so emotional."

"I'll be right there," Greg said. "I'm on my way."

"We'll be waiting for you, Gregory."

And then the phone call was over.

* * *

He parked in front of the two-story house. It was painted light gray and looked much as it had the last time he'd been there. There was a chain link fence now. He remembered there being a taller, wooden fence the last time.

He sat in his car for what seemed like a long time, trying to get up the nerve to go inside. And then he took a deep breath and opened the driver's side door. He slid out and stared over the top of his car at this house from his past.

He and Marlene had lived in the upstairs part for a few months before they'd been able to afford their own apartment. Back before Becky was born. There was no way he would have lived with *his* parents. But the Friedlands had been different.

They still were. Somehow he'd been able to drag himself *here*. He remembered driving on the curve past that other house the night before. Being unable to stop. This house was different.

He saw a face looking out of one of the upper windows. Could it be Becky?

It was all happening so fast. Was there really any way he could go back and correct all that he'd done wrong? Was there really such a thing as redemption?

The front door of the house opened and he got back into his car. He drove away before anyone could come outside.

This isn't going to work, he thought, keeping his eyes on the road ahead. *It was stupid of me to come back.*

* * *

Greg was back on the blue beach, staring out at the ocean. Listening to the waves.

The last he remembered, he'd been in his car, driving away from the Friedlands and Becky. Trying to get far, far away.

He hadn't made it.

Others had come here too. He could see them off in the distance. The blue clay seemed to stretch forever now. The beach was a thousand times bigger than the last time he'd been here.

He stared at the ground, not five feet from where he stood, and he knew that the great glowing thing was under there, wriggling. He just *knew.*

He could feel it in his mind, begging him to dig it out.

He moved toward it and dropped to his knees. There was no point in fighting anymore. He'd had to come back here, whether or not Becky had been waiting. She wasn't the real reason he had to return. He'd been summoned *here* all along. *To the beach.*

He dug with his hands, just like in his dream. The clay came away easily, but it stuck to his hands and he had to shake them now and again before he could continue.

It waited for him patiently. White and bloated and glowing. Ready for the next stage in its development, whatever that might be. It had been waiting a long time. And it wasn't alone. There were many of them. Some within the clay. Others in other parts of the city, beneath the ground. He realized that he'd been aware of them all along, since childhood.

He looked down at the bright, fleshy body. It almost looked like a grossly obese human being without arms and legs. Its small head rolled about on its immense shoulders, with wild, darting eyes. Its mouth worked frantically behind a layer of film that covered its face. Its skin appeared to have a gelatinous texture, like that of a jellyfish.

The way it glowed so brightly, it was a beacon in the night. Influencing this place. Exerting control from beneath the ground.

Pulsating with ancient poisons.

He resisted the urge to reach in and lift the thing out of its hole. He couldn't bring himself to go that far. Besides, it would get out by itself, in time. It wasn't going to be like this for much longer.

He walked out to the edge of the ocean. His back to the thing, trying to pretend it didn't exist. But knowing that it was more real than the beach. More real than *him*.

"Hey, mister, what did you dig up over there?" someone asked. And he turned to see the girl in the red bikini again. She was blinking her eyes, even though there was no direct light on them here, except for the gentle light of the moon.

"Something awful," he said, but he could tell she already knew what it was. That she'd known about it for a long time too. If not consciously, then on some instinctual level. Just like him.

Some people were just sensitive to such things.

"No," she said. "Not something awful. Not awful at all." She said it as if she were trying to convince herself of something she could never believe.

"Come on," he said softly. "Let's move down the beach a ways."

He took her arm and they walked further down the shoreline, away from the hole he'd dug. She looked back at the pit one last time, at the way the glow illuminated the blue beach around it. He could feel her looking, but didn't join in.

"Come on," he said again, tugging her forward.

She walked beside him. Somehow, they were holding hands. He did it more to move her along than anything else, but to both of them, it was reassuring.

"How long have you been here?" he asked her.

"I don't know."

"Yesterday, you had friends with you, didn't you? Where are they now?"

"Out there," she said, looking out across the expanse of blue clay. And he could see spots along the beach where other holes had been dug. Where other sources of light had been uncovered.

Something about the way the lights dotted the beach made him think of Christmas.

He turned and stared out into the ocean again. At the crashing waves. And he knew he'd be on this beach forever now. That there was nowhere else he *could* go.

The girl wandered away from him. And he almost reached out for her, but he didn't.

He found himself craving the taste of whiskey, as everything suddenly got very bright around him.

Holiday House

BRIGHT RED AND GREEN BANNERS, proclaiming *Merry Christmas,* hung from the walls, and a fully decorated Christmas tree took up a full corner of the room, even though it was the middle of July. Hundreds of Christmas cards, most of them yellowed with age, covered at least two of the walls like wallpaper.

Another room was full of Halloween decorations. Yet other rooms were shrines to Easter and New Year's. And there was a birthday room.

Marybeth didn't really notice them anymore. They were just normal rooms now. She had no desire to put anything away. Time was eating its own tail, and by the time she really thought about it, the holidays would be back, and their corresponding rooms would be current again.

Besides, the truth of the matter was Marybeth was too old to care anymore.

She walked past the Christmas room on her way to the kitchen. Once there, she sat down at the kitchen table, the white linoleum stained with yellow spots, and poured herself some cereal. It was always the same, corn flakes. There was a time when she'd buy certain brands, but these days it was the generic brand the supermarket put out. They all tasted the same anyway.

On the other side of the wall, in Genevieve's room, Marybeth's sister was having sex with William Lansing. He came over every Monday, Wednesday, and Friday morning, even though he was supposed to be happily married. Marybeth could hear their sounds, like always. They certainly didn't take any pains to be discreet. But the noises didn't bother her that much anymore. There were days, though, when Marybeth wished she had a William Lansing of her own.

And there was something else about William. He was Genevieve's link with the outside world. Someone who actually came over of his own volition. Something this house was starting to lack. *Visitors.* Genevieve had William, but he was only over a few hours a week, all added up, and had a life of his own. However, Marybeth had no contact of her own with the world outside. No one came to see *her*. It hurt the most late at night when she couldn't sleep. She hardly ever slept anymore.

While there weren't many visitors from outside, Marybeth did get the occasional visitor from *inside* the house. Ghosts, she supposed they were. There was no other name for them. On rare occasions, they wandered the halls, and seemed harmless enough. She was sure that her mind wasn't playing tricks on her, that the apparitions were real. But they never spoke, and they certainly never offered even a hint of intimacy.

"Hiya, Marybeth," a masculine voice said from behind her, and it was good old William Lansing, patting down his silver hair and tucking his shirt in his trousers as he walked through the kitchen to the back door. "I hope you're finding this morning to be a lovely one."

"It's good enough, I suppose," Marybeth said, forcing a smile. She prided herself on the fact that she still had all her own teeth.

William nodded and kept on walking. He had a real estate business not fifteen minutes away by car. In fact, the first time he'd come here was to try to convince her and Genevieve to sell the estate, but once he'd realized that would never happen, he seemed content to make do with Genevieve's affections. At least his visits here weren't a total loss, and if anyone asked, he probably just told them that he was wearing the old Walecock sisters down with his salesman's charm.

He was gone and the screen door slammed behind him. It was only a few minutes later when Genevieve came out, still in her nightgown, her hair like white flames. "What's for breakfast, Marybeth dear?"

"The same as there is for every breakfast. Cereal. I hope that's to your liking."

"It will have to be," she said, and sat down at the other end of the table. "I hope we weren't too loud this morning."

They were always too loud. It was quite clear they enjoyed putting on a show for lonely old Marybeth, acting like sex-crazed kids again. At first she resented it, but she'd since gotten used to it, and even found a vicarious thrill in the ritual.

"No, you were just loud enough," Marybeth said, suppressing a smirk. "We're almost out of milk."

"I'll have to call the market. I hope they send that nice new delivery boy again."

"I'm surprised you haven't seduced him too," Marybeth said.

"I'm trying," Genevieve said with a wink. "Some things take time."

They both smiled at that, on the verge of laughing, but not quite getting there.

"Are you going to go outside today?" Genevieve asked. "We haven't been out to the beach in ages."

"I don't know," Marybeth said. "I wasn't planning on it. I like it better inside."

"But it's so hot in here. At least there's a breeze outside today."

"Maybe. It's been a long time since I left the house."

"All the more reason to come with me, silly."

"Let me think about it."

Marybeth thought about the strange blue beach down at the end of the dirt road that ran alongside their house. She hadn't seen it in nearly a year and it might be nice to go take a look again. For old time's sake.

Marybeth hadn't even noticed that Genevieve had left the room again. Genevieve was on the phone, placing an order for groceries. Marybeth could hear her in her bedroom, saying, "Milk, eggs, apples." It went on for a while and just sounded more and more like a mantra until Genevieve stopped talking and hung up the phone.

"Marybeth?" she said, coming back into the kitchen. "I told them not to rush. They'll have someone bring the groceries over later in the afternoon. In the meantime, how about that walk?"

"So soon?" Marybeth asked.

"No time like the present, sister dear," Genevieve said. "And I see you're already dressed. Just give me a little bit of time to get ready, and we'll be off."

"Okay," Marybeth said, not sure if she really wanted to go, but not wanting to put up a fight so early in the morning.

"Fine," Genevieve said, and went back into her bedroom to get her clothes, and then she walked back through the kitchen and down to the hall that led to the big bathroom they shared. The one with both a bathtub and a shower. There were other, smaller bathrooms on the second floor, with just a shower, and even more above that, but they never used those anymore. In fact, they rarely had any reason to use the upper floors at all.

Marybeth finished eating and rinsed her bowl in the sink.

She wandered into the Christmas room again. The multi-colored lights on the artificial tree always seemed to calm her. She felt like she'd gone back in time to some Christmas morning of her youth.

"Look at me, lost in the past," Marybeth muttered to herself. "I'm turning into Miss Havisham."

She had to laugh at that. It had been such a long time since she'd last read Dickens.

She sat on the chair across from the tree and started to nod off by the time Genevieve came looking for her.

"Are you ready?" Genevieve asked, poking her head in.

Marybeth's eyes shot open. Had she really fallen asleep so quickly? "Yes, of course."

"You always come here, to this room," Genevieve said, looking around at the lights and the banners and the layers of old cards on the walls. "I always know where to find you."

"I like it here."

"Time to get some air."

Marybeth got up out of the chair, and could already hear Genevieve going through the kitchen to the back door. There was a six-year difference in their ages, but it felt like a millennium now, as Marybeth got to her feet and started walking. *My God*, she thought. *It's like the tortoise and the hare around here. And I've become a tortoise without even realizing it.*

When she got out onto the back porch, Genevieve locked the back door, even though people rarely came out this way anymore. It was a force of habit more than anything else. Then she came up beside Marybeth and took her hand. "I've got you," she said.

There was a pathway behind the house, out to the beach, that only they knew about. It wouldn't do to wander along the dirt road everyone else used. Well, everyone *used to* use. It wasn't like the beach had an abundance of visitors anymore. Walking along their special path always made Marybeth feel like they were children again, off to have a summer adventure. Going over to the beach seemed so wonderful then. Like having a tea party on the moon.

* * *

"It never ceases to amaze me," Marybeth said, staring out over the expanse of blue clay. She squeezed her sister's hand. "I bet there's no one else in the world who has a beach like this behind their house."

"It's a particularly bright blue today," Genevieve said. And they both looked at each other and smiled. They were just outside the perimeter of the beach, and they immediately took off their shoes and stepped onto the clay with bare feet. It was soft and pliable.

Marybeth swore she could feel the sole of her foot tingling as she walked forward toward the water.

The only sounds were the crashing of the waves against the rocks, and the occasional cry of a seagull.

"I don't know why it's been so long since we last came here," Marybeth said.

"I come here a lot more than you do," Genevieve said. "You just don't seem to be interested anymore. But I'm glad you agreed to come with me today."

"Me too," Marybeth said.

They held hands as they walked across the clay beach. They walked far enough into the water to cover their ankles.

"Remember when Mama used to pack a lunch and we'd come out here? There were people who used to come out to the beach then. And afterwards Mama would complain about the clay. How it got all over everything."

"I remember," Genevieve said.

Turning back from the water, scanning the length of the beach, Marybeth noticed some odd holes dug in the clay. They seemed to be far apart, but there was a kind of pattern to them. They were quite large, big enough to be graves.

Marybeth remembered a story their father used to tell them, about "bottle people" who lived under the clay, sleeping there like subterranean insects waiting to emerge with the spring. She knew it was just a story, but looking at the holes, she felt strangely uncomfortable.

"I wonder what caused those big holes?" Genevieve said, talking loudly to be heard above the sounds of the surf.

"I have no idea," Marybeth said.

* * *

On the way back to the house, Marybeth noticed that someone had spray painted words across the wall of what remained of the old gardener's quarters. She hadn't noticed the graffiti before. It read: *Salvation is Obsolete.*

"What a bizarre thing to write," Marybeth commented, pointing it out to her sister. Genevieve pretended not to notice.

The house was coming up ahead. It was so big it even towered over the trees. There were so many rooms, there was no way they could occupy all of it. Even if they turned each room into every holiday imaginable, incorporating the holidays of all the different religions, and even minor holidays like Arbor Day or Groundhog Day, it seemed that there would still be plenty of rooms left over. As it was, most of them were unused, their doors pulled shut, more lost in time than even the holiday rooms.

The Walecock Estate, Marybeth thought, looking up at their grand old home. What a great place this was once, a historical place. Their parents had thrown spectacular parties here, and everyone important had come, even some celebrities of the time. Their grandparents had done the same. There was a rumor that Samuel Clemens, Mark Twain himself, had once slept in this very house during a lecture tour of New England so very long ago.

Now it was a mausoleum. Marybeth could see the paint was chipping and some of the windows were cracked. It was in need of restoration. Too bad the money wasn't available for such extravagances. Their savings weren't what they used to be, and getting the roof replaced two years before had taken up a good chunk of the money that was left.

"All the memories here," Genevieve said, noticing that her sister seemed lost in thought. "It's amazing all the things that have happened here, in our very home. It's hard to believe it was all real."

"Yes," Marybeth said. "That's what I was thinking exactly."

"Sometimes I wish we could throw a big party here, like the old times," Genevieve said. "Like when we were children. Dancing and music and wonderful food. No one has even stepped into the ballroom in ages."

"That's because nobody ever comes here anymore," Marybeth said. "It's sad."

"William comes here," Genevieve said. "And the delivery boys." She meant it as a kind of joke, but she could tell Marybeth didn't understand, or wasn't listening again. So she said, "Yes, you're right. It's not the same. The time for balls and dancing is long gone."

* * *

"The groceries should be here soon," Genevieve said, looking at the wall clock. "We were gone a good two hours."

"It's the longest walk I've been on in ages," Marybeth said. "I think the air did me some good, but now I'm exhausted."

"Go sit down and catch your breath," Genevieve said. "I'll put the kettle on."

"Okay."

Marybeth wandered back to the Christmas room again and sat down in her favorite chair. It was then that she heard the humming. It came and went constantly throughout the day, every day. She was so used to it now that most days she didn't even hear it. And she'd long since stopped wondering what was causing it.

There were some days, though, when the humming seemed to give way to the voices. She hadn't heard them in a while, and Marybeth had never told her sister about them. She didn't want to sound that dotty. It was something better kept to herself.

Marybeth let the humming lull her to sleep, until she was awakened by the kettle's whistle. Soon after, Genevieve came into the room, holding out a teacup. "Here you go."

"Thank you."

"Do you ever think this room is a sad place?" Genevieve asked, staring at the tree and its multi-colored lights. There were plenty of boxes of replacement lights packed away in the closet in case any of them burned out.

"No, not at all. It's the exact opposite of sad."

"Not for me. It reminds me of all those Christmases we had without Daddy."

"You still miss him, even now."

"Of course, don't you?"

"Yes," Marybeth said, taking a sip of tea. It was just the way she liked it. "I miss both of them. But it's been a long time now. The pain isn't as much as it once was."

"You're right," Genevieve said. "But it never really goes away, does it?"

Marybeth had to think about that one. It had been such a long time since their parents had lived here. And their father had died young, only forty-three when he had the heart attack. Mama had lived for two decades after that, but she'd always been sickly.

Now it seemed like she and Genevieve had lived here on their own forever. Their memories of their childhood and their parents almost seemed like someone else's life.

Genevieve looked like she was in a trance, staring at the Christmas lights, and Marybeth took the moment to look at her face. She'd been beautiful once, the most beautiful girl Marybeth had ever known. There was enough of that left so that it wasn't totally gone, despite her age. Sure, her hair had gone white, and there were a few wrinkles here and there around her eyes. But for the most part she was still the same beautiful girl that Marybeth had envied when they were young.

Genevieve had never lacked for suitors and had been married twice. But neither marriage had lasted longer than a year. And she'd always come back here. To be with her sister again.

They'd both been adrift in thought when they were brought back to the real world by the sound of someone knocking at the back door.

The doorbell mustn't be working again, Marybeth thought. *We'll have to get that fixed.*

Without a word, Genevieve left to go see who it was.

* * *

Marybeth must have nodded off again. It was warm in the Christmas room.

She wondered how much time had passed since Genevieve went to answer the door, and forced herself up and on her feet. Marybeth went out to the kitchen.

There were bags of groceries on the table, still unpacked. And the door to Genevieve's bedroom was closed. She could hear sounds from there. Familiar sounds. Perhaps Genevieve had finally seduced the delivery boy after all. Or maybe it was William, come back for a rare midday quickie.

How I envy her, Marybeth thought as she started unpacking the bags and putting things away. *She never had any problems getting the boys. They came looking for her in droves. It was like she had some magic power I was never privy to.*

Marybeth thought back on her life. She'd spent it all here. In this house. Never marrying, never going away. After their mother died, she rarely left the house at all. She didn't often feel like a prisoner, though, unless she thought about it too much.

She realized that the blue beach was the most exotic locale she'd ever been to.

It was then that the sounds from Genevieve's bedroom changed. What had sounded like the sounds of lovemaking changed to shouts and the sound of crying.

Marybeth went to the bedroom door and listened, trying to hear what it was all about. William must have returned and they were having some kind of lover's squabble. Except it really didn't sound like William's voice. It was younger. Stronger.

Angrier.

As she stood there, ear close to the door, Genevieve screamed and then went silent.

"Oh my God," Marybeth said softly to herself, torn between trying to open the door and help her sister, and fleeing the house entirely. Instead, she found herself frozen there, listening to the sounds of someone scurrying about behind the door.

The only phone in the house was in Genevieve's room. There hadn't been a phone call for Marybeth in years.

She finally got her feet to move again.

* * *

"Where do you keep the money?"

She was in the Christmas room again, nestled in her chair. Somehow, she'd thought he couldn't reach her there. That she really had escaped into the past.

She stared up at him as he approached. The delivery boy from the market. Genevieve still called him "the new boy," but he'd been here at least a dozen times, and had always seemed so quiet and well behaved. Not a dangerous boy at all. But here he was. There was something different about him now. His eyes were wild and there were bloodstains on his shirt.

"Didn't you fucking hear me?" he asked. "Where do you keep the money, you old cunt?"

The harshness of his words scared her. She tried to get her tongue to work. "The bank," she said.

"No, the other lady, she said you had some here," he told her. "Lots of it. But she wouldn't tell me where it is."

"No," Marybeth said. "We don't keep any here."

"You're lying," the boy informed her. Well, she thought of him as *a boy*, but he had to be in his mid-twenties. At what point did they really stop being boys and become men? The process seemed to take longer these days.

Despite his handsome face and the fire in his eyes, there also seemed to be something lacking there. Like he was missing something that would have made his mind complete.

What was this talk about money in the house? Marybeth wondered. What story had Genevieve told him to get him into her bed?

"Get up," he said, and she saw the knife then. She'd been so intent on his face that she hadn't even noticed it until now. "Get up now and show me where the money is."

Marybeth started to cry, because as soon as she saw the knife she knew she was completely alone in the world.

In the corner, behind the Christmas tree, she could have sworn she saw one of the ghosts peeking out at her, with large, concerned eyes. A girl with a perpetually dirty face. Marybeth had seen her before, had even tried to talk to her, but the girl was very shy and certainly could be of no help to her now.

The delivery boy was close enough to touch her now, and his free hand grabbed her arm, just above the wrist, where it rested on the arm of her chair.

"I said get up!" he shouted, and pulled hard on her arm. She let out a cry as she was jerked out of the chair and to her feet. It happened so suddenly, she almost lost her balance.

He held her hand then, and it reminded her of the walk she had taken earlier in the day with Genevieve, when they, too, had held hands. And now she was gone; she was sure of it. Perhaps it was her ghost Marybeth had seen behind the Christmas tree. Maybe it had been the ghost of Genevieve when she had been a child, if such a thing made sense. But it probably didn't. Besides, could someone become a ghost so quickly after dying?

And she'd seen that girl a few times before when Genevieve was still alive.

"I'm not going to ask you again," he said.

The humming returned now, if it had ever truly gone, and it was louder than before. It sounded like a voice in her head. Between the humming and the boy touching her, she wanted so badly to scream, to shout her head off, but she didn't. She tried her best to remain calm, even though she knew that chances were good she'd be dead soon too.

"In the basement," she said, repeating what she thought the voice in her head was saying. "We keep the money in the basement."

"Show me how to get down there," the boy said, pulling her along.

* * *

The house was very old, and Marybeth knew there were hidden mazes behind the walls. A whole other house nobody knew about. She'd explored some of it as a child, finding passageways completely by accident. But she'd stopped exploring ages ago. It didn't matter anymore. They didn't use most of the rooms that were in plain sight, why look for more?

She knew the basement was much of the same. That there were hidden rooms down there as well. Passageways that led to places she'd never investigated. Perhaps if she could get him down there, she could stall for time.

But time wouldn't help her. It would just prolong the inevitable. He wasn't going to leave without his money, and there wasn't any money in the house to give him. What little remained of their legacy was in the bank. Unlike the stereotype of batty old women, they'd been as practical as possible to make what they had last. No hidden loot under the mattresses. There was some jewelry, but it was mostly Genevieve's, and he would have found that while searching her room.

Marybeth had no hope of overpowering him. And no one would hear her screams. Not in this house in the middle of nowhere. Even William Lansing wasn't due back until Wednesday.

"Is this it?" he asked her when she stopped walking. He made sure she saw the knife again.

"Yes," she said, pulling the bolt aside and opening the door that led downstairs. She flicked the light switch on the wall as they went below. It wasn't as bright as she remembered, and she made sure to watch her steps as she descended.

"An old house like this. You must have tons of hiding places."

"Yes," she said, knowing nothing she could say would save her.

She glanced at his shirt, at her sister's blood.

He noticed her eyes. "Keep going," he told her.

At the bottom of the stairs, they found themselves in an enormous room in the shape of a hexagon. Marybeth remembered once that her father had said the shape of the room was a kind of trap to catch "bottle people." He only said it once, and it had no real meaning at the time. She wondered why she thought of that now.

"So," the man said, squeezing her arm tighter and raising the knife toward her throat. "Where's the money?"

The humming surrounded them now. Marybeth had heard it on the way down the stairs, but it was louder now than it had ever been before. And with it came the voices. She could hear them clearer now, talking in unison, but she could not decipher the language they spoke.

There were doors along the walls, doors without knobs, and she was going to point to one of them, to get him to go looking, and take him and his knife away from her, when one of the doors opened of its own accord, and something approached them from the far wall. It was large and glowing and it moved strangely. At first, she thought it was another ghost, but she could tell that this one seemed solid. It was large and translucent, with a white light that glowed from within, and it hovered over the floor like a balloon. Its small, almost human head rolled atop its frame, with darting eyes. She instantly thought of the "bottle people" her father used to talk about so very long ago. But this looked more like some kind of jellyfish than a bottle.

As it got closer, Marybeth noticed there were blue smudges on it, which had to be clay from the beach beyond the house. This thing must have come from *out there*. There must have been a passageway somewhere along the far wall that led outside.

Its features were hard to decipher. They came to her in flashes, like a series of snapshots, and it was impossible for her to take it all in at one time, and something about that hurt her eyes.

The boy dropped his knife. There were tears streaming down his cheeks, and then he suddenly seemed very far away. The glowing thing stopped perhaps a yard away, but did not touch them.

He released her hand and dropped to his knees. He began to sob. Marybeth was surprised to hear him howl with sadness.

There was movement inside the creature's belly. Faces.

Her mother was there. Her father too. And the nameless ghosts Marybeth had seen wandering the rooms of the house. The shy girl who had been hiding behind the Christmas tree upstairs, and the other ones. The ones who never spoke to her, but knew they were being observed. All of them pulsated within the translucent skin, as if the thing were a bottle for souls.

Genevieve was there too. Marybeth saw her now, peeking out from behind the others. There was a confused look on her face. Perhaps her death had been too recent for her to fully assimilate it yet.

She looked down at the wailing man. He was pounding on the floor with his fists, and then he just collapsed, sprawled across the basement floor, unmoving. She knew if she looked at the creature's stomach again, she would see him there now too. But she could not bring herself to look.

She was afraid she would be next, but the thing did not advance on her. In fact, she could hear it humming softer as it slowly moved away. And then the humming stopped. Marybeth reached out for the staircase behind her, and her hand closed upon the railing. She turned and made her way up the stairs as quickly as she could.

At the top, she closed the door and pulled the bolt to lock it. Her breathing was labored. She was much too old for this much excitement and she feared her heart would fail her. But it didn't.

She had no idea what she had seen downstairs, but she knew it had something to do with the holes on the beach she'd noticed earlier, and she knew that it was not yet time for whatever that being had been to claim *her*. She had some time left. Time to get her things in order.

Marybeth went into her sister's room. The boy had torn the room apart looking for his precious money. It took her a few minutes to find the phone, but when she did, she dialed 9-1-1.

She could not bear to look directly at Genevieve where she lay on the floor, across from the bed. But she saw her blood on the sheets.

"This is Marybeth Walecock. A delivery man has killed my sister trying to rob us."

The police told her to stay where she was. That someone would be coming shortly.

Marybeth sat on the edge of her sister's bed and covered her eyes. Wishing herself away. Anywhere else.

Not even the Christmas room could comfort her this time.

Animal Biographies

INSIDE THE HOUSE, SEVEN people were pretending to be bees, busy within a hive. They crawled around on the carpet, buzzing. Mitch went outside. His heart just wasn't in it. He stood in the back yard, next to the grill, and watched the steaks burning. He watched the grease feed the flames. The meat was blackened. The edges danced with fire. Mitch watched the meat burn and wondered what it would be like to be the sun. The heat of the day helped his imagination.

After a while, he went back into the house, deciding that the steaks were a lost cause. The others were still playing their game, now pretending to be clams in their shells. They were all rolled up in balls and didn't make a sound. Occasionally, someone would throw open their arms like a clam opening its shell, and then close up again.

In the bedroom, everyone's coats were in a pile on the bed. No one wore coats on such a hot day, but, for some reason, everyone brought one. Mitch and his wife, Julie, had taken all the coats and put them on the bed. There were a couple of light jackets, a few heavy winter coats, a parka, even a rabbit fur coat. He had no idea why they were there, but he figured it had to do with one of their games. He resisted the urge to jump on top of the pile.

Mitch left the bedroom and went out the front door, avoiding the others. He went out into the street. No cars were coming. It was a quiet Sunday afternoon, and he hadn't heard any cars drive by for hours. He got down in the middle of the street and tried to imagine himself as a dead animal, crushed by a passing car.

As he lay there, his eyes closed, trying to imagine himself dead, he felt the asphalt vibrate beneath him. He sat up. A car was approaching. He got to his feet and walked over to the sidewalk.

The car's driver had seen him lying in the street, and slowed down as he got nearer. The driver stared at Mitch as he drove by. Neither man said anything.

Mitch went back into the house and tried to join the others, even though he had no idea what they were doing now. No one seemed to notice his comings and goings; it was as if he were alone in the house, as if the others were just furniture, which *was* something they sometimes pretended to be.

They were so engrossed in their games. It was as if they were in another world, and he was looking at them through binoculars. Or a telescope.

Benny was the first one to break character and sit up. Almost immediately, he began talking, talking about some mountain ranges in another country. Everyone else sat up, listening intently. Mitch was on the couch, not really paying attention to Benny's words, but envying how the others gave him their full attention.

Benny told them about various kinds of rocks he'd found in these mountains. Mitch hadn't known that Benny knew anything about geology, and yet Benny talked in very specific terms, explaining what minerals certain rocks were made up of, and what signs told him how old they were.

Mitch got sick of the talking, of the drone of Benny's voice, and he got to his feet and went out into the back yard again.

The meat on the grill was engulfed in flame now, looking almost dangerous. Mitch got the garden hose, turned it on, and went over to the grill. He sprayed it until the flames were extinguished. Then he turned the hose off and coiled it up near the side of the house like a snake.

He looked down at the hose, and pretended that it *was* a snake, and that, if he made any sudden moves, it would strike. He stood there perfectly still, as if in the midst of a stand-off. He stood there until he got bored and walked away.

Mitch went over to the grill and examined the meat. It was burnt to crisps. He poked at twisted, black pieces with his finger, as they floated in the black water that now filled the grill. A few pieces had fallen to the ground.

In the house, Benny was pretending to be a rock. Someone poked him and he shouted. He wanted to get into a rock-like state and his concentration had been ruined.

Mitch heard the shouts as he stood looking at the grill. He didn't really care about their games. The one they played most was called

Animal Biographies. Someone would pick an animal, and then try to imagine what it would be like to *be* that animal. And the others would ask questions. They would discuss the animal's life. Its fears and desires.

Mitch thought it was a stupid game, but he never said that to the others. Not even to his wife. They seemed to really enjoy their games, and even though he didn't share their enthusiasm, he didn't feel he had the right to ruin it for them.

He picked up a few pieces of charred meat and then went back into the house. He threw the pieces into the kitchen sink, turned on the garbage disposal, and listened to them get ground to bits. Then he went and stood in the threshold, looking into the living room, and watched the others play their game.

"Mitch," Benny said, noticing him for the first time in ages, "why don't you come and join us?"

Mitch realized that he had been staring at Benny's lips. He saw them move before he absorbed the words.

"No," Mitch said. "I'm lousy at these games."

"Come on," Benny said. "You just don't try hard enough to get into it. You're too caught up in reality to really enjoy yourself."

Mitch felt a sudden need to participate, to be accepted by them. He went into the living room and got down on the carpet with the others.

"Animal Biographies," someone said behind him.

Mitch turned and saw it had been Julie. It was funny how he hadn't noticed her before. He had been concentrating on Benny.

Julie was on her hands and knees, and she was topless. Handprints on her breasts revealed that someone had been trying to milk her.

They were all in various stages of undress.

"Yeah," Benny said. "That's what we're playing. Pick something and tell us what it's like."

Mitch felt foolish. He didn't want to do this after all.

"It doesn't have to be an animal," Benny said. "Hell, I was pretending to be a rock before."

Mitch looked around at the others, thinking that they were idiots. He wondered how he got involved in all this. But it wasn't such a mystery, really. They were Julie's friends, and they had been playing these games since long before he met her. At first, Mitch had thought the games were fun, strange yet strangely exciting. But after they got married, the games seemed to happen more often. Instead of once a month, they got together once a week. Sometimes even more often.

He was starting to doubt their sanity.

And his own.

"While you were all in here," Mitch began, "I went outside and stretched out on the street, pretending to be an animal that had been hit by a car."

"Really?" Julie asked. There was an excitement in her voice that he hadn't heard, directed at him, in a very long time.

"Yeah," Mitch said.

"What was it like?" Benny wanted to know.

"It's hard to explain, really," Mitch said. "I sort of felt nothing. It was peaceful. Then a car came along and I had to get out of the way."

"What kind of animal were you pretending to be?" Julie asked, tying her bikini top back on.

"I really didn't have anything particular in mind."

"That's too bad," Benny said. "About the car coming. It sounded like an interesting experience."

"Yeah," Mitch said, feeling awkward. For a few moments, it had been nice to have their attention, to be like Benny. But it wore off fast. "Well, that's all for me. I guess it's someone else's turn now."

"I'll be next," a girl named Felicia said. She removed what little clothes she had on and got down on all fours, pretending to be a dog in heat. She let out a high-pitched yelping sound, and then began to describe what she thought a dog in heat felt like. As she talked, it was obvious she was having difficulty concentrating on her words, and she began yelping again.

The men in the room had erections and were forming a line behind her. The closest, Benny, grabbed her roughly and began to mount her. Mitch considered joining the line, but instead he got up and went outside.

No one noticed him leave.

Beyond the Haze

WHEN I FINALLY FIGURED out where the singing was coming from, we were at the top of the hill, looking down at the abandoned airplane hangar. The hangar had been there for as long as I could remember, but I didn't know anyone who could remember when it was actually in use.

Maybe back when planes were a brand new thing and you had to turn the propellers with your hands to get the engines started. Like in the old movies. Maybe that's when this place saw some activity.

Now it was just deserted property. Why hadn't they torn it down and replaced it with something useful? I'd always thought it was the perfect spot for a baseball diamond.

So here we were, the four of us, at the top of the hill at midnight, and there was strange singing coming from the deserted airplane hangar. I guess it wasn't deserted anymore.

Harry was drunk out of his mind by then, the worst of us, and he wanted to go down to the airstrip and play some football. He'd even brought his ball. We hadn't played football together in years, but this was a special night. Harry had found out the divorce was final earlier that day, and he wanted to celebrate with a night out with the boys. We'd been happy to oblige. It had been a long and messy divorce, and we were all glad it was finally over.

I was relieved when Harry suggested the football game. At least he'd stopped ranting about "that cunt" by then.

Tom raised the bottle of Wild Turkey to his lips and tipped it back, trying to catch up.

"Might as well play one last game," he said, wiping his lower lip.

"What's that sound?" I asked, taking the bottle from him. I wasn't sure yet if they heard it too. I think I was more sober than they were; my senses were clearer.

"What sound?" Harry asked, looking around. "I don't hear anything."

"That singing," I said. I'd heard it back at the car, when we'd first gotten out and started heading downhill, but I didn't feel confident enough to mention it until now.

John tried to focus. "Yeah, I hear it too," he said. "Faintly."

"What the hell is it?" Harry asked, staring down at the hangar. He obviously heard it now. "Is it coming from *that* place?"

"I think so."

"Let's go find out," Harry said. He tossed the football up in the air and caught it again, and then began to run. We did our best to keep up with him.

Light came from some lamp posts here and there around the site. They'd been there as long as I could remember too.

None of us had ever been athletes. We hadn't had any desire to join the football team when we'd been in high school, that was for sure. None of us had fit in anywhere and just kind of drifted into each other's orbit. It was funny how strong a bond we'd been able to maintain. Sure, there were times when we wouldn't see each other for years, but we always stayed in touch; we always knew what the others were up to. Our friendship had outlasted most of our jobs and marriages.

In the old days, we liked to have a game just among ourselves. It didn't matter if we sucked or not. It was just for fun.

When we reached the airstrip at the bottom of the hill, the singing got louder. Now there was no mistaking it.

"Must be some kind of late night choir rehearsal or something," John said. He was normally the *quiet* one of the group.

"Let's get a closer look," Harry said. He'd dropped the football by now and had lost all interest in a game. Which was fine by me. I joined in because that's what we did, but I really didn't care one way or another. Somehow the Wild Turkey bottle had come back to me, and I found that a lot more interesting.

We ran along the airstrip, chasing one another. For some reason we knew we shouldn't shout out or anything. The only sound we made was that of our feet running along the asphalt, and even that was muffled by the weeds.

When we reached the building, it looked to be closed up pretty tight. There were windows on the side though, so we went around to find them. They were filthy, and no matter how many times we wiped them with our hands, we couldn't get a clear look inside.

There was light. We could see that much. But nothing else. No shapes, no shadows. Nothing.

"I can't believe we can't see anything," Tom said. He had the bottle by then and poured some whiskey on his handkerchief. He wiped harder at the glass.

"The dirt's on the *inside*," I told him. "You can't clean it from out here."

"Whatever," he said, but he'd already figured out it was futile and had given up.

"Only one way to find out then," Harry said, taking the bottle from Tom. "We have to go inside."

"You sure about that?" I asked. "What if they see us?"

"Who?" Harry said. "It's not like this is a private house or anything. It's an abandoned building. Public property. No harm in just checking it out."

"I guess not," I said, not really sure of his logic. But hell, we were all drinking, and it made sense at the moment. It didn't occur to any of us that maybe someone had bought the property and this place was off limits to trespassers. Not the way we felt that night.

"There's a door right over here," John said, leading the way.

It was locked, but Harry didn't waste any time jimmying it. I remember he was a whiz at getting laundry machine coin boxes open back when we were kids. It kept us in candy and comic book money.

The first thing we noticed when he got the door open a bit was the haze. There was this strange mist in the air, making it hard to see. You could still see the light, but not much else. This made me think that it wasn't dirt that kept us from seeing in the windows, but this thick haze.

"What the fuck is this?" Harry asked. "I can barely see in front of my face."

"Maybe we should just go back to the car," Tom said.

We could all hear the singing now, and it was much louder, but muffled for some reason. I knew it had something to do with the haze.

"Yeah," John said. "Nobody's seen us yet. Maybe it's a good time to cut out."

They felt it. I could feel it too. A sense that we shouldn't move forward. That we should cut our losses and just get out there, while the going was good.

Harry was so numbed out; he probably didn't feel it. Or maybe he just didn't care. He was always doing things to show the rest of us how fearless he was.

"No," he said. "I want to see what the singing is all about. Are you guys with me or not?"

I can't imagine any of us would have felt right leaving him there. We stuck together, even when it was stupid to do so. There'd been a few run-ins with the law because of this code we had. But nothing serious, so far.

"Come on, Harry," I said, trying to reason with him. "There's nothing here to see. Let's do something else."

"This place has got me curious," he said. "I want to see what's going on."

There was a chance that someone might see us now if we went inside. I thought there was something brazen about going that far to see what the singing was all about. But we were all liquored up and Harry was good at getting us to go along with what he wanted to do, even now. He was just the same when we were kids. Funny how some things didn't change.

He moved forward and we were close behind. And then we lost sight of him as he went into the haze and disappeared. We kept moving and followed him inside. I'd like to say we'd follow Harry to hell and back, but that's a lie. There were limits. But that night, the limits weren't all that clear.

There was a moment or two when we lost track of each other, and we called out so that we knew we were all still there, but we could barely hear each other over the din of the singing. It had gotten much louder, almost deafening, and at one point I had to cover my ears.

And then we came to a place where the haze was gone.

We saw each other first, and I felt a wave of relief knowing that we hadn't lost anybody, that there was an end to the haze and it was just some kind of weird phenomenon we didn't have any explanation for. That it wasn't anything dangerous. Here we were, just as we'd been before we'd walked through it. Despite the sense of dread some of us had felt following Harry inside.

But then, after we saw each other, we looked around and saw the rest of it.

Bodies. It looked like hundreds of them. They were all impaled on sharp shafts that jutted up from the floor. Or was it *dirt* beneath our feet? I couldn't see for sure. The bodies reminded me of accounts I'd read of the kinds of things Vlad the Impaler did to his victims. The real-life guy who was the inspiration for Dracula.

I'm not really sure if *bodies* was the right word in this case though; they weren't actually *dead*. They should have been, the way those strange shafts ripped through them. But, you see, the sounds we'd heard, the singing, was coming from *them*. Except, now that we were inside the hangar, I wasn't so sure it was singing anymore. It could have been the wailing of people being tortured. People in pain. But there was also a *melody* to it all.

The hangar was full of these people. More than it would seem could fit in that place. And yet, there they were. Their sounds louder than ever.

"What's going on here?" Harry said, trying to talk over the wails. We could hear him faintly. I could tell he wasn't fully grasping what was happening. Maybe he thought he'd passed out and was having some kind of dream.

Tom and John just stood there, as shocked by the sight as I was. It really looked like a scene out of hell. Except it was here, in front of us. And none of us remembered dying.

"We've got to get out of here," Tom said. I tried to see his lips as he spoke, but the light from outside was dim. It really wasn't easy to hear each other in this howling place. But I knew that he was right. We shouldn't linger there any longer than we already had.

"No," Harry said. "We have to help them," and he'd already started moving toward the impaled people, moving awkwardly, not sure how to go about it.

"We have to leave," Tom said, walking back toward the haze, back toward the way out of this place.

I grabbed his arm. "Help me with Harry," I said. He shook his head. Then he pulled his arm away and kept walking.

He didn't make it very far. Something large and sharp came up from the floor without warning and forced its way through his body as he stood there. It was an angle that was painful to look at, and he started screaming almost immediately.

"Holy shit," John said, frozen beside me. We watched as Tom wriggled in agony, trying to get free of the thing that tore through him, literally nailing him to the spot.

I looked over at John, hoping he might have an idea of how to proceed, and seeing that he was as clueless, and as scared, as I was.

All through this, Harry continued to try to pull people free of their shafts. He'd seemed to have forgotten we were there with him. Or maybe he just assumed we were trying to save people too.

But all John and I were concerned with, at this point, was saving ourselves.

I tried to go out the way we'd come through, but I couldn't *find* the way we'd come through. Every time I stepped through the haze, trying to find an exit, I found myself bumping into a wall. At one point, I walked into the mist for what seemed like ten minutes, until I ended up right where I'd started.

"I can't find the way out of here," John said, his mouth close to my ear. "What the fuck is this place?"

There was a new sound then. And I knew without looking that Harry was now in the same position as those he'd tried to help. I turned and saw him impaled, kicking his feet, trying in vain to free himself.

"We have to help Harry," I said. "And Tom."

"No, we have to get out here before it happens to us," John said, as desperate and confused as I was. "There has to be a way out."

I turned. Harry was still struggling, and now he'd joined in on the screaming. He was a part of this great agonized choir. And so was Tom. He was over to the side, blood trickling from his lips as he howled.

"What are you doing?" John said, grabbing my shoulder. "If you stay too long, it'll happen to you too."

But even as he said the words, a shaft slid up from the floor, plunging through him. It looked as if it entered in through his anus and ripped up through the top of his head. It all happened so fast, he didn't even have time to struggle. Blood poured out of him like some kind of obscene fountain. But he wasn't dead. His mouth was moving, though his lips were stained with red. His eyes stared at me, pleading.

He tried to speak, but couldn't form the words. Blood spattered his clothes. And then he suddenly started *singing*, like the others.

I turned toward the direction I thought was the way out. The haze obscured the dimensions of the room. I had a general idea of how big an airplane hangar should be, but I was disoriented. There was nothing about this place that was logical. The rules of physics did not seem to apply here. There were so many more impaled bodies in here than there should have been. The more I looked, the further they spread.

I thought of why we'd come here. Harry had been in a funk; the divorce had clearly broken something inside him despite his bravado. Now, the late night football game we'd planned seemed so far away.

I stood there, staring, not knowing which way to go. Part of me wanted to just run as fast as I could, but another part of me knew that sudden flight would probably mean a collision with an unseen wall. But I had to try again to get out of this place. I couldn't let what happened to my friends happen to me.

It was then that I heard the hiss of a shaft shooting up through the floor. Not that I could actually *see* a floor. A layer of haze covered where I'd been walking. Haze and, I knew, blood.

The shaft penetrated my skin, and as I struggled to pull away, to move before it ripped through my torso, it moved faster, surging more forcefully through me. It wasn't painful, not really, but I knew what was happening to me. I could feel the pressure of the shaft parting my flesh and ripping through my organs.

I stared into Harry's face. His contorted, howling face. And I realized that I, too, was howling. But it didn't sound like howling to me anymore. It really did sound like singing. My voice joined the others', and it was almost beautiful, the way we cried out in unison. Our voices embraced and enhanced each other's. Turned many sounds into one.

And then I felt my mind open. The shaft had probably pierced my brain by that point. These gigantic thorns ripped through us as if they had their own agenda. As if this were all planned somehow, and they weren't simply random, mindless things, but *living things*. I could feel movement inside me, pulsating energy. I felt my mind open to the other victims around me, and I could hear their thoughts, and they could hear mine. And there were two choruses being sung then. One by our mouths, and one in our heads. All in unison.

The haze seemed to be churning toward us, making it harder to see one another, but we each knew the others were there. The haze didn't block out the sounds, or the thoughts. It simply enhanced them. Nothing else mattered.

I could feel my blood dripping down my back, and it was the most wonderful feeling in the world.

Crocodiles

SOMEONE WAS POUNDING NAILS in the kitchen when Dave woke up. The *pound pound pound* was like the steel-toed boot of God kicking his brain awake.

"What the hell," he said as he pulled himself out of bed. It was seven o'clock on a Saturday morning and there was no reason for this kind of shit. The landlord was going to hear about this.

It's not like he could sleep late every day. Besides, this was his place, he paid rent. He had every reason to assume he had enough rights to prevent just anyone from coming into his apartment and pounding on the fucking walls.

Dave entered the kitchen and saw a tall man bent over the open oven door. He was looking inside.

"Excuse me," Dave said. "But what the fuck do you think you're doing?"

The man rose to his full height and turned to face him. He had long hair. His face looked pretty young, maybe in his early twenties. He was larger than expected and had a hammer in his left hand. He stared at Dave. It looked like he wasn't sure whether or not he should brandish the hammer as a weapon.

Dave looked around at the big-headed nails that had been hammered into random places on the wall.

"Look, this is my place. What are you doing in here?"

The man did not say a word. He just stood there, staring. His face was devoid of recognition or understanding.

"Where do you get the fuck off just breaking into someone's place and making a mess of things?"

Dave moved forward and pushed out with his hands, pressing the bigger man backwards against the nearest wall. Size didn't particularly matter now. Dave was building up a head of steam and didn't care about anything except getting this intruder out of his apartment.

He was surprised how easy it had been to push him. The guy looked pretty formidable, but he didn't put up a fight. And he hadn't even thought to use the hammer to defend himself.

Dave stared up into the blank eyes, his face just inches from the larger man's chin. *This guy must have a screw loose or something*, he thought.

"Give me the hammer," Dave said, holding out his hand.

The man hesitated, then handed him the hammer. There was a slight glimmer of curiosity in the man's dark green eyes.

Dave tossed the hammer across the room. It slid beneath the dining table.

"You better get out of here before they have to carry you out in a body bag," Dave said.

The man smiled then. The biggest, broadest smile Dave had ever seen.

And his teeth, they looked like the sharp little daggers that lined a crocodile's mouth.

The man said nothing, just stood there, grinning.

Dave suddenly felt light-headed, afraid his legs would give out.

"Back off!" a voice said from behind him. He turned to see another man enter from the living room. The man was Dave's height and came at him with his fist raised, knocking him to the floor. "Get the fuck away from him!"

Dave stared up at his attacker.

"Who are you? And what are you doing in my place? Did the landlord send you?"

"Your landlord doesn't know I exist," the shorter man said. "And he's all the luckier for that. You, on the other hand..."

"Look, I don't know what this is about, but I want you both to leave my apartment."

"Must be nice to want," the man who'd punched him said. "I'm the Carotid Kid, and this here is my buddy, Smiley."

Dave looked at Smiley, who was no longer smiling. The man's mouth was now closed and looked very grim. As for the Kid, he didn't look particularly youthful. His face was old and tired-looking, despite the fact that his punch had packed quite a wallop.

"Why are you here, in my house?" Dave fully expected to be hit again.

The Kid knelt down beside him. "You ask way too many questions."

"How would you feel if strangers broke into your home? Put nails in your walls? Hit you when you asked any questions?"

"Shit," the Kid said. "Someone did that to me, I'd kill them without giving it a second thought."

And then he delivered a second punch to Dave's head. This time, he lost consciousness.

* * *

When he woke up again, his hand was incredibly sore, and hurt more when he moved. He looked down. Someone had nailed his hand to the floor, right through the palm. There was a pool of blood around it.

He groaned.

"Oh, so you're awake again, are you?" the Kid said.

Dave noticed there were more nails in the walls. They seemed to make patterns, but he had no idea what they meant.

Smiley was over by the window, looking down at the traffic below.

"Please, don't hit me again."

The Kid seemed to think about that, then he looked at his watch.

"Take whatever you want.".

"I really don't want much right now," the Kid said. "Except for you to shut the fuck up. Do you think you can handle that?"

Dave nodded slowly.

"Good. So keep your trap shut, or I'll put a nail through your other hand."

The Kid walked over to Smiley and whispered something in his ear. The bigger man turned and looked at Dave and smiled, showing off his weird crocodile teeth again.

Dave closed his eyes and prayed he'd lose consciousness again.

* * *

"Time to go," the Kid said, kneeling on the floor. He had the hammer now. He used it to pry up the nail in Dave's hand. Taking it out was even more painful.

Smiley grabbed his other arm and pulled. Dave did his best to cooperate, afraid that if he resisted, the big man would rip his arm out of its socket.

"Where are we going?"

The Kid looked him up and down.

"You have a real talent for saying too much," the Kid said. "I have to admit, it's a very annoying habit."

Dave tried to control himself, but his hand hurt like hell and he was getting very sick of not getting any answers. "Look, you broke into *my* apartment, you beat *me* up, you put a nail through *my* fucking hand. I think I have a right to at least ask *why*."

The Kid smiled then. His teeth were normal. No tiny daggers there. Dave thought he was going to say something to him, but instead he turned to Smiley and said, "Let's get out of here. Throw his ass in the trunk."

He turned back to Dave. "You going to behave while we're outside, or do I need to put you out again?"

"I'll be quiet."

"Sure you will," the Kid said. "A talkative guy like you has no problem keeping quiet. But you see, I don't trust people too much. Must have been my mother, she lied to me all the time. She used to love to tell me that every guy she brought home was my daddy. So I think everyone's lying to me. And I don't know you, so that makes me even more distrustful."

"I'm not lying."

"Listen, you want to know why they call me the Carotid Kid? You want to know how I got my rep? Because I'd be more than happy to show you. There ain't nothing in my contract that says I've got to bring you in alive."

Contract? Bring you in alive? What was this all about? It at least provided some motive for all this, but it created a whole new set of questions.

"I'll behave."

"Damn right you will," the Kid said, and struck Dave in the head with the hammer.

* * *

.

When he woke again, Dave felt a lot groggier than before. He figured, at this point, he probably had a concussion.

He opened his eyes and had to close them again. The sun was too bright.

"He should wake up soon," the Carotid Kid's voice said. "I didn't hit him that hard."

He heard the sound of something moving in water, and slowly opened his eyes.

And stared right up into the sun. He closed his eyes again and considered whether to try and sit up. Did he want them to know he was awake?

And what horrible things did they have in store for him?

His hand ached again. When he tried to move it, ever so slightly, pain rippled through him. He tried hard not to cry out, but it felt like his hand was nailed in place again.

There was another sound—of movement in water. Someone swimming, perhaps.

"Fuck this," the Kid's voice said, and then there were noises that were harder to decipher. And a bucketful of cold water splashed over Dave's head and torso, forcing his eyes open. He sat up as much as he could.

"He's awake now."

Dave was right about his hand. It was nailed to some kind of deck, with a large pool in the middle of it. Two large shapes swam around within it. *Alligators.*

"How you feeling?" the Kid asked.

Dave stared up at the man. Smiley was nowhere to be seen. The Kid still had the hammer. In his other hand were some nails.

"Why?" Dave asked.

The Kid looked over at the pool and nodded his head. "It took me awhile to track you down. It had been a long time, and she had no idea where you'd gone. Across the country, as it turns out."

"Who is *she?*"

The Kid laughed at that one. "Someone who can't let go of the past, I'd say. The more I know about her, the less I get it."

"You're going to feed me to the alligators? Some kind of punishment for a past crime I never even committed?"

"I ain't a lawyer, and I ain't your judge either. I'm just someone who does jobs for people. Sometimes I just track people down so someone else can get their licks in. Other times I take care of things myself. But it's just a job, that's all. Don't take it personal."

The Kid stared off into the distance. There were age lines etched in his face. He might have actually been a kid once, but Dave thought the guy looked about fifty.

"And they're not alligators," the Kid said. "Alligators have rounder snouts, and other stuff—hell, I don't claim to be an expert on this shit. But these here are *crocodiles*."

One of the crocodiles was swimming around the perimeter of the pool in an almost restless way, like it was killing time. The other one was close to the edge, staying very still, staring at Dave.

"So you're going to toss me in?"

"Actually, I've got shit to do, and time is money," the Kid said, and stared at the motionless croc. "How long is this going to take anyway?"

The animal continued staring at Dave, and then slowly pulled itself up out of the water. Its front claws were on the deck. It pointed its narrow snout in his direction, as if it recognized him.

Dave tried to pull on his nailed hand, but he didn't have the courage or tolerance for pain to pull hard enough to rip it free. Besides, even if he got loose, he'd still have to contend with the Kid and these oversized reptiles.

The Kid whistled and rolled his eyes. "Fucking cat and mouse."

The crocodile's face began to change then. Slowly. The snout receded. The head shrank, becoming more like a human head. Dave watched in mute fascination.

Brenda. The name came to him even before she was done changing. He recognized the eyes, the small, upturned nose. He hadn't seen her since they were kids, but there was no mistaking her. She was older now, but just as beautiful as he remembered.

She must have seen the recognition in his eyes, because she smiled.

"It's been way too long," she said, her lower body still submerged in the pool. Her upper body was exposed, naked. Her breasts were larger than he remembered. She had developed a bit more since he last saw her. Her nipples pressed against the deck, just out of sight.

He didn't think to ask how she had been a crocodile, or how she had transformed like this. He found all these things impossible to accept. But now, seeing her, he blocked out the impossible and focused instead on the familiar.

"Yeah, it's been twenty-five years," he said, still tense with fear.

"You remembered."

"Some things you don't forget."

"How fucking heartwarming," the Kid said. "Can we get on with this?"

Brenda shot him a look. "I'm paying you well. Keep your pants on."

The Kid walked away from them and went back into the house through sliding glass doors.

"Brenda, what's this all about?"

"We didn't part on the best of terms," she said. "I was pregnant with your child and you decided to skip town."

"I know, Bren, but God, we were only fifteen. No way I could have been responsible at that age. I begged you to get rid of it. To go on with your life."

"I couldn't tell anybody," Brenda said. "I was so ashamed. But I wanted you to stand by me. It would have been easier if you'd just stayed."

"I was young and stupid," he said. "That's the only excuse I had. I hated that town enough, without feeling even more trapped. I couldn't wait to get away—what happened just made me want to leave all the more. To the point where I just couldn't resist the urge any longer."

"You were young," Brenda said. "Sure, I understand that."

"Then why have me brought here by two violent psychopaths? Why have me nailed to this deck so I can't get away?"

"I wanted you to meet your son," Brenda said.

Dave looked at the other crocodile. It had drifted to another side of the pool and was staring at him. He watched it transform into Smiley. The young man threw back his mane of wet hair and smiled at him with those dagger teeth.

"My son?"

"You know I never would have had an abortion," she said. "Of course he's your son."

"But why?" he stammered. "How?"

"There were a lot of things you didn't know about me back then. Things I never would have told you. And a lot of things that have happened to me since. It's too much to talk about now."

"And that's why you had me brought here, why you had me tortured by this sadist? *To introduce me to my son?*"

"I've put it off long enough," Brenda said. "A boy has a right to know who his father is."

"So I can go now?"

"What?"

"I've seen him," Dave said. "Now I want to go home."

"You don't understand," she said. "It's been twenty-five years. He's been waiting to meet you all this time. This is an important moment. Didn't you ever wonder what had happened to us after you left? What happened to *me*? If your son was born alive and healthy?"

Dave squirmed, but every time he moved the nail in his hand shot waves of pain through his arm. He saw that the Kid was walking along the perimeter of the pool now, watching him. He was afraid the man would come back and maybe knock him out again. He was sure his head couldn't take too much more of that before it cracked like an egg.

There were scrolls hanging from the fence that surrounded the deck. He hadn't noticed them before, but he did now. On them were the same strange patterns as the nails back in his kitchen walls. He was sure of it.

"You didn't care," Brenda said. "You didn't give us a second thought when you left. It wouldn't have mattered to you if we died!"

She was climbing the rest of the way out of the pool now, and there was something happening to her skin. She was becoming fully crocodile again as she crawled toward him. Even if he could get his hand free, there was no way he could get out of her way fast enough.

Blam!

Brenda stopped and turned her head. Dave looked in the same direction. It was the Kid. He was standing on the deck, over the place where Smiley had been grinning at them. He wasn't grinning anymore. Smiley was floating face-down in the water, half human, half crocodile. Blood blossomed from his head where the Kid had shot him.

Reverting to her crocodile form, Brenda raced back into the pool and swam to where her son was.

Her *dead* son. And *his* too, Dave realized.

At first it appeared that she was trying to help him, even though he was obviously way past dead, and the water was getting murkier with blood by the second. But then it was apparent the blood had driven her into some kind of frenzy. She was splashing around, ripping pieces of her son off with her powerful jaws.

"She's eating him," Dave said softly.

The Carotid Kid had his gun out again and was firing at her as she tore her offspring to pieces. He hit her in the head with his second shot. She stopped thrashing and moved in his direction. His third shot stopped her progress, and her life.

The echoes of the shots still reverberated in his ears while the Kid casually walked around the pool, stopping just out of his reach. He put his gun on a picnic table between the pool and the sliding doors. He reached into his pocket, pulled out a pack of cigarettes, and lit one.

"You smoke?"

"No," Dave said, but he considered starting now.

"They sure got a lot of blood in them," the Kid said.

"Thanks for stopping her," Dave said, feeling weird to be thanking the man who brought him here, who had knocked him out twice.

"Unnatural freaks," the Kid said. "Her money was good, but I just got sick of how this scenario was turning out. I gotta stick with humans over reptiles, you know."

He stood there, smoking his cigarette, staring out into the pool where two forms floated, one half human and the other all crocodile, both spilling their blood into the water like ruptured oil tankers.

"You know, I thought they'd revert to human form when I shot them. Like werewolves do in the movies. But they stayed exactly just the way they were before they died."

"Do you have any idea what they were?" Dave asked.

"Naw, but I've seen a lot of crazy shit. They ain't that special."

The Kid took a final pull on his cigarette and then tossed the butt out onto the pinkish waters.

"Does this mean I'm free to go?"

The Kid looked at him. His tired eyes lit up, and he almost laughed.

"Shit, what do I care? My job's done. I've been paid. No reason to stay around here moping."

Dave looked at his hand. "Can you get me out of here?"

The Kid grabbed the hammer, which was on the picnic table next to his gun, and tossed it over to where Dave was. It banged onto the deck a few feet away. He could reach it but he'd have to really stretch for it.

The Kid turned and walked back toward the sliding doors.

"Wait," Dave said, struggling to get his fingers around the handle of the hammer. "Can you give me a ride back home? I have no idea where we are."

The Kid turned back. "Look, I just gave you your life back. I could have easily put my last bullets into you. Just be grateful for what you've got. If it's an inconvenience finding your way home from here, just remember. At least you're alive to go home.

"Oh, and what you do from here on in is up to you. But I don't recommend you mention anything about me being here if I were you. To anyone. Remember how easy it was for me to get into your apartment this morning? You wouldn't want to meet me again like that, would you?"

He stared right into Dave's eyes. Dave forced himself to shake his head.

"You fuck me over, and you'll find out, once and for all, why they call me the Carotid Kid."

The man walked back into the house.

Dave waited a few minutes and then reached out, finally getting a hold of the hammer. It took him a long time to dig the nail out of the deck.

The Click of an Unhinged Jaw

SOMETIMES IT FUCKING SUCKS being an eleven-year-old girl. Sure, I know being a kid is supposed to be the best time of your life, and youth is wasted on the young, and all those tired clichés, but to be honest, I never really felt all that comfortable being a kid. First, there were other kids, who I hate. And the fact that no one takes you seriously, which is my dilemma. Yeah, *dilemma*. I know words like that because I read books. A lot of books. They're what I have instead of friends. It used to be books and my sister, but my sister is gone now, and Mama works two jobs and I hardly ever see her. And I know I shouldn't say "suck," or even worse, "fucking," but I'm trying to make a point. Trying to *emphasize* something, and while it might not be polite, it makes my point about how awful it is to be eleven, and frankly, if I'm the narrator of my own life, I'll say whatever I want to. Although, I do try to use it right, for emphasis, and don't swear just to swear like some kids do.

Back to my sister. I mentioned that she's gone, and that's on account of she's dead. Murdered, actually. They haven't caught her killer, and don't seem to have much to go on, and from what I can tell, the police and everyone else just gave up, and now I'm the only one who still wants to find out who killed her. I've always been fascinated by detectives, and there are some who are girls like me, like Nancy Drew and Veronica Mars, even though they're older than I am. The thing is, my sister, Charlotte, wasn't just murdered. It was the strangest murder anyone had seen in a long time; they told me so. Because when they found her, she didn't have a head.

I guess they figured out who it was because of her fingerprints, but I could have told you just from the way she was dressed, with the green sweatshirt she liked so much with the picture of a lion on it. She had gone out jogging—like Veronica Mars, she's older than me, or she was—and she disappeared for a few days, and then they found her body in the woods. Without a head. I know what she was wearing because they called Mama to identify her body at the morgue, and I was in the car with her, and she didn't have time to drop me off home first. They wouldn't let me in to see the corpse, because I'm too young, but Mama told me what she was wearing, and we both agreed, yep, it had to be Charley. That's what Mama and I called Charlotte.

The police questioned a lot of people, and it was on the news, and then time went on and they gave up and then everyone tried to just forget about it and move on. I know Mama never forgot, because she never seemed the same afterwards, like when I talk to her a lot of the time, she seems to be in a trance or something, and she doesn't hear me, although she pretends like she does, and I trick her and say something that proves she wasn't listening after all.

So I'm doing everything I can to solve her murder. But it's not easy when you're eleven. Like I said, no one takes you seriously, even when you're trying to conduct a serious investigation and gather up all the facts. A lot of people won't give you the facts, because either they don't think you can handle it, or they just don't think it's worth their time to tell you. So right from the start, I was at a disadvantage. But being a girl never stopped Nancy Drew, and it won't stop me.

Like I said, trying to investigate a murder when you're eleven sucks. And I don't think an eleven-year-old boy would have much more success, although maybe a little, because boys tend to get away with stuff more than girls. Which I always fucking hated.

Okay, okay. I'll cut down on using the "F" word so much. I know it's not ladylike. But I'm trying to *emphasize* how this whole thing is like banging my head against a wall. And *that* hurts. Besides, I can say whatever I want when I'm alone. By the way, Mama says I'm *preternaturally* mature for my age. That's a pretty big word, huh? I looked it up. I don't think I'm some kind of genius kid or something, but I am pretty smart. So if you're thinking *she doesn't sound like she's eleven years old*, well then, too bad for you.

I wasn't super close to my sister. There was an age gap—she was like seven years older than me—so I guess we didn't have a lot in common. Except for books. She used to read a lot too, and a lot of the times she would give me her books after she was done with them, and not all of them were geared to the YA audience, if you know what I mean. She made me promise not to tell Mama, but that wasn't a hard promise to keep, because Mama is hardly ever home, and I don't think she cares what I read. Which is good, because even though I'm eleven, I really don't consider myself a kid anymore. I mean, physically I'm not a woman yet, but I've got a highly evolved mind. I'm sure you can tell that by now. I'm not some dumb girl who spends all her time on her phone texting her friends because, as I stated before, I don't really have any friends. But I use my phone for lots of other stuff, and it even helps with my murder investigation. But I think that's probably obvious.

Anyway, I started out by reading everything I could find online about my sister's murder, and then about any murders that were similar, especially if they weren't too far from where I live. And then I even went down to the public library, and read more stuff there, even though no kid I know ever goes to the library anymore and it's mostly older people trying to use the really old computers there because I guess they can't afford to buy their own or something.

I found out a few things that way. First, there were a few similar murders not far from here, over several years, and they were all girls—I guess I should say young women—like Charley. Second, they have no idea how they lost their heads. It's like they just popped off like a doll's head, and the neck wound was closed up, or something like that. I read some theories about "some kind of acid" that might have been used to obscure how exactly the heads were removed. I thought that was pretty weird, and I guess I'm not alone, because whenever some forensics person was asked about it in the news, they mentioned how weird it was too. But they knew it was murder because people just don't go around losing their heads, and it's pretty hard to do something like that to yourself.

Oh, I don't think I ever mentioned my name. I guess that's not polite. My name is Pauline Rush. If I had any friends, I'd insist they call me Pauly. Charley called me Pauly. But no matter how many times I tell Mama to call me that, she never does. She's stubborn that way. If you're wondering about my dad, he's not dead or anything. He just has another family in Florida somewhere, and he stopped visiting us a while ago. I guess we just weren't a good enough family for him, so he made another one that he liked better. I don't know *why* we weren't good enough for him. I think Mama takes that personally, but I was too young to have formed my personality back then, so you couldn't tell if you liked me or not yet, and so I don't think it was me who drove my dad away. Not that I care, mind you. Mama says he's an asshole for what he did to us, and I agree with her. On holidays when he calls us, I have to really pretend not to hate him, and try to be polite, even though it's really hard, him being such an asshole and all.

Mama said he really wanted to come out when Charley first disappeared, but she talked him out of it and said he would just be in the way. And he had been gone so long, what good would it do to come back now? He didn't know anything about her life or the people she knew, and he was just using it as an excuse to try to get close to us again, so he could leave a second time and hurt us some more. I agree with Mama. But then they found the body and he had to come out for the funeral, where we all gathered in a room with a coffin in it. They said Charley was in the coffin, but the lid was closed, so you couldn't be sure. They could have lied to us and just put an empty coffin there. Even with the coffin closed, it was pretty awful. Dad had brought his new wife, but not his new kids, and after Charley was buried, they came back to our place and Mama and Dad had the biggest argument I ever heard, and said some pretty awful things, and then Dad went back to Florida and I hope he stays there forever.

So, back to the name thing. You can call me Pauly if you want. The Rush part is easy to remember too, because my dad really liked an old rock band called Rush and he used to play them all the time back when he lived with us, although I don't remember it that much. Mama tells me he did that, and because of that she hates the band Rush, but I think they're okay. I listen to them sometimes on Spotify. I like the music a lot, but sometimes the singer's voice gets on my nerves and then I listen to Lorde or Billie Eilish instead, or better yet, some of the female rappers who rap about dirty stuff. I don't understand everything they say, but I like it. I think it's funny.

So I read up on everything that was reported about Charley's murder, but it didn't help that much. There weren't a lot of answers in all that. Everyone else seemed as baffled as I was, and though there were other murders, they didn't happen very often, and then time would go by and people would forget about them again.

So I started to take little trips. I went to the place in the woods where they found Charley's body a few times. I don't know the exact spot, but I think I have a good idea, except looking around there never seemed to help much. Then again, the reports said she wasn't killed there anyway, that she was killed somewhere else and then left in the woods. I went on Charley's Instagram page, and I did some investigations of her friends, to see if anyone sounded suspicious. But most of her friends were pretty dumb and they posted about stupid things. Charley posted a lot of stupid things too, and her friends liked them. I guess that's what people do when they have friends, but it just seems like a waste of time to me.

I haven't been completely honest. I *had* friends once. Sure I did. But last year some of the girls started to be really mean to me online, bullying me, and it just went too far. I closed my account so they couldn't find me, and I made up another name. A fake name. I even put in a picture of some rando I found in a Google search. So they wouldn't know it was me. So I could spy on them, but they wouldn't know who I was. That didn't stop all the bullying, of course, those girls were still mean to me at school, but at least I was able to stop *some* of it. Some of the girls were so stupid that they started to think the fake name I used was their friend. That was really funny. Most girls my age are so dumb.

Which is why I don't need any friends. They are just jealous because I am smarter than them, and I don't care about their stupid friendship. I don't need them, and they hate me for that. But I keep telling myself that school won't last forever, that I'll be a grown up someday, and I can do whatever I want. Mama says I should try harder to make friends, and I lie and tell her I'm trying, but I'm really not.

Besides, I have more important things to do than make friends. I'm going to find out who killed Charley, and I'm going to expose them to the world. And when I find them, I'll be a hero, and I'll have done something even the police couldn't. That will show those stupid girls who used to be my friends. That will show them I don't need them at all.

* * *

There are some benefits to having a mother who works two jobs. It gives me the ability to come and go as I please. I used to have a babysitter who watched me when I wasn't at school, but Mama said I'm old enough to take care of myself now, and besides, paying for a babysitter was a waste of money we didn't have. When Mama was a kid, they had things called "latchkey kids" who spent time home alone when their parents worked, and while it's frowned upon now with most of the kids having to take dance and play soccer and join afterschool clubs, I don't have to do any of that because I told Mama I really don't want to. I'm sure if she didn't work so many hours she would be just as involved in my life as the other kids' parents are, so I'm kind of glad about the two jobs.

That's why I was able to go examine the place in the park where they found Charley's body, and why I've been able to go back there every day after school to be observant and see if anything strange is going on.

It's like belonging to an afterschool club called the *Solve a Murder* club, except I'm the only member.

And today, I think my *diligence* has paid off. I was watching from my usual place, out of sight from the main trail, and I saw two strange ladies sitting on a bench talking. I don't know why they seemed strange; they didn't look like homeless people or anything, but something about them set off alarm bells in my head, so I decided to keep watching them. They're not in the park every day, but I saw them one other time this week, and there is something "off" about them, as Mama would say. I took pictures of them with my phone, but there's nothing I can really do with the pictures yet, because I don't have any proof they actually did anything.

But I know they did. They must have done *something*.

And why do they spend so much time in the park? It's not like they're jogging, and the park isn't all that nice. It's kind of crappy actually. But at least there's enough woods around it so I can hide and watch them.

* * *

Mama asked me what I do after school and I told her I do my homework and play video games, and then she let it go. She asks this every once in a while, and I always give the same answer, and she always has the same reaction, like she just asked the question to hear herself talk. There's no real importance to the question, which doesn't make me feel as bad when I lie to her. It's obviously not important, so why waste time feeling guilty about it?

Mama sure does work a lot of hours. Sometimes I see her for a late dinner, and sometimes when I go to bed, she's still not home yet. But I go to bed anyway, and pretend to be asleep when she gets home, because I want her to trust me and I don't want to worry her. She has enough on her mind these days.

* * *

Well, something finally happened today, and I want to write it down so that I don't forget any of it.

I was watching those two strange ladies from my hiding place. Like I said, I'd seen them twice before in the park, and I knew there was something different about them. I'm glad I followed my instincts.

Today, they were sitting on a bench, arguing about something. One of the women is tall and has long black hair, and the other one is a little shorter with short brown hair, and they stopped talking long enough to watch another woman jogging in the park. The jogger was wearing sweatpants and a hoodie, and I didn't see her face very clearly, and then the two women on the bench stood up and watched her go by. And then they started jogging after her. There was no one else around.

Anyway, I left my hiding spot to see them better, and I saw the taller woman touch the jogger's head, and she went sort of limp, and the two women carried her down a hill to a shack at the edge of the park. That shack has been there forever, and I even went in there one time when I had a friend named Janet. We went inside and looked around, but there was nothing much to see, and it wasn't even a good clubhouse, because there were spider webs everywhere and lots of spiders, and I just hate spiders. I'm sure there were snakes and rats in there too. I never went back in there. It used to be a shack for custodians, or something like that, but no one uses it anymore.

They went inside the shack, the two strange women supporting the jogger between them. Like I said, the jogger was kind of limp. But she still moved a little, and I think she even said something once, but it wasn't very loud. She seemed confused, but she didn't struggle or try to get away.

There's a hole in the back wall of the shack. It's at a special angle, so it's hard for someone to see you if you they don't know what to look for. I was using that to watch them.

The tall woman was holding the jogger from behind now. The hood on the jogger's hoodie was pulled down now and I could see her face better. She looked sort of familiar. I didn't know her name or anything, but I had seen her jogging in the park before. It was chilly today, which explained why she had her hood up.

I heard the taller one say something then. It sounded like, "It's your turn now."

Then the taller one grabbed the bottom of the hoodie from behind and pulled it up and over the woman's head. The jogger was only wearing a sports bra under that. The shorter woman took off her coat and her shirt too, and I started to feel really weird about what I was watching.

One time, Janet and I were surfing the web when we were friends. We were in my room and Mama was working, as usual, and Janet went to a site I'd never heard of, and we watched people get naked and do really weird things. I didn't like it all. It wasn't long after that that we stopped being friends. I've thought about going back to the site once in a while, I'm not sure why, but I never did. I really don't want to see that again. Grownups are really ugly without their clothes, and the whole thing was pretty gross, and my stomach kind of hurt when I watched it.

Anyway, I thought that these women were going to do something like I saw on that site, because they were taking off their clothes, although they didn't take off their underwear, and then the shorter woman's head started shaking. It was the strangest thing I had ever seen. It shook really hard, and then her neck got longer, and then...

I don't know how to explain it. It really scared me. But her neck got long and then it broke away from her body. Her body just stood there, where it was, but her head was moving separately now. The head had a long body like a snake now. The snake had been inside the woman's body and came out now. I told you it was hard to explain.

The taller woman held tight to the jogger from behind, and the snake woman slithered—that's what snakes do, right?—up the jogger's body, until the head was right near the jogger's head, which was limp and had fallen forward.

The snake's head opened its mouth—it was the woman with short hair's mouth, like I said, not a real snake's head—and I heard a weird click, and the mouth opened wider, and two of its front teeth had gotten longer and sharper, and the teeth went into the top of the jogger's head like two long icicles.

The jogger started to move then. I guess she was struggling, but she was very weak, and it wasn't much of a struggle, and the taller woman held her elbows from behind, so she wasn't going anywhere. I was sure if she wasn't so sluggish, the jogger could have handled them. She was in great shape. But they had done something to her. Maybe drugged her somehow.

The snake woman's head just stayed like that, with her fangs in the jogger's head for a few minutes, almost like it had fallen asleep, and then it seemed to wake up and move again, and its jaws opened wider—there were more clicks—and wider still. And then it took all of the jogger's head inside its mouth.

And just as suddenly as the jogger had started squirming, she stopped.

As I watched this, I knew the same exact thing had happened to Charley. I was watching someone get murdered the same exact way she had been murdered, and it scared me so much, I closed my eyes. But I knew I had to open them again. I had to see what happened next.

* * *

Sorry, I had to stop writing for a while. As I wrote about it, I saw it all over again, and it just scared me too much.

So, the woman with the snake's body swallowed the jogger's head, and by now her snake body had wrapped around the jogger's body, but the tall woman was still holding the jogger upright so she wouldn't fall down.

It reminded me of those nature shows when they show a python swallow a whole cow and then its body is the shape of the cow as it digests it. She was that kind of snake. Her jaws were open so wide, and there was a big bulge in her long neck now, and then the jogger's head somehow came loose from its body. The taller woman let go then, and the jogger's body fell to the ground, with the snake body wrapped around it.

The bulge of the jogger's head had moved down a bit on the snake's body—it was digesting it—and the snake body slowly let go of the jogger.

The taller woman was watching her friend now.

From where I was hiding, I could hear them talk.

"Good," the taller one said. "We'll be good for a while."

"What do we do with her?" the other one said. I don't know how she spoke when she was digesting the head. It did sound like someone who talks when they have a mouth full of food though.

"Leave it here. We don't have to worry so much now. We're leaving town as soon as you're able, and we're never coming back."

And then a big spider crawled right next to my face, and I screamed.

* * *

I'm not afraid of much. I'm very brave. But spiders are my kryptonite. I am just so scared of them, and I don't know why. I tried to let one crawl on my arm once, I tried to overcome my fear, but I ended up bawling and running away. It's just a fear I can't get rid of.

Of course, when I screamed, they knew I was there, watching them. The taller one ran out of the shack and had grabbed me by the arm before I had a chance to get away, and she dragged me into the shack with them.

* * *

So I'm standing in the shack, with the tall woman holding me from behind, and I just know I'm next. I know that I'm going to die the same exact way my sister died, and they would find me in the woods somewhere without a head.

I looked down at the headless body of the jogger. Even though it had no head, it wasn't bleeding, and I knew it had something to do with the acid they mentioned in the paper. Some acid that made it difficult for them to determine how the head was removed.

I looked at the big bulge in the middle of the snake body where the jogger's head was being digested. Then I heard the crackling of skull bones being crushed by snake muscles, and then the bulge flattened.

The snake's human head was tilted up, ever so slightly, and I could see its eyes were looking up at me. Meanwhile, its human body was still where it had been, standing, rigid. Intact and untouched. Just without a head.

Waiting for its head to come back. The wound where the head detached itself wasn't bleeding.

"She knows everything," the taller woman said. She was holding my arms and it hurt. She was *trying* to hurt me.

"Yeth," the snake woman said, still sounding like there was something in her mouth.

99

"We have to get rid of her."

The snake head stuck out its tongue and it vibrated, and I know that snakes use their tongues like we use our noses, to smell.

"No," the snake's head said. "We can't."

"Why not?"

"Innothent," it said.

"How old are you," the taller woman said, shaking me hard. "Ten?"

"I'm eleven," I said. I felt like I'd been insulted.

"Too young," the woman said.

"Innothent," the snake head repeated.

"Look, we're not allowed to kill you," the taller one said. "There are rules."

"What is that?" I said, staring down at the snake woman.

"*Gulars*," the taller one said from behind me. "Both of us. But we've fed now and we're leaving. You won't see us again."

"Where'd you come from?" I asked.

The taller one didn't say anything for about a minute; then she said, "Same place as everyone else."

That didn't make sense to me. But it was the only answer I was going to get.

"Why do you just eat the heads?" I asked.

"It's a brain thing," she said. "We need them. The venom starts the process and then we break them down. You eat your way, we eat ours."

I didn't think she would answer that one. I was surprised that she did.

"Don't tell anyone about us," the tall woman said. "They won't believe you anyway. They never do. It's too freaky."

"They'll make fun of you," the snake head said.

"But if you do tell anyone about what you saw today, we'll know. We'll know and we'll come see you when you're sleeping, and we'll eat your head too. Rules or no rules."

"Yeth, we will."

And then the tall woman hit me hard in the back of the head.

* * *

When I woke up, I was in my hiding place in the woods again, at the edge of the park. Where I had spied on them before the murder. The fact that they put me there proved they knew about my hiding place, and they knew I had been watching all along.

And if they knew that, they might just know how to find me when I'm sleeping.

I couldn't take the risk, you see. I knew that another headless body was in the shack, and if I told the police, I would be a hero, just like my plan. But I also knew it would open *a can of worms*. I always liked that phrase. I can picture the worms wriggling as they spill out of an old tin can.

I knew several things.

I knew that if I said anything about the second body, the police would question me. If I told them what happened, they wouldn't believe me. It was a hard story to believe, even if an adult told it. But me, an eleven-year-old girl? They were never going to believe a story like that.

And then I thought, what if they thought I killed the jogger? It might be hard to believe a kid like me could kill a grown woman. And what did I do with the head? But I didn't want to risk it and spend the rest of my life in jail.

So I got up from the ground and looked around. Nobody was in the park.

And I went home.

Mama doesn't have to work her night job tonight, and I'm going to make her a special dinner in the microwave. These bean burritos she really likes. They'll be ready when she comes home.

I'll tell her that school was just fine, and everything's okay.

When they find that body, I'll act surprised and scared. I'll even cry because it will remind me of Charley. And no one knows the killers aren't still in the area, so I'll have to pretend I'm a little scared to be alone. But not scared enough so that Mama makes me have a babysitter again.

I solved Charley's murder. But I can't tell anyone. And I don't get to be a hero like I wanted. But they didn't kill me, at least. And I know they're gone.

I looked up *gulars* online, but I couldn't find anything about snake people.

I keep checking the news on my phone, for more bodies turning up without heads. But I don't think I'll hear about new cases anytime soon. Not around here, at least.

I never used to be scared of the dark. I'm brave. And I know they won't come back for me, as long as I don't tell. But I wonder if writing it down in my diary counts. I've been thinking of throwing this away or burning it. But as long as no one reads it, I should be okay.

I hope.

Sometimes the Good Witch Sings to Me

T HE ENTIRE RIDE HOME, after he buried the wicked witch, Jerry Cuttle kept asking himself, *How much longer can I do this?*

Sitting in his driveway, tired and dirty, he felt as if he couldn't move. As if he were completely paralyzed. But that didn't last long. The desire to be clean motivated him to get out of the car.

When he got inside, the phone rang. He stared at it, thinking about how badly he wanted to take a shower. The phone rang again.

He was so afraid it was the witch, calling him from the grave.

He didn't dare answer it.

Jerry stood frozen, staring at the phone. It didn't ring a third time.

I'm safe, he thought. *Thank you, Glinda.*

Then he went into the bathroom to wash off the dirt and blood.

* * *

As he stood under the hot water, Jerry Cuttle thought about the first time Glinda appeared to him. It was after his first suicide attempt. He had taken a bottle of pills and laid in the dark, waiting to sleep forever. And she appeared before him. All white and shiny. Just like in *The Wizard of Oz*, a movie he had loved since he was a child. She waved her magic wand over him and spoke to him in that high, child-like, sing-song voice:

"Wake up, Jerry. You can't die today."

He opened his eyes and looked at her. He wasn't an idiot. He knew that *The Wizard of Oz* wasn't real. That it was just a movie. And that the characters in it were just actors. Glinda was played by a woman named Billy Burke. She was either dead now or very old.

And yet, here she was, young again, in full Good Witch regalia, standing over him, telling him he couldn't die.

"I c-c-can't?" he asked, not believing his eyes. Surely this was a hallucination. And if he just closed his eyes again, he would fall into a deep sleep, and none of this would matter. Perhaps he was dreaming, even now, though he wished the dream didn't seem so real. Here was the same crappy old house, the same sick feeling in his stomach. Why couldn't he feel wonderful in his dream? Wonderful in death?

"No, silly. You can't die yet. You have so much to do."

This struck him as laughable. He had been a failure his whole life. What on earth, of any importance, could someone like him have to do? His job? It was a dead end, and no one would even notice his absence. His personal life? It was virtually non-existent at this point. All he did was work and come home. And wish he was dead.

"No," he said. "No point." The discomfort in his stomach was getting worse. He really didn't feel like talking. He just wanted to die in peace.

"Of course there's a point," Glinda persisted, refusing to let go. "I have great need of you."

"Need?"

He had needed so much in life. Money, love, respect. Things that always eluded him. Need? *He was made of need.*

"Yes, you must help me. I have a mission for you."

She leaned over him, looking into his eyes. "A wonderful mission. An adventure."

Then she pressed down on his stomach, and the pills all came up in a surge of vomit.

He sat up on the couch, coughing and wiping his mouth. She stood to the side, watching him with a slight smile.

"Now you can live," she said. "And help me get rid of the bad witches."

* * *

It hadn't been easy at first. He had never killed anyone before. And even though Glinda had tried to make it clear to him that he wasn't actually killing a person at all—that he was killing a creature of pure evil—there were certain barriers he had to overcome before he could accept his mission.

He searched the streets for old women who fit the bill. It was actually much easier than he thought. There was no shortage of vile old women, wandering around, glaring at passersby. Most of them were homeless. Glinda spoke to him and told him which ones were witches. Bad witches. So many of them were evil. It was almost unfathomable how they simply walked among us, performing their unholy rites, putting curses on innocent people who didn't stop to acknowledge them or give them a handout.

"That one," Glinda would whisper in his ear. "She needs killing."

* * *

After he showered and dressed, Jerry burned the clothes he had worn when he had killed the witch, in a metal garbage can in the back yard. Returning to the house, he heard the phone ringing again. It didn't scare him this time.

"Hello?" he asked. A part of him still expected to hear the old woman's voice on the other end, cursing him for his deed.

"Jerry?" a man's voice called out to him. "Is that you, bro?"

It was Henry. His brother. Somebody he hadn't heard from in years.

Jerry hesitated. There were old wounds between them that hadn't healed.

"Jerry? You still there?"

"I'm here."

"You still mad at me for taking off?" Henry asked. "You going to hang up on me?"

Jerry swallowed. Then, "I won't hang up."

"I'm sorry. I heard about Mom. I'm sorry you had to handle it alone."

"That was the idea, wasn't it? When you left?"

"I had a lot going on in my life. Bad stuff. I couldn't handle any more. The only recourse I had was to get away."

"Bad stuff?" The anger welled up inside him. "You think you were the only one dealing with bad stuff?"

"Some of us can handle it, Jerry. Others can't. I had to get away to stay sane."

Sane. Jerry thought of what he had been doing that morning and wondered what the word meant anymore. If he didn't have Glinda to guide him through the pain, he wouldn't know what to do anymore.

"My wife and kids leave me," Jerry said, "and I move back here. With her. And she's always dying, taking years to die. Always in pain. And you think you had it bad."

"It's over now," Henry said. "She's not in pain anymore."

Henry's words were insensitive, but true. But he hadn't earned the right to say them. He hadn't suffered through the final days. He had been a safe distance away.

"You don't have the right to talk about her," Jerry said. "You didn't have to deal with it all."

"Listen, I was going through some bad problems. Booze, drugs. You knew that. I had to clean up my act. Get my life in order again. There was no way I was going to do that and watch Mom disintegrate. It just wasn't possible."

Once again, what Henry said made sense. He had been struggling with his addictions all his life, since they were kids. As they got older, Henry seemed to be getting worse. Unable to hold down jobs for any length of time. Incapable of any lasting relationships. Even with his family.

But, Jerry thought, *what about* my *pain? What recourse did I have?* With Henry disappearing all the time, he had always felt the need to be the responsible one. The one who held everything together. He always hated Henry for that.

"Are you still there?"

"Yeah, I'm here," Jerry said, trying to keep any traces of anger out of his voice. For all his faults, Henry was still his brother. And he was weak. Jerry couldn't really hate him for that.

There was a silence. Jerry waited for his brother to continue the conversation, although he already knew what this was about. He refused to make it easy on Henry.

"Jerry?"

"I said I'm here, Henry. It's good to hear from you, after all these years. But let's get down to brass tacks. Why are you calling?"

"You're in the house all alone now. The house we grew up in."

Jerry didn't answer.

"Things are bad. I need someplace to stay. To get my head together. I need some kind of sanctuary."

"And now that Mom's gone, it's safe to come back home?"

"It's not like that, Jerry. I just need somewhere to get my head together."

"You said that already, Henry."

"I want to come home, Jerry. That used to be my house too. I want to be brothers again. I want to try to make things right between us."

I can't have someone else here now, Jerry thought. *Not with my mission. It's hard enough without someone watching my comings and goings.*

But a part of him wanted to recapture the past. The two brothers had been close once. So many years ago. And he really didn't want to continue with the mission anymore.

Standing there, the phone receiver to his ear, Jerry thought he saw Glinda in his peripheral vision, darting toward a shadowy corner. Waiting for him to finish the call.

"Jerry," Henry said, his breathing sounded labored. Like he was on the verge of tears. "Please. Give me another chance."

"Fuck off," Jerry said, and hung up the phone.

* * *

The first time Jerry killed a bad witch, it took days to get up the nerve.

The first thing he had decided was that he would not use a gun. Guns made him nervous. He had a big hunting knife. One of the few things his father had left him. When they were kids, he and Henry used to go hunting with their father. Back before he had a heart attack and died at the age of 45. He just went into the office one day, sat at his desk, and never got up again.

Their father was a strict man. Jerry and Henry hated going hunting, but their father would not hear any protests, and they knew better than to even try. One good thing about his death was that they didn't have to go hunting anymore.

Until now. Now, Jerry finally found a use for the old hunting knife.

He had never been in the military, but he had seen a lot of movies. Mostly bad B-movies that showed him how to grab someone from behind and slit their throats. In the movies there was lots of blood. So he knew what to expect. He grabbed the witch in a stinking alleyway, the one Glinda had picked out for his first kill, and slit her throat from ear to ear with the big hunting knife. She made an odd, gurgling noise and struggled at first, but it didn't last long. And suddenly, he had rid the world of some evil. The witch had been disguised as a pathetic homeless woman with hard eyes and no teeth. He had watched her for days before killing her, wheeling her cart full of garbage bags all around the city.

It had been fairly easy to kill her, and leave her body among the piles of trash and feces. It did not look like anyone had been in the alleyway for years.

It wasn't as easy to forget. He knew she was evil. Glinda reassured him he had done the right thing. But it didn't make living with it any easier. He had killed someone, even if she was a force of evil. He hated the bad witch for forcing him to do such a horrible thing.

He remembered asking Glinda, why couldn't he just throw water on them, like in the movie? Water disintegrated the Wicked Witch in the movie.

"This isn't a movie," Glinda told him. "You can't get rid of evil that easily in the real world."

Sometimes he woke from his sleep hearing that gurgling noise. The noise of someone drowning in their own blood.

* * *

After he had killed his seventh witch, Jerry tried to take his own life again.

He took the hunting knife he had used to cut witches' throats and put it up against his own throat, determined to press it as hard as he could and let all the life leak out of him. It was a very sharp blade; he made sure to sharpen it every day.

He gently pressed the blade against his throat, and was about to apply pressure, when Glinda appeared before him and touched his hand. She drew his hand and the blade away from his throat.

"No," she told him. "You can't do this. Not now. You have so much evil to get rid of. Please."

He looked into her face. She didn't look like she did in the movie just then. Her face was younger, more attractive. A beautiful face, that made him miss his estranged wife all the more. He hadn't even tried to pursue another relationship since she had left. He loved her so much; he couldn't even think of replacing her. Even now, he couldn't understand why she had just up and left him like that.

But here was Glinda, young and beautiful and here with him. She cared about him. She didn't want him to die.

She looked like a golden angel before him. He felt the urge to kiss her.

"Glinda, I can't do this anymore. It is not in me."

"Of course it isn't, sweet Jerry," she told him. "That's because you are *good*. If you enjoyed this, you would be as evil as they are. I am so lucky to have found someone as good as you to help me in this mission. You have been wonderful. The world is such a better place now, because of you."

"I love you, Glinda," he said softly.

"I know," she told him. "Your actions have shown you to be a warm, loving man, Jerry. Don't think I don't appreciate that."

His hand was down at his side. The knife was gone. He saw it on the other side of the room. On the dining table. He didn't have an urge to go get it and draw it across his throat anymore.

He leaned in to kiss her. But she was gone.

* * *

Somehow, he was able to function at his job. It wasn't something he had to think about too much. And if he was quiet, or distant, it made sense. His mother had died. He was separated from his wife. He had reasons to be distant.

Sometimes co-workers tried to seem sympathetic. They would invite him out for lunch or drinks. But he had always begged off. Nobody ever pursued it too much.

He kept working. Kept up appearances. There was no reason not to. Bills had to be paid. And it gave him something to do until the next mission.

* * *

"Jerry, please don't hang up."

Henry sounded like he was about to cry again. His breathing was very heavy. It was almost like an obscene phone call.

"I know I've been a fuck-up all my life," Henry said. "I know I've left you holding the bag all our lives. That I've been a disappointment to everyone. Especially you."

"No," Jerry said, trying to reassure his brother. But it didn't sound convincing.

"I really want to make it up to you. I want to show you it's never too late to change. I've been clean for three months now, and it's getting easier. I just need some place I can feel safe. That's all."

"It's not a good time, Henry," Jerry said. "I'm on the verge of getting back together with Celia. It's touch and go. I don't need the extra stress in my life right now."

"I grew up in that house too. I know you have room for me. I don't see why I can't come back there."

"Mom left the house to me. You were long gone. You don't have any rights to the house. And it's a real bad time, Henry. You've had places to stay all these years, can't you find somewhere else to get your head together? Can't you give me the space *I* need right now?"

"Please, Jerry. At least promise me you'll think about it."

"When things are better, I'll call you back. I promise. Give me a number where I can reach you."

"Really, Jerry? You promise?"

"Of course. When things are better here, I'll call you. Hell, if I get back together with Celia, I'll probably be going back to my own house. You can stay here then."

"You don't realize how important it is to me, to hear you say that."

"But you need to give me time, Henry. You need to make other arrangements for now. Until things are better for me. You owe me that much. After all these years."

"Sure, Jerry. I owe you that much. Thank you so much for reconsidering. Now let me give you my number here, okay?"

"Sure thing."

Henry gave him the phone number. Jerry did not write it down. He made no attempt to remember it. He knew he would never, ever call back.

"Got it," Jerry said.

"You don't realize how much this means to me, Jerry."

"I know. I've really got to go now, Henry. I'm expecting a call from Celia."

"I'll let you go, bro. I really hope you two can work it out. It must be killing you to be apart from your family like this."

Henry actually sounded as if he sympathized with his brother. Like he cared.

After all these years of nothing.

"Thanks a lot, Henry," Jerry said, sounding very sincere. "Really."

And he hung up the phone.

Then he threw the phone across the room.

* * *

The ninth time he killed a wicked witch, she scratched his face. Jerry was convinced that she had injected some kind of poison into him with her nails. He was sure that he would die. He even looked forward to it. For the release.

But he didn't die.

The next morning, he woke up alive and healthy. Like any other morning. He woke to the sound of gurgling, which faded out and was replaced with the buzz of the alarm clock.

He made excuses for the scratch on his face. It wasn't very deep, but it was ugly. He said his cat scratched him. He didn't have a cat, but nobody at work knew that.

In time, it would heal. And he would try very hard to forget about it. But he couldn't. He couldn't forget any of them. They were evil and had to die, but he never got used to it. And it never seemed easier.

He had read that serial killers find that killing gets easier as they continue doing it. But he wasn't a serial killer. He wasn't killing *people*.

He was killing evil monsters that fouled and corrupted the world.

That was why it never got easier. Because he didn't want to keep doing these things. He wanted it to stop. He wanted to go back to his life the way it was.

Jerry had not heard from Celia in months. And he made no attempt to contact her.

Despite the fact that he was ridding the world of evil, dirty creatures, Jerry felt dirty too. He took long showers every morning, and at night. To wash the dirt away. But he never felt clean.

He didn't want to get any of that dirt on Celia, or the kids.

* * *

The third time he tried to kill himself, the car was running in the garage, and the door was closed. He sat behind the steering wheel, with the windows open, and closed his eyes.

After a while, the engine shut off. Glinda was sitting beside him in the passenger's seat.

"You really have to stop trying to kill yourself," she said, in that childish, sing-song voice of hers.

"Glinda, I can't do it anymore. I'm not the right person for your mission. I'm weak. And all this is killing me."

"No," she said. "You are doing good. You are much stronger than you think you are. I know you feel sorry for the bad witches, but you mustn't. It is their bad magic that makes you feel this way. But you must resist it. They know you're on to them, and they're trying to stop you. If you give in to it, they will be safe again. And we're getting so close."

"So close?"

"To ridding the world of them. They are the cause of everything bad in the world, don't you see? All the violence and inhumanity. It comes from them. The bad witches have taken over the earth. And you are my knight, freeing the world from their reign. Don't you realize how important all this is? How much good you're doing?"

"When you say close. Do you mean this is almost over?"

"There will be a time when your work will be done," she said. "I promise you that. But don't give up. We can't let them win now. They thought they were invincible, but now you've scared them. Made them realize their days are numbered."

"It's so hard to go on, Glinda."

"I know. I'm sorry this is so hard for you, Jerry."

"So hard," he repeated.

"I love you, Jerry. I love your goodness."

She kissed him softly on the cheek.

"Poor, poor Jerry."

He stared out the windshield. He sat there for about five minutes before he realized she was gone.

He got out and closed the car door. Then he went back inside the house.

* * *

"Jerry, is that you?"

"Celia?"

"Jerry, I was worried. The kids have been asking about you. They want to know why you haven't come to see them in so long. I've been trying to call you. I know we're separated, Jerry, but I never said you couldn't see the kids."

"I can't, Celia. Not now."

"What is it, Jerry? I know you took it hard when your mother died. Are you okay?"

Hearing her voice. It created so many conflicts inside him. He wanted to beg her to take him back. He wanted to tell her never to call him again.

"Jerry?"

"I can't talk now, Celia. Tell the kids I miss them. But..."

"Jerry, they want to talk to you. I'll put them on the phone."

He heard her go away for a moment. He hung up the phone.

The phone rang soon after, but he didn't pick up.

* * *

"I'm so tired, Glinda," Jerry said. "I don't want to do this anymore."

He could see her hovering above his bed.

"Glinda, do you hear me? I can't keep doing this. It's killing me."

She stared down into his face. Her face was young and pretty. She looked sad.

"Glinda?"

She covered her eyes. She seemed to be crying. He could feel himself on the verge of tears too. He wiped at his eyes.

She was gone.

* * *

Someone was ringing the doorbell. It took all his effort to get out of bed and go to the door. All his energy went to the effort it took to go to work every day and appear normal. Once he got home, it all drained out of him.

"I'm coming," he said. As he moved toward the door, his movements seemed to rejuvenate him somewhat.

He opened the door. It was Henry.

He hadn't seen Henry in years, but it was obviously him. The once-young face was harder now. Weathered. But it was the same little boy he used to wrestle with. Who used to cry with him after their father would beat them both with his belt.

"Hello, Jerry."

"Henry," Jerry said. "I didn't realize you were coming. I thought you were far away."

"Not that far," Henry said. "I'm sorry, Jerry. I know I told you I'd wait. Give you time. But I haven't heard from you in so long. I thought maybe it would be better to just come in person, instead of calling you on the phone. Phone calls are kind of cowardly. I needed to see you face to face. To apologize like a man."

Jerry stood in the doorway. "It's been a long time, Henry. It's like seeing a ghost."

"I know. It's been way too long."

Jerry stared at him. Picturing the child's face. Superimposing it over the man's.

"Can I come inside?"

Jerry stayed where he was. "No, Henry."

"Why not? I want to talk to you. I need so badly to set things straight between us."

"Not yet, Henry. Not now."

"Please," Henry said, and tried to push past him. Jerry struck him in the head with his fist. Hard. He remembered his father hitting him that way once. And the memory was like a flash of fire inside him.

"Jerry!"

His brother looked startled, stumbling backwards.

"Not now, Henry."

"Why?" Henry said, clutching his forehead, his eyes puffy with tears.

"It's not a good time. It will never be a good time."

"Please. I came all this way to talk to you. To make things right."

"Things can never be right. It's too late, Henry. It's too late and you can't fix things now. You were a fuck-up your whole life and you'll always be a fuck-up. And I don't want to ever see you again."

"Please, Jerry. You don't know what you're saying. You've been under a lot of stress and you don't know what you're doing."

"Get out. Or I'll hit you again."

Henry hesitated. Then he turned and walked back toward the street. There was an old, beat-up car in front of the house. It looked as used up as Henry did.

Jerry stood in the doorway, watching him go. Thinking that at some point his brother would turn back and say something. One last parting thing. Something for Jerry to remember this moment by. But he didn't. Henry just got in his car, started it, and drove away.

Jerry stood like that, in the doorway looking out onto the street, for what seemed like a very long time. Then he went back inside.

* * *

He pulled the old homeless woman back into the alleyway and put the knife to her throat. She struggled and grunted and tried to scream, dropping her torn, worn valise—something she'd no doubt found in some dumpster and clung to herself as if she were a tourist and it was her only piece of luggage.

He pressed the knife hard against her flesh. It took only a moment. He was getting to be very efficient. Maybe it was getting easier after all.

She was gurgling as he let her fall to the ground.

Then he pressed the knife to his own throat. He didn't give himself a moment to think about it. He pulled the sharp blade against the flesh of his neck, and felt his blood come pouring out.

It's over now, he thought. *I don't have to do this anymore.*

He stumbled back against the alley wall and slid down to the ground, one of his legs on top of the dying witch, who was still twitching in a puddle of her blood.

He saw Glinda in front of him. Or at least he thought it was Glinda. He couldn't be sure anymore. She looked like Billy Burke in *The Wizard of Oz*. But that was just a movie.

"Poor, poor Jerry," she said, hovering over him.

"I can't do it anymore," he told her. His words sounded like gurgling.

Glinda looked very sad. She knelt before him and took his chin in her hand. She looked right into his eyes and started to sing to him. A lullaby. To put him to sleep.

Jerry closed his eyes. Her song was very sweet. And even though he knew he was going to die, her song consoled him.

And he knew that, despite his inability to go on, he had made the world a slightly better place.

Rotten

THE FIRST THING I noticed upon entering his hotel room was the smell. My hand went immediately to my face, without even a conscious thought. It was a strong, sickly sweet smell that he had tried to cover up with lots of cologne. Not that it helped much.

He was sitting in a chair in the middle of the room. The lights were off and the shades drawn. There was a single candle burning on a table, close enough to illuminate him slightly, to show me he was there. But not enough to show him clearly. He was wearing a bathrobe and pants, and a strange, veil-like thing over his face.

I had a hard time believing this was the same person I'd grown up with. Been kids with. The older brother I'd always idolized. There had to be some kind of mistake.

"Is that really you, Cliff?"

"Yeah, little brother, it's me. It's been a hell of a long time, hasn't it?"

It *was* still him, despite all the mystery. I would recognize that voice anywhere, even thought it was a bit weaker than I remembered. It was the same voice that I had heard on the phone earlier that day, when he had called me at work and insisted I come here alone. It's funny, I had always thought he would make a great radio announcer, but he had always been too restless, too indecisive to settle down someplace and get a real job. He had been traveling constantly all his adult life. I'd only seen him on rare occasions. Like this one.

"What's with the candle?"

"I picked up a bit of sensitivity to light during my travels. It's something I've gotten used to. I hope it's not too much of an inconvenience."

"I just wish I could see you, is all." I moved closer but he held up his hand.

"Please," he said. "That's close enough."

"What's wrong? And what's that horrible smell?"

"All in due time, brother. There's a seat right next to you. Why don't you take a load off?"

I have to admit, ever since our parents had passed away, I'd felt kind of adrift. Here was my only living relative, and I only saw him once in a blue moon. I guess down deep I kind of resented him for it. For not being more a part of my life. When we were kids I always looked up to Cliff. He was so big and strong and sure of himself. I don't remember too many people ever messing with old Cliff. I always felt better, knowing he was there for me.

Maybe in a weird way, I wanted some of that back.

My hand went to my face again, bringing me out of my reverie. The smell was that bad. I hated to complain about it, to make Cliff feel uncomfortable, but it was just too much. I tried to breathe through my mouth, and I could still smell it.

"Is there anything we can do about the smell in here?" I asked him.

"Not really. Sorry."

I tried to keep from gagging.

"You'll get used to it. It won't seem so bad in a few minutes."

I hoped he was right, but I didn't believe it.

"During my travels," he said, "I acquired a bit of an illness. I figure it got to me in one of the more tropical climates I visited. I have to admit, it was quite unexpected. I've always had one hell of a constitution. Even things like seasickness and Montezuma's Revenge never affected me. In fact, I hardly ever got sick at all, even when we were kids. Remember? Not really sick. Until now."

"What are you trying to say, Cliff? Are you dying?" I felt weird asking it, but I just had to know.

"It sure looks that way, Danny. Your big brother is in bad shape. Not much life left in me, I'm sorry to say."

"Are you sure I can't turn on a light, Cliff? I'd really like to see you clearly."

"Please don't," Cliff said, and his breathing was loud enough to hear for a moment. "I just couldn't handle that right now."

"So," I said. "You have no idea how this happened to you?"

"Well, I guess I have an idea," he said. "But it's not one that makes sense. It's just too far-fetched."

"You can tell me, Cliff," I said. And suddenly it was like we were kids again, and I was begging my big brother to let me in on a secret. "You can tell me anything. What do you think caused this to happen?"

"Voodoo," he said, "or something like it. Some kind of ancient magic that we can't even comprehend."

"Please," I said, trying to sound like I'd believe anything he told me without reservation. That he didn't sound crazy at all. "Tell me all about it."

Cliff shifted around in his seat. I could tell that one of his arms was pretty much useless. Even the light of the candle seemed to make him uncomfortable; he noticed my scrutiny, which made him fidget around even more.

"Have you ever killed a man, Danny?"

"No, of course not."

"Well I have. It happened in Morocco. A man accosted me and demanded my wallet. When I put up a struggle, he pulled a knife on me. It degenerated from a robbery to a matter of life and death in the space of seconds. Somehow, I turned the knife on him, and saved my own life. In the process, I took his."

He shifted around some more.

"I was arrested but it didn't take long for the police to determine what had happened and they let me go. It was self-defense, after all, and it seemed to me that they couldn't wait to get rid of me. But outside, a handful of people had gathered. I didn't know who they were, but somehow they knew me.

"A woman among them was their spokesperson. It turns out she was the sister of the man I'd killed. She kept shouting something at me I couldn't understand. She was clearly angry with me. I went inside and brought one of the cops back out who could translate for me. He told me she was putting a curse on me. She said that I was a rotten human being for killing her brother, and that, being rotten on the inside, it only made sense that I be rotten on the outside too."

I tried to find his eyes behind the veil, but they avoided me.

"I didn't think anything of it until a month later, when my condition started to manifest itself. It started as a terrible itching, and then the itch would go away and be replaced with numbness. I was in London at the time. No doctor I went to could explain what was happening to me. Some of the flesh on my arm had started to decay.

There was talk about removing the limb, but by then the decay had spread to other places, and it didn't seem to matter anymore. I was rotting, yet I was still alive. Nobody had ever seen anything like it.

"I came back to America to meet with some specialists, but I'm no closer to a cure. And right about now the only thing that makes sense to me is to go back to Morocco and find that woman, and beg her to remove the curse."

"So you really believe this is because of what she said to you?"

"What else can it be?" he said. "The doctors can't seem to find any answers. It's not that flesh-eating virus you keep hearing about on the news; it's not anything they can identify. But it's not contagious, at least. I know, I even spent some time in quarantine. The doctors tell me this is something totally outside of their knowledge. So I don't see that I have any other choice than to beg a stranger to remove a curse. That is, if I can ever even find her again."

"So you're going to go back there?"

"Yeah," Cliff said. "I'm leaving tomorrow morning. But I wanted to see you first. I figured I'd say goodbye before I left. We haven't seen each other in such a long time, and you're all the family I've got. Besides, I was in the city. I really had no excuse not to contact you. It's not like we hate each other, after all."

"No. But something still went wrong, didn't it?"

"I guess so," Cliff said. "But I can't for the life of me ever figure out what that was."

"I think it was this restlessness of yours, is all. It's not easy to keep up with you. Or to stay in touch in any kind of real sense. I think we simply drifted apart because of that."

"So you don't think it's a serious rift," Cliff said, "something that we can't fix?"

"No, of course not. I mean, obviously I'm concerned about your condition. But it really is good to see you again."

"Same here."

"You're sure the doctors can't do anything to help you?"

"I've been to the best. Spent a lot of the money I'd accumulated over the years," Cliff said, shifting around again. "No dice."

"And you really believe this is all because of some curse?"

"I've come to believe that there's nothing else that can explain it."

"Of course there is. It's some weird disease you caught somewhere that the doctors just don't know anything about yet. Something random and horrible that happened to you, but not because some woman wished it on you."

"Believe what you want. I just wanted to tell you the story. So you know why I'm leaving again."

"Do you really feel up to traveling right now?" I asked. "You don't look well."

"No kidding?" Cliff tried to laugh but it didn't sound right. "Look, at this point I don't have time to hesitate. Would you like to come with me?"

"I can't," I said. "I've a got a family, Cliff. Responsibilities. I can't just up and leave."

"I knew you'd say that. But I wanted to ask at least. It really is good to see you again, little brother. It's too bad we haven't had much time to talk since we grew up. I guess we really are strangers after all."

"No, Cliff," I said. "We're not strangers. We can't have changed that much since we were kids."

Cliff shook his head ruefully.

"What have you been running from all these years?" I asked, and immediately regretted putting it into words.

"I don't know," he said. "I like to think that I've been running *to* something. But I never did find it."

"Have you ever met anyone who you wanted to settle down with? Who you wanted to raise a family with?"

"Nope. That's not my bag, little brother. Never was. You and I could never agree on what we wanted out of life. Settling down, having the kind of life you do, it would never work for me. It would kill me."

"It's not as bad as all that."

"Just goes to show how different you and I really are," Cliff said, his voice taking on a distant quality. Then he seemed to become aware again. "How are the wife and kids, by the way?"

"Everyone's fine," I said. "I was wondering if you'd mention them."

"I've got a lot on my mind these days, Danny. I'm rotting to death, if you didn't remember."

"Sorry."

"It doesn't matter. Nothing matters anymore at this point."

"Don't say that."

"Aw, I'll say whatever I want," Cliff said, clearly irritable. "I get tired a lot more quickly these days. I really need to get some sleep. I hate to cut our little reunion short, but do you mind..."

"No problem," I said. "I'm really glad you called me and asked me to come. It's been such a long time."

"It's too bad something like this had to be what finally brought us back together."

I went to move closer to him; my instincts had taken over by then. My arms went out to hug him.

"No!" he shouted. I must have looked startled, because then he said, "I'm sorry. It's just that, like this, I can't stand to be touched."

I pulled back from him. "I understand."

"Listen, if you want, turn the lights on for a moment before you leave."

"Huh?"

"Turn the lights on. Take one last good look at me. Might as well."

I stood up and went to the wall switch. I could barely make it out in the dim candlelight. I turned on the overhead light and stared in the direction of the man in the chair, who had been bathed in shadows. Suddenly the shadows weren't there anymore.

Neither was Cliff. Well, not the Cliff I knew. He was barely recognizable in his current state, and *barely* is the key word here.

He flung the veil to the ground. "I don't need this anymore," he said. "Besides, it's so damn uncomfortable."

I nearly collapsed then. His face was a patchwork of pink and pale flesh that didn't adequately cover his skull. Sections of bone protruded here and there. His nose had disintegrated into pieces that didn't quite fit, and his lips were mostly gone. Only his eyes seemed intact, despite their squinting painfully in the artificial light.

His hands were sheathed in gloves, and I knew that, beneath the material, they were probably in even worse shape than his face.

"I didn't realize it was so far gone. Are you sure it's not leprosy?" I asked, staring at the wreck of a man before me who had once been my big brother. Knowing full well that I had no medical training and wouldn't be able to tell, for the life of me, what the telltale signs of leprosy were.

"No, it's not leprosy. I told you. It's something they can't diagnose. It's baffled a lot of doctors. I've done everything I could to reverse this condition, met with every specialist I could find, spent almost every penny I have, and it's all been useless."

"How long...?" I asked.

"Please, can you turn off the light again? It's hurting me."

"Okay." I hadn't moved. I was still by the wall, my hand still by the switch. Seeing him, I'd been frozen in horror. I wasn't even aware of the smell anymore.

I shut off the light.

"Thank you, Danny," Cliff said. "I thought you should at least see me clearly one last time. There was no way I could adequately explain how bad it was otherwise. It's been almost a year now. And I have to admit, at this stage, it's getting painful just to keep breathing."

He took a drink from a flask. I didn't know what it contained, but liquid morphine came to mind.

"It's traveled to just about every part of my body," he said. "And it's just going to get worse. Unless I do something. Unless I get that woman to take her curse off me."

"You really believe she's the cause of all this?"

"I do. Maybe I'm being a superstitious fool. But it's all I have to go on. I'm sorry about the circumstances, Danny. But I really had to see you again."

"I'm glad you did," I said, although, to be honest, I can't be sure I meant it. I certainly never wanted to see my brother like this.

"You've really got to leave now, Danny. I'm sorry, but I'm on the verge of

collapse here."

"Okay," I said, suddenly feeling shame wash over me for judging him so harshly over the years.

I left the way I had come, without another word. It was a little difficult finding the door in the dim light. I guess I was still in a state of shock. It took me a few minutes to catch my breath in the hallway outside his room. I could still see that tattered face of his in my mind's eye, as clear as my own hand in front of me.

* * *

I went back home, to Janeen and the kids, and tried to forget about what I'd seen, but it would take time. A lot of time.

"What's wrong?" Janeen asked me at the kitchen table. She could tell I was disturbed by something. She'd been trying to get me to talk about it ever since I got home, but I had trouble putting it into words.

"It's Cliff," I said. "I saw him today."

"Your brother?" she said. "That's wonderful news. Why didn't you tell me before? We haven't seen him in such a long time. Why didn't you bring him home with you? We could have had dinner together."

"He's sick," I said. "Really sick. I think he's dying."

My eyes started to well up with tears and she came over to me and put her arms around me.

"I think it's cancer," I said. I couldn't tell her what I'd seen. Not yet.

"I'm so sorry," she said. "I know how close you two were when you were kids."

We held each other close.

"Where are the boys?" I said. "Why aren't they down here for dinner?"

"I tried to tell you before," she said. "But you were clearly distressed. They've come home early from school with the chicken pox. But they're boys, they'll be okay. All kids go through it eventually. It's just been tough keeping them from scratching all the time."

* * *

I didn't sleep all night. I kept seeing that face every time I fell asleep.

I got up early and left before anyone else got up. I usually said goodbye to Janeen and the boys, but I had so much on my mind. Driving usually helped me to relax, and it was early enough so that the traffic wouldn't be very bad.

When I reached his hotel, I realized I'd intended to go there all along. I had to see Cliff again. Even though he'd become something out of a nightmare. He was still my brother.

"I'm here to see Cliff Carnes," I told the man at the front desk. "He's my brother."

"I'm so sorry. Mr. Carnes left a few hours ago. He had a very early flight."

I could tell from the man's reaction that he had *seen* my brother. Or at least smelled that awful smell.

"Are you Danny Barnes?"

I nodded.

"He left something here for you."

He handed me an envelope. It had my name on it. I didn't even recognize Cliff's handwriting at first. He hadn't written anything to me for over a decade. It was little more than a scrawl.

"I'm sorry that you missed him, sir."

"I am too," I said, and I went back to my car.

It took me awhile before I had the courage to open that envelope.

The letter had been written on a laptop and printed. I was afraid I wouldn't have been able to read it if it had been in the same handwriting that had been on the envelope.

Danny, I read to myself. *I'm so sorry you had to see me this way, but there was no other choice. I had to see you one last time before I went back. Just in case I don't succeed.*

There's one thing I couldn't bring myself to tell you in the hotel room. When that woman put the curse on me, it wasn't directed at me alone. She wished it on me and all my family. I know you'll think this is stupid, but I had to see you in person, to prove to myself that it wasn't true. You're all the family I have left, you know. I'm so glad that nothing has happened to you. I know this is probably proof that the woman's words had nothing to do with my condition. But at this point, I will do whatever I have to do to stop what is happening to me. I hope we'll meet again someday, and all this will be behind me. Love, Cliff.

She wished it on me and all my family, Cliff's note had read.

My first thought was for my sons. Danny Junior and little Anthony. Home with the chicken pox. *They* were Cliff's family too. The same blood that ran through our veins ran through theirs.

But there was no connection. There *couldn't* be. I was letting my imagination run away with me. Kids getting chicken pox was a completely normal thing.

And then I thought of Cliff's face again.

I had no idea how to reach him again to find out if he'd been able to accomplish anything in Morocco. He had been in such bad shape, I wondered if he'd even live long enough to get back there alive.

Sitting there in my car, I began to cry. It was the first time I had cried in years, and I couldn't control it at all.

I cried out for my brother, who I'd idolized while we were growing up. Who I'd so badly wanted to be like when we'd been kids.

And through the tears I realized, as I scratched my arms and bits of skin and blood speckled my pants...

I'd gotten my wish.

Venus

VENUS REMEMBERED A TIME *when he was tall and blond and sitting in the high wooden lifeguard's chair. The brisk scent of salt in the air, the constant white noise of the waves. He, waiting for someone to cry for help. The wave of a drowning hand. But none came. He got the worst sunburn he'd ever gotten in his life that summer.*

Willie and Eva were over at the game where you throw baseballs at arrangements of old-fashioned milk bottles when the carnival barker came over to them.

"You won," he said softly, close to Willie's ear.

"Huh?"

"Every night we have a random drawing," the barker said. He was about the same height as Willie, with a similar build, but his features were old and hardened. For some reason, he reminded Willie of his grandfather. His mother's father, who had died, back when Willie was small, of cancer.

A closer look told him that the man didn't really look like his grandfather at all.

"I don't remember buying a raffle ticket."

"You didn't," the barker said. "Every night we pick someone. Someone who came to see the sideshow. We pick them for a special attraction."

"What is it?"

"It's a secret. Only for you. You have to come and see."

Willie looked over at Eva. She smiled weakly.

"Can I bring my girl?"

"Of course," the barker said. "You two came in together. You can certainly bring her in. This is a special showing, just for the two of you."

"Can't you tell me any more?"

The guy turned then and started walking back toward the sideshow tent.

Willie looked at Eva. Then he threw the last baseball in his hand, knocking over a pile of bottles.

"We have ourselves a winner!" the short, muscular man behind the counter said. "Pick anything from the second row."

"You seem to be doing a lot of winning tonight!"

"What do you want, Eva?"

She pointed at the stuffed red devil. The guy brought it over and handed it to her.

Then they started walking in the direction the barker went.

* * *

They had been inside the big tent before. It wasn't much of a sideshow. A man covered in tattoos from head to feet. An obese woman who swallowed swords. A dwarf who spat fire. "Giant Carnivorous African Toads" in a cage, with a video showing one eating a rabbit. There was a sign that said *Do Not Put Hands In Cage*. The toads were big but looked lethargic, sitting in black, slimy-looking mud in cages that were clearly too small for them. They didn't move. It was hard to believe they could overpower anything.

It was a pretty ragtag bunch. Nothing all that shocking. Not like the old days when they called them freak shows. Willie had read about those things, and had always wanted to see the real thing. But that was an attraction relegated to the past.

The barker smiled, seeing them enter the dimly lit tent.

"You came," he said. "I knew you would."

"So what's this all about?" Willie asked.

"Nothing to it. Once a night we pick a customer for a special viewing. And tonight, you're it."

"A special viewing?"

"Something that's not for public consumption. Something that's too special and too rare for just any eyes. You and your lovely girlfriend have been chosen to see something few people have seen."

Willie looked at Eva. She cocked her head. She was as curious as he was.

"Follow me."

The barker took them through a space between tents. They saw the dwarf and the tattooed man playing cards on a bench. They looked up when Willie and Eva went by, but didn't say a word. Then they entered another, smaller tent. They could feel a breeze but it was pitch black inside.

And then the light clicked on overhead.

Stretched out on a king-sized mattress was a gigantic woman. Three times the size of the woman who had swallowed swords. Her body was hard to distinguish beneath all the rolls of fat. But they could see two things right off the bat. She was naked. And there was a sign around her neck that said *Touch Me.*

"Go ahead," the barker said. "She won't bite. Her name is Venus."

Willie looked at Eva. They weren't sure what to do.

"Look, I'll leave you alone with her. Just, please, no pictures. I know it's tempting, but I want to keep this one special. One of a kind. But do whatever you like to her. She can't complain. And she wrote that sign herself, so you know she's giving you permission."

"I don't get it," Willie said.

"There's nothing to get, son. It's all clear as crystal."

And then the man left the tent.

Willie looked around. The tent was made of canvas, overlapping sheets of red and green. He did not see any holes or anywhere that people could peek in at them. The tent was closed up tight. There was one single, bare bulb hanging above their heads.

"I bet there are cameras somewhere," he said. "They're watching everything we do."

Willie's eyes went back to the sign around the giant woman's neck. At least, he *assumed* she had a neck. He couldn't be sure.

"Let's get out of here," he said.

"No," Eva said. She wasn't afraid of anything, and she wasn't about to change now. "This is a special attraction just for us. I want to look at her."

She moved around the mattress, looking at the woman's huge, dimpled arms, her thick, tree-trunk legs. Her humungous breasts that hung to either side of her. Eva stopped and looked between her legs. But whatever was there was obscured from view by her mammoth thighs.

"What's that smell?" Eva asked.

"Smells like flowers, I think. Really nice ones," Willie said. Then he pointed. "There are flowers in her hair."

In fact, it looked like her hair was made of flowers. A whole multi-colored bouquet of them.

"I think she's dead," Eva said.

Flies buzzed around one of the woman's breasts.

"What kind of thing is this to show two kids?" Willie asked.

"I don't know," Eva told him. "This is fucked up."

"Maybe we should leave."

Willie looked at the woman's face. Her eyes were closed, her mouth expressionless. The sign around her neck:

Touch Me.

And he reached forward and touched one of her breasts. Fondled the nipple. It didn't feel exactly like skin. It kind of felt like flower petals. Soft, but almost waxy between his fingers.

Eva buried her hand between the woman's legs, feeling around amidst the fat.

"What are you doing?" Willie asked.

"What do you think I'm doing? I'm trying to see if she has a pussy," Eva said. "I'm doing what the sign says."

"You're going to get us in trouble," Willie said. "I just know it."

Eva pulled her hand back. She wasn't sure if she'd touched anything like a vagina. It all just felt like more fat.

The woman's eyes opened then.

"She's alive," Willie said.

Her face was expressionless.

The smell of flowers increased, filling the air. And then the woman opened her mouth.

Willie was closest to the mouth, and he smelled it stronger than Eva did. It was the most wonderful thing he'd ever smelled before, and it rose in waves over him, making him want to move closer to her.

"What are you going to do, Willie? Are you going to kiss her?"

* * *

Venus remembered being young and running along the beach in a bikini, without a care in the world. She was in love for the first time. Really in love. And he was running beside her, tall and muscular, with close-cropped hair and a snake tattoo on his left arm. He was completely devoted to her, and that made her feel wonderful.

The waves roared as they came ashore.

* * *

The woman looked pale and a bit greenish in the light of the bare bulb.

Eva watched as Willie got closer to the woman's head, and put his mouth close to hers. He *was* going to kiss her.

"Give her some tongue," Eva said. She was grinning now. This was starting to become fun.

She dug around in her purse and pulled out her cell phone. She stood back and took a picture of Willie kissing the woman's lips. The barker had said no pictures, but he wasn't here now, and how would he know? She could not think of one person who wouldn't use their phone to take a picture in this situation.

She thought Willie would complain. He tended to be a bit uptight, too much of a rule-follower, and it annoyed her sometimes. But he didn't even seem to notice her now.

When Willie's done, I'll go over near her head and take a selfie, she thought.

The mouth opened wider. There weren't any teeth that Eva could see.

Willie pushed his entire face into the mouth, and kept pushing.

"What the hell are you doing?" Eva asked.

He said something, but it was muffled. She thought he had said, "This is incredible."

* * *

Willie had never smelled anything so wonderful in his life and he wanted to be closer to it, he wanted to smell it even stronger. It was something beyond sweetness, something beyond hunger or desire. It was instinctual. He wanted to submerge his whole body in the smell.

And the deeper he pushed himself, the more it bathed all of his senses, grabbing him like a drug, bringing him into a pulsing nova of ecstasy.

When he pressed his face into the mouth as it grew wider, he felt her tongue upon his flesh, sticky and wet, attaching itself to him. It felt like it was pulling him in. He did not resist. The more he succumbed to the feeling, the more intense it was. The more he wanted it.

Needed it.

* * *

Eva watched in horror as Willie's entire head disappeared into the mouth of the humungous woman.

"What are you doing?" she shouted as she ran over to him. Now his neck and shoulders were inside the mouth, and he was wiggling in further.

She grabbed his hips and tried to pull him out. She couldn't tell if he was going in voluntarily or not, but this had to stop.

He pushed her away with his lower body, kicked at her, and climbed in deeper.

The woman's head was totally twisted out of shape, and there was a huge bulge in her neck region where Willie was moving inside her.

Eventually, his entire body was inside, his legs kicking Eva away.

"Willie!" she shouted. Her attempts to pull him out had been useless. There was no stopping him. And the woman was not going to let go.

Eva stood there staring as the huge lump that was Willie moved toward the woman's stomach, and then the shape became more indistinct. Like he'd fallen into a well in the center of her.

She stared into the woman's open eyes. "Give him back!" she shouted. "Spit him back out."

But the eyes just stared up at her. Glassy and unmoving. Not quite alive at all.

"Oh my God," Eva said, looking around the otherwise bare room. *I've got to find that barker,* she thought. *He's got to help me get Willie out of there.*

But before she could leave the tent, Eva was overcome by the strong scent of flowers, and something more. Something that stirred her hunger and her emotions, making them cloud her thoughts. The scent grew stronger still.

The mouth opened again.

There was something inside of it. A tongue made of rose petals.

Eva put her head close, breathing in the rush of scents, focusing only on the beautiful tongue. She had never wanted anything so desperately before in her life.

* * *

Venus was on the Ferris wheel. He was holding Eva close, kissing her. He finally got up the nerve to squeeze her breast and she didn't push him away. Instead, she leaned in and kissed him deeper. Coming to the carnival was turning out to be a great idea. They had been friends for a long time, but he had always hoped for something more. The fact that she appeared to feel the same filled him with joy.

Her hands tugged at his pants. They were at the top of the wheel and stopped. He had no idea how long they'd be at the top, waiting for the wheel to turn. But he hoped it would last forever.

He felt a mixture of desire and fear as he felt her mouth on him.

* * *

Eva saw a glowing green tunnel before her. It smelled wonderful, and she found that she was incredibly hungry. She knew that if she just got in a little deeper, she'd find something wonderful to eat.

She reached her arms as far as they would go before her, and wriggled her body forward. Slowly, she moved along the tunnel, getting closer to whatever was creating the intoxicating smell.

Sliding further, she could feel her shoes fall off as she pulled her legs all the way in and pushed forward on her knees. It gave her just the momentum she needed.

* * *

The barker checked his watch and decided enough time had passed. He went back to the tent and cautiously peeked inside. No sign of either one of the kids. But there were two large lumps in Venus's belly that reminded him of an anaconda devouring an antelope.

He went outside again and found the garden hose. He twisted the faucet and went back in, spraying Venus's body. He moved the hose up and down, making sure he soaked her well. The moisture helped with her digestion.

Then he went outside and shut off the hose.

When he came back in, the lumps were smaller, but it would take most of the night for them to vanish completely.

He picked up the small purse and the stuffed red devil that had fallen to the ground. Then he saw the pair of woman's shoes. When he reached down for them, he saw the cell phone. There was a picture on it. Of the boy putting his face inside Venus's mouth. He had told them no pictures! He put the phone in his front pocket.

"Good night," he said softly, as he switched off the bulb above her bed.

He closed the canvas flap behind him and went to help his crew close down the carnival.

* * *

Venus was seventeen years old, pretty and petite. She watched in horror as Willie climbed inside the strange obese woman in the tent. She tried to pull him out, but he kept pushing her away.

She watched as he disappeared inside, determined to go outside and scream for help. But something stopped her. A wonderful scent that filled the tent. That pulled her closer to the woman stretched out on the bed.

Venus looked down at herself with a young girl's eyes and thought she was the most beautiful thing she had ever seen.

Still Life with Soul Juice

CARLOS SCRATCHED THE BITE on the inside of his arm. He'd been getting a lot of them lately.

"Another one?" Misty asked.

"Yeah," he said. He scratched it so hard that his nails drew blood. "Fucking bugs."

"I don't have any bites on me," she said. "Maybe they just like you."

"I guess I'm just too fucking sweet to resist," he said. "That's why *you're* here, right?"

She didn't say anything. She just looked at the painting he was working on. A great swirl of reds and blacks so far. He kept stopping to scratch his bites.

"I never see the fucking things," he said. "Do you?"

"I see the roaches well enough," she said. "But I don't think it's them. Roaches don't bite, do they?"

"I don't think so," Carlos said. "Maybe we just have really hungry ones."

"I guess they took a look in the fridge," she said, then walked away, went into the other room.

He scratched at his arm and some pus mixed with blood ran down his elbow. "Shit!" he said. "Where the hell did you go?"

Misty came back in with some mercurochrome. "Maybe this will help."

"It couldn't fucking hurt. I'm bleeding here."

"Poor baby," she said, and poured some of the liquid on a piece of gauze. "Where's the cut, loverboy?"

He showed her his arm, and she started cleaning the wound.

"You're fucking Florence Nightingale," he said as she worked.

"*I am not!*" she said. "I never touched the lady."

"Yeah, yeah, real funny," he said, sounding annoyed.

"I just realized, I'm here because you have such a great sense of humor," she said, and stepped back. The gauze was stained with blood. "Maybe you should put a band-aid on the damn thing."

"Where do I start? They're on my back, down my arms. I look like a fucking *junkie* with all these marks all over me."

"I guess you wouldn't consider going to the doctor."

"Why the fuck would I? I know what it is. Some kind of fucking bug bites. Why should I pay some doctor to tell me the same exact thing? Or maybe he'll look at them and really think I am some kind of addict. I don't need that shit."

"But they look like they're getting worse," she said, trying to sound concerned. It was getting harder all the time.

"Don't you think I *know* that?" he asked her. "Don't you think it's fucking obvious to me?"

"You should get one of those bug bombs or something. Maybe call an exterminator."

"Fuck that. I have a painting to finish. All that can wait for now."

"You're in one of your moods."

"Moods? I'm *creating* something here. How is that a fucking mood? I need some peace and quiet is what I fucking need. If you can't be quiet and stay out of my way, then I need you go away for a while."

"Yeah, yeah."

"Just go take a hike, okay? This isn't a spectator sport."

"Okay," she said, and went to get her coat. She came back to give him a kiss. Not because she really wanted to, but because he'd go ballistic if she didn't, and she just wanted to get out of this place with as little hassle as possible.

"I'll come back later."

"Do what you want," he said, stepping back and looking at the canvas. Trying to get back into the groove, trying to decide what he was going to do next.

"Sure," she said, and left. Out in the hallway, she really wondered if she was ever going to come back to this dingy place.

* * *

Blood dripped from his arm as he painted, but Carlos was oblivious. Before him on the canvas was a gigantic vagina, open with the crown of a baby's head beginning to emerge. The source of life. Streaked with red and black.

And then, it began to change. To become something less distinct and more primal. He was entering a fever-like state at this point, and was getting lost in his art.

He stood back. It was the most beautiful thing he had ever seen. But it was far from done. It needed more color.

He went searching for more paints.

* * *

Midway through the painting, Carlos passed out. He woke up to find himself on the carpet, paint spatters on his clothes, and some kind of creature weighing heavily on his chest. It had large red insect eyes and a spear-like snout. His hands reached out and touched it, and it felt like a mouse's body did—a thin, furry layer of skin stretched tightly over muscles and bones. Although in this case, he wasn't exactly sure what he felt beneath the skin (did insects have bones?).

His first instinct was to scream. Whatever was on top of him was wrapping its thin, spindly legs around him and he could tell it was some kind of giant bug, about the size of a large dog. Because of the snout, his first thought was it was some kind of giant mosquito, except it didn't have any wings.

"Don't struggle," the thing said softly, near his ear. He couldn't see a mouth. "Don't move a muscle."

"What are you?" Carlos forced himself to ask. "What do you want from me?"

"Soul juice," the thing said. "That's what I want."

He knew then that this was the thing that was leaving the puncture marks on his body, that it must have been feeding on his blood as he slept. He was amazed that it had finally revealed itself.

"Blood," he said. "You drink my blood."

"No," the thing said. "Your soul juice. I've only taken a little at a time, enough to sussstain me, but I'm ssso very hungry. I need more."

"You're going to kill me."

"No. We can help each other, you and I. You will feed me and I will give back to you. I will give you what you need to create."

"Give back to me?"

"Yes," the thing said. "You provide me with food. I provide you with a fire in your belly. A desire to create your beautiful paintings."

"Food? What kind of food?"

"You will know when the time comes," the thing said. "But keep in mind. If you do not feed me with others. Then I'll have to take my nourishment from you."

It released some kind of vapor then, which smelled awful and which sent him drifting off to sleep.

* * *

Carlos woke up again, and saw that Misty was back. He was stretched out on the floor, and she was in the bed, sleeping. She hadn't even tried to wake him up and get him into bed with her.

Then again, he was sure she was cheating on him with some other guy. Why else would she come back late all the time? Where was she going?

He sat up and looked under the bed. The beast was under there. Poking its elongated snout at him. He could see it wriggling there, in the shadows, and he wondered how long it had been here, in this apartment. He wondered how many times it had been under the bed when he slept, when he and Misty made love.

The thoughts filled him with revulsion.

The thing looked at him with its bulging, segmented eyes and moved forward toward him. Its thin legs softly clattering on the floor. Not enough noise to wake her, but enough to make him sit up and consider running away from this place, never to come back.

"Now," it said in his brain. "No time like the present."

And it climbed up the side of the bed, pulling itself up the length of the sheets hanging over the side, and it clambered toward her sleeping form. It crawled on top of her and hugged her with its legs.

"Wha-" Misty said, and then began to struggle. He could hear the creature in his head saying, "Help me, you have to help me," over and over. And just to shut it up he grabbed a hammer off a table behind the canvas, and he went over to the bed to hold her down. She struggled, calling out his name.

"Keep her still," the thing pleaded.

Carlos hit her in the side of the head with the hammer.

Once.

Twice.

By now, the creature had pulled the sheets away from her. She always slept nude. And it struggled a bit as it pushed her over onto her back.

She was still conscious, but clearly dazed by the hammer blows. Blood trickled down her neck and onto the cloth, making red Rorschach blotches.

He'd hit her harder than he meant to. Blood and some brain matter stained his naked chest. Carlos dropped the hammer and held her shoulders down.

The thing scuttled down and brandished its sword-like proboscis. It reared back and then plunged its nose into her stomach. Into her belly button. Ramming its nose deeper and deeper. Misty groaned in pain, and thrashed about weakly.

Then the thing lifted its head, its nose ripping her flesh, opening her up like a piñata. But instead of candy spilling onto the ground, her internal organs bulged out of the long, deep wound. The creature thrust its razor-sharp nose into her again, tearing through still more tissue. Misty struggled and Carlos held her tight, although, by this point, she wasn't putting up much of a fight. Her eyes were wide and staring up at the ceiling as the thing eviscerated her at the foot of the bed. She was gurgling in the back of her throat, trying to scream.

"Why don't you just put her to sleep, like you did me?" Carlos asked.

"Because it tastes so much better when you humans are awake and trying to fight back," the thing replied. "I put you to sleep because I wasn't sure if I could overpower you. But now, with your help, I subdued *her* easily."

She started to spasm, and he lifted the hammer again and smashed in her cheekbone, closing one of her eyes harshly. Then the loss of blood took its toll and she drifted away. The separation of the soul and the body.

"No!" the thing cried out in his head. "We mustn't let the soul get away."

A long tongue jutted from the tip of the pointed nose now, lapping up blood, licking the red off of exposed organs.

"So you do feed on blood," Carlos said, stepping away from the bed.

"No," the thing told him. "Not blood. What's *in* the blood. What's still leaking from her. *Soul juice.*"

He felt it nudge him in his mind, and he felt himself moving toward her, climbing onto the bed, imitating the creature's actions. He reached in and pulled out one of her kidneys and began to lick it clean, tasting the coppery taste of blood at first, and then something else. Something tangy he couldn't quite name. And he knew that the only reason he could taste it, that he was aware of it, was because the creature had done something to his mind to make it more aware.

"Go to sleep now," the thing told him, as Carlos smelled the rank vapor again. "Let her essence sink into you. And I will clean all this up."

Carlos stretched out on the bed beside her mutilated body, lying across a giant blood stain that grew larger and larger. He could feel the wetness beneath him on the sheets, and hear the slurping sounds of the giant insect-thing that was still licking up as much of her soul as it could.

"When you wake, you will be full of the desire to paint," the creature told him. "You will be caught up in a frenzy of creativity, and you will let it guide you. But until then, close your eyes."

It spoke in his mind with the voice of a hypnotist, and he had no desire to resist.

* * *

Carlos woke up on the floor, achy and covered in paint. He rose to his feet and stumbled to the bathroom. He was naked and multi-colored. His head was throbbing. He took a couple of Percocets and washed his face. The paint on his body had already dried.

He went back out into the main room of the apartment, which he'd stripped of furniture long ago and filled with drop cloths and canvases. And the painting awaited him. He didn't remember making it, but it was clearly his style. And something extra.

Something amazing. It was the most beautiful thing he had ever seen.

A bright green vagina, the crowning head aglow, a thousand rays of color to greet its arrival into the world. He knew its name immediately.

The Birth of Birth.

* * *

After he got used to the painting enough so that he could finally pull his eyes away, Carlos looked around the room. No sign of Misty. The thing that had killed her had told him the truth—it got rid of the body. There were big splotches of dried blood on the sheets, but he'd get rid of those.

Even the hammer he'd used to smash in her face was licked clean of blood.

* * *

"It's the most incredible thing you've ever done," his agent, Jaze, said, standing in front of the painting, taking it all in. "I'm sure we can sell this one quickly."

"I almost hate to see it go," Carlos said.

Sun was coming in from the room's lone window, illuminating the colors. It looked like a rainbow had exploded and thrown its guts against the canvas.

"Let me make some calls," Jaze said. "You got any more like this one inside you?"

"I hope so," Carlos said.

* * *

Carlos woke to the sound of feet running across the ceiling.

He opened his eyes slowly. The thing was watching him and crawled down the wall to get a closer look.

Carlos sat up. "What are you anyway?" he asked.

It was in the corner of the room, staring up at him. At first, he wondered if it was the same one he spoke to before. It didn't say a word. Didn't talk in his mind.

"I am your muse," it said eventually.

"Yes," he said, relieved there weren't more than one of these things.

"You like the painting then? The one you made with soul juice?"

Carlos scratched his arm. The puncture wounds on his body were healing now. "Yes. It is beautiful."

"You'd like to make more like that?"

Carlos nodded.

"Then I will inspire you."

* * *

"You Carlos?"

A man was sitting on the front steps of his building with a little kid. Carlos had just come back from the grocery store and was carrying two bags.

"Yeah."

"I'm Frank," the man said, standing up. "Is Misty around?"

"She's out right now. Can I give her a message?"

"This is Frank Junior," the man said. "He's her son."

Carlos looked down at the boy who was wearing a black T-shirt and jeans, just like his father.

"Yeah?"

"I need to leave town for the weekend. I was hoping his mother could watch the kid for me."

Carlos had heard Misty mention her son a few times, but he never knew where the kid lived, how often she saw him, or why he wasn't with her. He never asked. He figured it must have been painful stuff if she never talked about it. She talked about everything else.

This kid. He didn't know a thing about him. And nothing about his father.

"Is she expecting you?" Carlos asked.

"Fuck no," Frank said. "Something just came up all of a sudden like. You know how it is."

"Yeah."

"So can the kid stay here or not? She hasn't seen him in a long time. I think she might be happy to spend some time with him."

Carlos nodded. "Yeah, I'm sure you're right."

"I've got to go," Frank said. He had short hair and his eyebrows were shaved off. He looked like he worked out a lot.

"Look, I really don't have time to babysit."

Frank got really close to him. "I know she lives here. And you don't have a choice. I gotta go, and she's the only one who can watch Frank Junior right now. He's her kid after all. Let her pretend to be a mother for once in her life."

Then Frank was going across the street to his car.

Carlos stood on the steps, watching the man drive away.

He looked down at the boy.

"Well, I guess you're staying here for a few days. You hungry, Frank?"

Frank Junior nodded his head.

"Let's go inside and see what we've got to eat."

* * *

Something was scuffling in the closet.

"What's that?" Frank Junior said, jumping at the sudden noise.

"The pipes," Carlos said, making a ham sandwich. "You want cheese on that?"

"Sure."

Carlos didn't have the heart to tell the kid his mother wasn't coming back. But this whole situation put him in a bind. There was no way he would be able to paint with a kid around. And what about the thing that climbed the walls?

"When's Mommy coming back?"

Carlos bit his lip and dabbed mayonnaise on the sandwich.

"Eat up, kid. You're going to have a long wait."

* * *

Carlos was sleeping on the floor when he woke up. The kid had been on the bed, but he wasn't there now. Maybe he went to the kitchen for a midnight snack.

He got up and checked the place, but no sign of Frank Junior.

Maybe he ran away.

Carlos heard the scuffling again and turned on a light. He went to the closet and opened the door.

The thing was holding onto the clothes hanging in the closet, its long sharp proboscis jammed down Junior's throat. The kid was sitting on the floor, looking up, except his eyes were closed. He looked like he was still sleeping.

"No," Carlos said. "Leave the kid alone."

"But his soul juice is so pure," the thing said in his head. "So sweet. I've never tasted anything like this before."

"Don't kill him."

"I don't want this to ever end. Leave him with me. Tell his father he ran away. His mother took him away."

"I can't do that. Don't make me do that."

He heard the creature moaning with delight in his head. He had no idea how to pull the kid out of there. The thing's nose was down his throat, making the boy look like he was being impaled. He was afraid if he moved the kid, he risked hurting him.

Instead, he stepped back and closed the closet. He shut off the light.

* * *

He woke with a start to someone tugging his arm.

"I'm thirsty," Frank Junior said. "My stomach hurts."

Carlos got up and poured him some orange juice. It was only five a.m.

The kid drank it down fast. Carlos watched him, looking for scars, scratches, any sign of harm. But he didn't see any. Frank Junior was wearing striped pajamas and tiger slippers.

"You want more?"

"Yes, please. I'm so thirsty."

Carlos couldn't shake the image he'd seen in the closet.

Frank went back to bed, curling into a ball beneath the sheets.

There was a drawing on the floor near the bed. Carlos picked it up. It was rough, but very good for a kid.

* * *

"What's with the kid?" Jaze asked, looking around the room at the finished paintings.

"He's Misty's," Carlos said. "This is the first time I've seen him."

"That's weird, I didn't know Misty had a son. Can I take these three? I know exactly where to bring them. I don't expect they'll take long to sell."

"Yeah, business has been good, hasn't it?"

"I'll say."

Frank Junior sat at the small kitchen table, watching them. Not saying a word.

* * *

Carlos woke and got up off the floor. On the bed, the insect thing was on top of Frank Junior. They were struggling. It was probably smothering him, with its needle nose buried in his flesh.

"Will you let me have him?" it said inside his head.

"I don't know."

"I gave you an alibi," it said. "I can end this tonight."

"He's just a kid," Carlos said softly.

"His soul is so sweet. I can't ration it out anymore."

"Give me one more day," Carlos said. "I don't know if I can go through with this."

"You wouldn't reveal me, would you?" it asked. "You wouldn't betray my trust?"

"No," Carlos said. "But give me another day to come to terms with this."

"I can do that."

The creature, like something out of a nightmare, moved away from the boy and slid off the bed. It went back to the closet, and closed the door behind it.

Carlos stared at the door for a long time before he went back to sleep.

* * *

They were in the park, eating ice cream cones.

"What's the thing that lives in the closet?" Frank Junior asked, staring up at him.

"What are you talking about?" Carlos said, trying to be gentle. He followed it with a little laugh.

"The monster," the kid said. "In your apartment."

"There's no monster," Carlos said. "You've got some imagination."

"Look," Frank said, pulling a folded-up paper out of his pocket and handing it to Carlos. "I drew a picture of it."

Carlos unfolded the paper and looked at the drawing. It was fairly accurate.

"That's a scary one," Carlos said. "You say you saw this in my place? In the closet?"

The boy nodded. The look on his face was confused.

"I've never seen it there," Carlos said. "He must be a good hider."

He handed the drawing back. The boy folded it and put it back in his pocket.

"When's my mommy coming back?"

* * *

Carlos woke to a sharp pain in his head. He opened his eyes just in time to see the hammer come down again and hit him in the face. He shouted and jumped back, putting his hands out, pushing Frank Junior away.

The boy stood there in the darkened room, holding the hammer. There was some moonlight from the room's only window. Just enough to make him out.

"What are you doing?"

"You have to be still," the boy said. "So it can drink from you."

"Put down the hammer, Frank."

"My mommy is never coming back," the kid said.

He raised the hammer again, but Carlos grabbed his wrist and shook it loose. The hammer clattered to the floor.

"You weren't strong enough," the thing on the ceiling said.

Carlos looked up. Its nose pointed at him.

"Why?" Carlos said. "I was going to go along with your plan."

"No," it said. "You were having second thoughts. So I decided to be the boy's inspiration instead. Have you seen his drawings? He'll grow up to be as good as you. Maybe even better."

"He's just a boy," Carlos said. "What will he tell his father when he comes back? That he has a new pet that he wants to bring home? A giant bug that drinks souls? You can be one big happy family?"

"I don't need you any longer," the thing said, and ran down the side wall.

"You said the boy's soul was too sweet to ration," Carlos said. "You said you couldn't resist any longer."

"I can ration it out a long time," the thing said as it moved toward the bed. "And he makes new soul juice. He's young and he can replace it as fast as I drink it. I don't have to be hungry anymore."

"And what about me? Are you going to feed off me like you did Misty?"

"I don't need you any longer," the thing said again.

Frank Junior was looking around on the floor and found the hammer again. He ran and struck Carlos in the side of the throat, trying to reach his face.

"Stop it," he said to the boy. "Stop it."

"Hit him," the creature said in his mind. In both of their minds. "Make him stop moving so I can feed. So *we* can feed."

Carlos wrenched the hammer away and hit Frank Junior with it. He did it without thinking, just to get the kid to move away from him, and he must have hit him harder than he meant to, because the boy dropped to the ground and didn't move. Blood began to pool around the kid's head.

He couldn't tell if Frank Junior was dead or just hurt.

He turned on the light and the thing ran under the bed.

"Come out of there," Carlos said, running toward the bed, turning it over. As the creature tried to get away, he struck it with the hammer, over and over, pulping its legs, pounding through its thin furry skin and crushing the bones beneath. Or whatever the thing had instead of bones. He could hear it crying out in his head.

He caught a whiff of the strange-smelling vapor that had previously put him to sleep, and he held his breath.

It tried to spear him with its nose, but he struck that with the hammer again. He put his knee on the nose, even though it cut into his leg, and he hammered the proboscis over and over until it separated from the head. And then he pounded the head until it stopped moving. Until the thin flesh of its body stopped moving with its breaths.

Its blood covered his chest, his face. He licked his lips, and it was the sweetest thing he'd ever tasted. Before he realized what he was doing, he buried his head in one of the creature's open wounds, sucking furiously at the nectar within.

When he was done, Carlos stood up and moved away from the thing, wiping his mouth with the back of his hand. He stared from it to the boy.

Neither moved.

Carlos reached over and turned off the lights.

* * *

Carlos was sitting on the steps in front of his building when Frank's father came back. He parked his car in front of the building and walked over.

"I'm here to pick up Frank Junior," the man said. "Tell him I'm here."

"You just missed him," Carlos said. "I'm really sorry."

"What the fuck are you talking about?"

Carlos could see the veins in the man's neck.

"They left. Misty took the boy and they went away. They were gone when I woke up this morning. They didn't even leave a note."

"She wouldn't dare," the man said. "She knows I'd hunt her down."

"I don't know what to say," Carlos said. "I'm as surprised as you are. Misty and I had been talking about getting married. I thought she was the one."

"You're not in on this?"

"I think she was afraid I'd tell you where she went," Carlos said. "She didn't tell me a thing about this."

"That bitch," Frank said. "That's what I get for trusting a former junkie. I figured I'd give her a chance to prove herself. Prove she could be a real mother again. But I should have expected this. Well, I'll make sure she doesn't get far. I know guys on the force. They'll find her."

Carlos was amazed how easily the man accepted his story. He hadn't even demanded to see the apartment. Not that it would have helped much if Misty and the kid were gone.

"You hear from her, you call me," Frank said, handing him a card. Some kind of carpentry business. "I'll make sure it's worth your while."

"Sure," Carlos said. "I can't believe she just left like that in the middle of the night. I didn't see this coming."

Frank Senior went back to his car. He pounded on the hood a few times before getting inside.

Carlos watched him drive away.

He stood up and went back inside.

He suddenly had the most wonderful idea for a painting.

A Full Canteen

THERE WAS STILL DRIED blood on Jeb's shirt as they rode. The sun reflected off the narrow stream flowing down the length of the valley. On both sides, there were mountains high enough to almost blot out the sun, but not quite. They had been traveling for three days, and their canteens had gone empty miles back.

Griff was in charge, stopping and making the others stop as well. He was a big man, with arms like tree trunks, and he stooped down to fill his canteen from the stream. The others stayed on their horses watching, waiting for their turn.

"It's been a while since we saw fresh water," Griff said. "But I knew we'd come across some eventually."

He took a long gulp and then bent to fill it back up again. He stood up and scratched his crotch through his dusty trousers.

"How much farther?" Jebediah Boones asked.

"Another day's ride," Griff said. "If that."

As Griff moved away from the stream, the other two got down off their horses and followed suit, taking long drinks and filling up their canteens as well.

Herv, the youngest one, looked up to Griff like some kind of father figure, and it could get irritating sometimes, the way he kept looking to the older man for approval. Jeb really wanted to give the kid a beating sometimes. Just for the hell of it. It didn't help that the kid had such a baby face, looking much younger than his twenty years. The truth was, Griff returned the attention most times, looking on Henry as a son he never had.

Jeb had no stomach for such bullshit. They needed to get their affairs in order. There was a bag of money to split up, and he was itching to go his own way. He didn't much like taking orders from Griff, and he was sure the older man and the boy wouldn't miss him much. But he wasn't going anywhere without his share.

Griff had turned out to be a good guide, though, getting them safely through the desert, and keeping them one step ahead of the law.

The last job they did had turned bloody. Jeb had gutted a man with his buck knife, from navel to collarbone. A security guard who had tried to be heroic. Griff had insisted he overreacted, putting them in jeopardy with his violence. But the truth was, either way, they'd be wanted men. And Jeb thought the guard had deserved it.

You can't show mercy to people who try to shoot you dead.

Jeb remembered vividly the way he split the bastard from belly to heart. The man's innards had hung out of him like living spaghetti. It had not been a pleasant sight.

Then again, Jeb Boones was not a pleasant man. And from what he remembered, Abe Griffin, who always went by Griff, hadn't been much better. When they were younger, Griff wouldn't have balked at what happened back there, but he seemed to have softened some. Taking a kid like Herv under his wing just emphasized the change. He never would have pegged Griff for a man who would have grown sentimental.

Jeb took another gulp from his canteen. He could feel the water coursing through him. It made him feel tingly inside. Must have been a side effect of being dry for so long.

"Shall we move on?" Griff asked.

"Sure." Jeb put the cap back on and put his canteen back in his saddlebag.

It was then that the kid started vomiting uncontrollably.

"What the hell is wrong with him now?" Jeb asked, climbing up on his horse.

"What's wrong, boy?" Griff asked, putting his arms around the younger man. "Are you okay?"

Herv pushed the larger man away, and Griff let him. Then the boy slipped down to his knees and pitched forward, washing his head in the stream.

"That's better," Herv said, wiping the wet hair out of his eyes.

"It's passed?"

"Not really," Herv said. "It's just not as bad now."

"You said you thought we were being followed back there," Jeb said to Griff. "If that's true, we don't have time to spend nursing a sick boy. Either he pulls his weight, or we leave him behind."

Griff was red in the face with anger as he looked up at him. "I decide who stays behind, not *you*. I'm certainly not going to abandon the boy for just getting a bit sick."

"Can we move on?" Jeb said, making his impatience clear. "It's touching and all, seeing how you fuss over him, but we don't have the time to spare."

"Okay, okay," Griff said, sounding weary. "You gonna be okay, boy?"

"Yes'um," Herv said. "I feel better now."

"See, he's going to be fine," Griff said. "Let's go then."

Griff went back to his horse.

* * *

An hour later, the boy fell off his horse, landing head-first into the rocky soil.

"Herv!" Griff shouted, stopping his own horse and getting down. "Herv, are you okay?"

The boy was vomiting again, uncontrollably. His body spasmed with each heave.

"Goddammit," Jeb Boones said under his breath.

As the boy wriggled in his grasp, Griff noticed that his arms and legs had begun to bleed. He had no idea what to do to stop the flow. There was just so much blood.

"My God," Boones said. "What the fuck is wrong with him?"

"Shut up, will you?" Griff said. "I've got to make a tourniquet."

"He's way past that."

And Boones was right. Already, the boy's arms and legs were separating from his torso, slipping off like false limbs. His stumps continued to bleed and his whole body wiggled like a gigantic worm.

"I've never seen such a thing," Griff said. "Boones, tell me what to do!"

"I wouldn't know where to begin," Jeb said.

Griff stepped back, awash in Herv's blood, and the two men watched as the boy rolled on the earth, limbless and bloody, vomiting still as he moved.

"He's a goner," Jeb said.

The boy stopped moving and was on his back. He opened his eyes.

"Griff," he said. "Are you there?"

"Of course, I'm here, son," Griff said. "Are you going to leave us?"

"I don't think so," Herv said. "I feel better now."

The bleeding and vomiting had stopped as suddenly as it began, but Herv was still limbless and a most disturbing sight to behold. His face was flushed and his eyes bulged from their sockets.

"You've lost your arms and legs," Griff said.

The boy groaned.

"Let's go," Jeb said. "Leave him here. He'll only slow us down."

Griff didn't respond. Instead he took some rope out of his bags and went through the laborious process of tying Herv to the back of his horse. Then Griff grabbed the reins of Herv's horse and pulled it behind them.

The whole time, Boones watched with glaring eyes.

I can't wait to be free of these bastards, he thought. *They'll get us killed yet.*

But his anger was tempered with fear. He had no idea what had happened to the boy, and didn't know if the same could happen to him and Griff.

The sooner I get away from them, the sooner I can forget what a spectacle that boy was, losing his limbs like that, Boones lied to himself.

* * *

A few hours later, they were still riding beside the stream, with no end in sight. There were still mountains on either side of them. The sun was sinking now, and they couldn't see it, though they could see its light.

"It will be sundown soon," Griff said. "We should set up camp."

"Yeah, might be nice to eat something too."

They had slowed down considerably since Griff had tied the kid to his horse. They had lost a lot of time.

* * *

"How's the kid?" Boones asked.

"Not good," Griff said. "He's shivering a lot. I think we're losing him."

"So what do you think did it to him? The water?"

"You and me seem to be okay."

"What else could it have been?"

"I have no idea. I've never seen or heard of anything like this before."

Griff opened the kid's sleeping bag and slipped Herv inside, wrapping him up to keep him warm. His eyes had rolled up into his head and his lips were blue.

"Looks like he's freezing to death," Griff said, wiping his brow. "But it's still hot as hell out here."

Boones nodded. "Good night," he said, getting into his own sleeping bag.

* * *

Boones woke to the sounds of Griff vomiting his guts up. He had walked a ways from the camp and was bent over, retching.

Boones grunted and went over to Herv's sleeping bag, and looked inside. The boy had changed overnight. He appeared to be melting, or at least turning to ooze. He looked like a giant slug. Boones made sure not to touch him as he wrapped him back up again.

He sat by the burned-out fire, watching Griff. Waiting.

The older man came back, wiping his beard. "This isn't good," he said.

"Nope."

"So what do we do?" Griff asked. "Wait to die?"

"We move on," Boones said. "It doesn't do us any good to stick around and wait for them to catch up with us."

Griff stared at the ground for a long time.

Then he dropped to the earth, wriggling, as his arms and legs detached from his body.

* * *

I've got a couple of freaks on my hands, Boones thought. *And it's only a matter of time before I join them.*

He had decided to take off on his own, but he didn't want to leave the other two in plain sight. They deserved that much, so he rode ahead a bit, looking for someplace to put them, and he found a cave. He came back and gathered up the kid, tied him to his own horse (there was no way Herv was going near *his* horse), and took him over to the cave. He carried the sleeping bag with the boy inside and put him on the ground. Then he went back for Griff.

The man struggled as Boones put him back in his own sleeping bag, and wrapped him up as well.

"What are you going to do with us?" Griff asked.

"I'm gonna leave you here," Boones said. "But I'll get you out of the sun, at least."

"You're going to take all the money, aren't you?"

"Yep. I don't think you and the kid will be needing it."

"You did this to us, didn't you?"

Boones stared into the other man's eyes. "Do you really think that?"

"The way you killed that man back there," Griff said. "I think you are capable of anything. And you've been jealous ever since Herv joined us. Jealous of the bond we had."

"Bullshit," Boones said. "I don't care about stuff like that."

"I'll admit it. He reminded me of my son, if Jake had grown more to manhood and hadn't died so young."

Boones nodded, but he had no idea the man had had a son once, that he had been part of a family. He couldn't picture Griff staying put in one place long enough to plant roots.

"But I never meant to shut you out. I just liked being a daddy to someone, you know?"

"I know," Boones said. "And I weren't jealous. I couldn't care less about you and the boy."

"You don't mean that," Griff said. "We were close friends once. We were like brothers."

"Once," Boones said. "But I've been thinking about splitting for a while now."

"I stood by you," Griff said. "All this time, I didn't split on you. No matter how vicious you got. How you put us all in jeopardy by not controlling that temper of yours."

"The bank guard deserved what I did to him," Boones said. "He would have shot me."

"I know, but you didn't have to gut him in front of everyone."

"I had to make an example of him."

Griff coughed. "I don't want to talk anymore."

So Boones tied Griff to Herv's horse and rode in silence as they went to the cave. He took Griff down and put him next to the boy, who wasn't moving anymore. Then he got Griff's horse and brought it back. He took all the food and supplies and money from the others' saddlebags and put them all in his, then he slapped Herv's horse, sending it on its way.

"You going to take my horse?" Griff asked.

Boones looked down at him. "You won't be needing him."

"I know, but if you pull him along beside you, he'll slow you down. You should let him go free too."

"I don't think so," Boones said. "If it takes much longer to find a town, I might have to eat him."

Griff could not tell if he was joking or not.

"But I'll think about it. The thing is, he's a strong horse, I might be able to get a good price for him in the next town."

"I never thought you'd do this to me," Griff said. "Leave me here to die. I thought we were closer than that."

"We were, but things changed. Besides, what can I do for you, really? If I took you along, *you'd* just slow me down too much."

Boones considered taking out his gun and putting both men out of their misery. He wasn't even sure if Herv was alive anymore, but he stopped himself. Ammo was in low supply and he couldn't go around wasting it.

He took out his canteen and opened it.

"You thirsty, old man?"

Griff grunted in anger, and wriggled in his sleeping bag.

Boones turned it over and let the water pour out onto the ground. The way he saw it, they all drank the water at the same time. They all should have gotten sick around the same time. But they didn't. First Herv got it, then Griff.

But he felt fine. Maybe it wasn't going to happen to him.

Either way, he wasn't going to drink any more water from the gulch stream. He had a spare canteen hidden away in his bags. It was about half-full of water from the last town they'd been in, and he knew it was safe. It would have to last until he found the next town.

Then he heard a gunshot.

* * *

Hiding behind a rock, he saw the posse way off in the distance. There was no way they had seen him or the others, and he had done a good job covering up where they had been. But there would always be tell-tale signs, and maybe they noticed where the campsite had been.

Posses tended to be made up of hotheads who were itching for a fight, so a gunshot wouldn't be totally unexpected. Then again, maybe someone was shooting at a rabbit for supper.

Either way, it wasn't the best time to be moving on, where he might be seen.

Boones grabbed the reigns of his horse and Griff's and brought them into the cave. It was big enough to accommodate them. And both animals were calm enough in their new surroundings. It would only be a couple hours until the posse had gone by anyway.

He went back to the mouth of the cave. At least there were some big rocks to obscure the entrance. He'd been lucky to find the place, and it was a perfect location for him to keep watch from.

"Looks like I'll be hanging around longer than expected," Boones said to Griff.

The man did not reply.

* * *

It was nightfall by the time the men had disappeared from view long enough for Boones to feel safe again.

Griff and Herv had stopped making any sounds, or moving, long before, and he was sure they were dead. It was too dark in the cave to tell for sure.

"Might as well eat first, and then try to make up for lost time," Boones said, and began to build a fire.

After he ate, he figured it wouldn't hurt to wait until morning, when the posse was long gone, to start traveling again. And he was really tired. He didn't want to be around Griff and Herv anymore, but the cave was a safe place, and he put his sleeping bag as far from them as he could.

Then he nodded off.

* * *

Boones woke to the sound of startled horses moving about. Griff's horse had already fled into the night, but his own horse was more securely tied to a rock and she whinnied and struggled against her reins, but couldn't get free. The fire was still lit, although it was slowly burning itself out. And there was a sound all around like something being dragged across a rock floor.

He looked over at the other sleeping bags, that were empty now, and then up, over his head, at the walls of the cave, and he saw them. Dozens of them. Slugs that slithered across the stone walls, all of them the size of men, all of them with strange faces that looked like wax dolls that had melted in on themselves.

He knew that Herv and Griff were among them.

He stood there in silence, watching them move about, and he took out his gun.

Boones aimed it at one of the bigger ones, and was about to shoot, when he stopped.

There was a tingling sensation in his arms and legs, and he couldn't be sure if it was real or if it was the fear playing tricks with his mind. Why hadn't he changed yet? He'd drunk the water too. It was just a matter of time.

He stood there, waiting, but he didn't start bleeding, and his arms and legs did not fall off. He didn't fall to the ground a limbless thing that couldn't upright itself.

The tingling intensified, but he was sure he was going to be okay.

I'm not going to become like them, Boones thought. *It's just the fear. It's all in my mind.*

But he couldn't be certain.

He put the barrel of the gun in his mouth and held his breath, waiting for some sign to let him know for sure whether he should pull the trigger.

The Sweetness and the Psychic

HE WAS MY FIRST REAL lead, sitting there in the middle of the motel room, hiding behind dark glasses and a worn fedora. I had tried to make him feel at home, but there wasn't much homey about the room. His name was Willoughby, and I didn't know a lot else about him. But I was grateful I'd been able to track him down, and that he had agreed to meet with me.

"So you can see me?" I asked, sitting across from him on the bed. He sat on the only chair in the room.

"No," he said. "Not like you see. Not with the *eyes*."

"Then how?"

"With the mind, brother. I can see every detail of this room; I can see *you* seeing *me*."

"And you can see the future?"

"Sometimes."

I wanted to believe him, but I wasn't sure how much I did. I reached out and held my hand in front of his face.

"Waving that hand," he said. "Like you don't trust me."

He could have felt a slight hint of air when I moved my hand; he could have heard it in front of him. I wasn't convinced yet.

"You know where the boy is?" I asked.

"I saw him last night. In a dream. A dream that was more than a dream."

There was a pause, and I waited.

"A dream that was a doorway."

* * *

When I first arrived in Rust Bottle, Missouri, I didn't have a hell of a lot to go on. One of my contacts had heard something. I wasn't sure if it was relevant, but I was desperate. I had been on this case for a week, without much to show for it, and the boy's father was getting antsy. I knew that if

I didn't deliver something soon, he'd shake me off and move on. As far as he knew, I was stringing him along.

My contact, Freeform Ed, was the one who put me into contact with Willoughby here. A blind psychic who had helped the police with a few cases. Supposedly legit. But I didn't believe in this kind of thing, and so his legitimacy wasn't a sure thing by any stretch. I'm a pragmatic man though. I'm skeptical, but I can be convinced if you get me results.

Willoughby didn't move a muscle, sitting there.

"Can I get you something to drink?" I asked.

"Some water would be nice."

I went into the bathroom and filled up the complimentary glass with water from the sink. It was slightly yellow. I wondered how much lead was in it.

I held the glass in front of him. He didn't hesitate, just reached out and took it from me.

"Bottled water would have been nice," he said. "This local water has a bitter tang to it."

"Sorry, I don't have any bottled water."

He nodded and took a sip. Then placed the glass down on the carpet beside the chair.

"So tell me where the boy is."

"I don't know that," he said. "Not an exact place where he is. But I do know how you can find that place."

"How?"

"I'm not in the business of giving information away for free," he said.

I got out my wallet and fished through the bills. When I took out three twenties and looked up, he already had his hand out, palm up, and I placed them there. He didn't move. So I added two more.

"There's two things I have to say to you," he said.

"I'm listening."

"There's a house on the edge of town here. The Dowager place. You'll find some answers there. Not all, but enough to point you in the right direction."

"The Dowager place. Is that the name of the street or something?"

"I'm not going to draw you a map. You'll know it when you see it."

"And the second thing?"

"If you taste the sweetness, I suggest you walk away."

"What?"

"Sweetness. If you taste it, leave."

"I don't follow."

"You will." He grinned then, and shifted enough to put the bills in his pants pocket.

"That's all you've got?"

"You'll call on me again," he said. "But yeah, that's all I've got. All you'll need. For now."

He got up, stood there a moment as if getting his bearings, and then he walked to the door. I was going to say goodbye, but he didn't stop. He just opened it and let himself out.

* * *

No one I talked to had ever heard of the Dowager place, so I just drove around in neighborhoods that seemed to be "on the edge of town." He said I'd know it when I saw it, but nothing caught my eye. Willoughby had conned me.

I went back to the motel room and cracked open a beer. It was a really hot day, and the AC wasn't very good. And it made a hell of a racket.

I drank a few more beers, and eventually was able to fall asleep.

* * *

The next day I filled up my gas tank and went driving around again. If I didn't find anything two days in a row, then I'd know for sure Willoughby was feeding me a line of bullshit. But I had to know for sure.

I went down a street that looked familiar from the day before, and then took a turn at the end. And then I noticed the ONE WAY sign and realized I was going the wrong way. I stopped the car.

And there it was.

There were strange markings spray-painted on a stone wall near the house. They looked like hieroglyphics or something. Writing out an old mummy movie. And that immediately caught my eye. The house next to the wall was old and in disrepair, and most likely abandoned. There was nothing to identify it as the Dowager place. The street it was on was called Lincoln.

The front door was locked, but it was an easy enough job getting in. It wasn't the most sophisticated lock I'd ever seen. I had my flashlight and I looked around the place. A few pieces of furniture, but not as much as there should have been. One room was completely empty, except for the dust on the floor. I had gloves on, but I tried not to touch anything. I did try the light switch, but the power wasn't on. I didn't open the blinds. That's why I brought the flashlight.

I didn't see anything that could be useful. I found a trapdoor that led up to an attic. It was too small to stand in, and I crawled around, shining the light, but there wasn't anything of worth.

I found the door to the basement, and went down there. There wasn't much down there either. A rusted old tricycle. A water heater.

On the water heater, there was something written in what looked like blood.

Help me.

* * *

When I didn't find anything else, I got out of there and drove into town. There was a diner where I had gotten a couple of meals, and it was decent enough. I ordered the pork chops and looked at the picture on my phone that I'd taken of the message on the water heater.

It wasn't a lot to go on.

But it had to mean *something*. It was ominous enough. A cry for help.

Was it the Bellerium boy? Had his kidnappers kept him in that house for a day or two as they planned their next move? It certainly seemed that way if Willoughby was to be believed. He said I'd find some answers. This was the closest thing to an answer I had.

The waitress, an older woman named Margaret with graying hair, who had probably worked in that diner all her life and would probably die there, brought my plate over and refilled my coffee cup.

"Sure looks like rain," she said.

"Yeah."

She walked away and I put my phone down and picked up a fork and knife. Started cutting up the meat. It was a little red and bloody inside. Too rare for pork. You had to be careful with that. So I called Margaret over and asked her to have the chef cook it a little longer.

She nodded her head and took it away.

I looked at the picture on my phone again.

Help me.

* * *

"Missouri, you say?"

"A small town called Rust Bottle," I said.

"And you have a lead?"

"Yeah, I do."

The man on the other end cleared his throat. "Mr. Bellerium will be happy to hear that. He hasn't gotten much in the way of good news."

"Well, don't build it up too much. Just in case it doesn't pan out."

"We take hope where we can find it."

I was talking to a Mr. Cook, Mr. Bellerium's assistant or lawyer or something. It wasn't clear what his role was, but he did most of the talking for Mr. Bellerium, who couldn't be bothered to have a conversation with someone like me, even if it was about his son's life.

Someone had kidnapped Bellerium's kid. They made it clear that they had him. The boy didn't just run away or anything. But there was no follow up. No request for a ransom. No instructions. Nothing. Bellerium was adamant that the police not be involved. I don't think Mr. Bellerium's line of business was something he wanted the police sniffing around. You'd think a man like that would have some crooked cops on his payroll who would be good at tracking lost people, but if he did, they hadn't helped him much.

It was clear that I was a last resort. That Bellerium had come to me only because he didn't know who else to ask. He knew I'd keep it quiet. I had issues of my own.

"You there, Mr. Rinder?"

"Yeah," I said.

"I thought you'd left the call."

"Just thinking, I guess."

"Mr. Bellerium instructed me to tell you that you have three more days. If you don't have something substantial in that time frame, Mr. Bellerium will have no choice but to terminate your arrangement and find an alternative resource to sort this out."

"I understand."

"You seem like a reasonable man, Mr. Rinder," Cook said. "I knew you'd understand. Call me again when you have more. But three days is all you have left."

"I'll call you every day with an update."

"No. Just call if you have something to give me. Don't waste either of our time. I'll call you on the third day if I haven't heard from you."

"Okay."

"Hopefully you'll have some good news soon."

He hung up first.

* * *

It was late and I couldn't sleep, so I took the chair in the room outside and sat in front of my room in the parking lot. It had rained earlier, but not for very long, and it had gotten comfortably cooler at night, and it was quiet. A lot of the other rooms were dark. I had a cooler beside me full of beer bottles, and opened one.

Something moved in the dim light of the lot. As it got closer, I saw it was a dog. He came up to where I was sitting and sat down beside me. I reached down and rubbed his head. He stuck out his tongue and panted. I got up, went into the room, and poured a glass of water. I put it down in front of him and he bent his head and lapped water from the surface of the glass.

I sat back down and petted his head some more.

There was a crescent moon in the sky. The dog was a mixed breed. He was friendly, but looked a little mangy. Neglected. If someone at the motel was his owner, they weren't taking very good care of him. Then again, he was probably a stray.

I didn't have anything decent to feed him. I'd get something in the morning.

The dog stretched out on the ground beside me and went to sleep.

* * *

I didn't know what else to do, so I went back to the house where I'd seen the *Help Me* message. I searched the place again, from top to bottom, and had no more luck than I had the first time. I went down to the basement again and the water heater was clean. The message had been wiped away. But that meant something.

It meant someone had been there since the day before.

Someone who might be aware that I was there now. Who might be waiting for me to leave again.

I looked at the picture on my phone. At the *Help Me* message. It had been real, all right.

As I stared at it, I started to get a strange taste in my mouth, in the back of my throat. A sweetness, just like Willoughby has described it. It made my eyes water. And it got stronger. *Sweeter.* I rolled my tongue around, licking my lips trying to get rid of the taste, but it wasn't going anywhere.

I left the basement and got out of the house. Went back to my car.

I sat there, watching the house. But no one else came by, or left the place. I was alone. The sweetness was still in my mouth, but it was diminished since I left the house.

It didn't go away completely until I drove away and was a good distance from the place.

I went and bought a bottle of bourbon to wash the taste away.

* * *

"I'm not so good with photographs," Willoughby said.

"I thought you said you could see with your mind," I said.

"I can see you," he said. "I can see the room around me. I'm just not good with photos for some reason."

"It's a white water heater," I said. "There are words written on it. Looks like blood. *Help Me.*"

"So I was right," he said, and smiled.

"And I felt that sweetness you were talking about. It was a strong sweet taste in my mouth."

"You left the house then?"

"Yes."

"Good. It's nice to know you were listening. That you're taking me serious."

"What was it?" I asked. "The sweetness."

"A warning," he said.

"The message proves someone was there. But someone wiped it off."

He nodded.

"I need more," I said. "This isn't much at all. It's certainly not an answer. You said I'd find some answers."

"Well, you're on the right track; that's an answer. The fact that you tasted the sweetness is proof of that."

"I've only got two more days," I told him. "And then they'll fire me. I'm running out of time."

"You've got a dog now," he said.

The mutt hadn't left since the night before, and I didn't have the heart to shoo him away. I'd gone to the store and gotten it some food. The dog ate like he hadn't had a meal in days.

I grunted. I didn't see how the dog mattered in what we were talking about.

"So how long you been this way?" I asked him.

"Been *what* way?"

"You say you're blind, but you can see me. You saw where I should go for the message. Have you always been this way?"

"For a long time," he said. "No rhyme or reason to it."

The dog went up to him and Willoughby rubbed his head. Then he got to his feet.

"So you're not going to help me anymore?"

"I didn't ask for money this time, did I?" he said. "I haven't seen anything else to tell you."

"So what should I do? I can't just sit here, twiddling my thumbs."

"Go back to the house tomorrow," he said.

Then he left.

* * *

I took the dog with me this time. I left him in the car with the windows rolled down. I figured if he ran away, there wasn't much I could do about it. It wasn't like I was planning to adopt him. I was just taking care of him while I was in town. He sat there, his head hanging out the open window, watching me.

"Good boy," I said.

I went back in the house. I didn't see anybody in the nearby houses, but if there were any neighbors, I'm sure they thought I looked suspicious. So far, nobody had called the cops. Then again, this wasn't the kind of neighborhood where people did that much.

I went to the basement first this time. There was fresh blood on the water heater. Words.

It Hurts.

I took a picture of it and went back outside.

The dog was gone.

* * *

I stared at the photograph of the note that had been left behind when the kid got grabbed. It read simply, *WE HAVE HIM.* The handwriting was odd, and looked somewhat like a child's, but it was examined and it was not the victim's. Aside from the fact that the kid was gone, this was the only evidence.

"What are you looking at?" Margaret asked. I didn't know she was awake. I'd swung by the diner on the way home the night before, and asked her to go for a drink. We had ended up here, talking most of the night. I told her a lot about my case. She was pretty knowledgeable about the town since she grew up here and never really left. For one thing, the house used to be owned by a family called Doger, not *Dowager*, and there was a murder. That was easy enough to check, and she was right. Mr. Doger killed his wife and kids six years back. No one had moved into the house since.

"You going back there today?" she asked.

I didn't have much of a choice. It was the only lead I had. All trails ended there.

"Can I go with you?" she asked.

I nodded. I didn't see any harm in it. Besides, since she knew the area, maybe she could fill in blanks I wouldn't know.

She got out of bed and I watched her bare ass as she walked to the bathroom.

I wondered if the dog would ever come back.

* * *

When we got to the Doger house, the first thing I noticed that was different was the stone wall near the building. The hieroglyphics had been covered up with about a hundred flyers, all exactly the same, all with a face on them. I had to go closer to see exactly what they were. Each of the flyers asked, "*Have you seen me?*" and the photo was the most recent picture I'd seen of Benjy Bellerium. Like the kind of thing you'd see on the side of a milk carton. I had no idea where the flyers had come from, but I took a picture of one of them up close, with my phone, so I'd have the phone number. Then I took another picture of the entire wall, showing the way they all covered it up like wallpaper.

I emailed both photos to Mr. Cook.

"What is it?" Margaret asked, coming up behind me.

"It's the kid I'm looking for."

"Then that's pretty damn creepy," she said.

And she was right. The fact that someone had created these flyers and then papered the wall with them, knowing I would be back here, gave me chills. I was sure then that I was being watched. There was a good chance that Cook already knew about this. *Someone* posted the flyers here. But how did he know the exact location? I hadn't told anybody about this place yet. And if they already knew about it, then why did they need me?

I reached out to grab one of the flyers, and something really weird happened. My fingers pressed the wall as I touched the paper, and I swear I could feel the wall moving *away* from me. As if recoiling to my touch. Like it was alive or something. It was subtle, but so strange that I kind of jumped back. Margaret asked what was wrong, but I didn't say anything. I was trying to wrap my mind around it.

I didn't wrap long. I left the wall and went to the house.

Margaret and I went inside and she stayed upstairs while I went down to the basement first thing. As I trained my flashlight beam on the water heater, I noticed it was wiped clean again.

Then I tasted a slight sweetness in the back of my throat.

Movement caught my eye. I followed it with the light. There was something on the ceiling, something big, moving very fast. I only caught tiny details, it remained one step ahead of my light throughout. I followed it to a far corner of the cellar.

When it disappeared, I saw what looked like a small human being on the floor below where it had been. I went closer, keeping the light on it. Examining the face, I saw it was Benjy Bellerium. He was incredibly pale and not moving, and I presumed he was dead. Then he stirred slightly. I reached down to shake him.

The sweetness returned then, stronger than before, filling my mouth and throat to such a degree that I felt like I was choking. I remembered Willoughby's warning about the sweetness, to leave when I tasted it, but I was determined to take Benjy with me. I grabbed his arm and shook him hard. He would not open his eyes.

I was squinting my eyes from the intensity of the sweetness that had become so dominant that it seemed to be blocking out my other senses. I lifted the boy from the floor, determined to swing him over my shoulder and carry him upstairs, but it was then that I saw the moving thing again.

It was bigger than Benjy and came out of a large, dark hole in the wall behind him.

I aimed the flashlight straight ahead, and it was the first time since I got there that I could really see it. Whatever shivers I got from the flyers outside were intensified a hundredfold now.

I was looking at something that looked like a gigantic cockroach, except it was even more repulsive, and it was a green that intensified and grew bright, as if lit from within. It was as big as I was and, as it lifted the front part of its body, I could see the nose and jaw of a human face under its carapace.

The jaw was moving, as if it were speaking, but I didn't hear any words.

But I did hear a scream.

I turned toward the staircase, and saw Margaret half-way down, repulsion in her face as she continued screaming.

At this point, I felt like I had been exposed to tear gas. The sweetness was overpowering and I dropped the boy, hurling myself in the direction of the scream. My eyes were only open a crack as I moved. The thing in the wall crept closer and then was running along the ceiling in my direction. I ran up the staircase, grabbed Margaret's arm, and pulled her upstairs. She helped me slam the door before it could reach us, which didn't really make sense, since it seemed to move much faster than we could. It had deliberately let me get away.

Which I suppose didn't matter, as long as I didn't take the boy with me. It clearly wanted him to stay put.

With the sweetness still tormenting me, I ran out the front door, Margaret following me. And it wasn't until I got outside that the vile taste began to subside.

We were both coughing. She tasted it too, but hadn't been as close to the source as I had been. Somehow, I hadn't blacked out.

I had three options at that point. The first was to get in the car and drive as far away as I could go. The second was to call Mr. Cook and give him all the details. I'm sure Mr. Bellerium could send some of his men to come down and fumigate the place, most likely with bullets, in order to get Benjy back. That would also mean my part of this would finally be over, and I wouldn't have to get my hands dirty.

But I opted for the third choice. Finishing this thing myself. I got my gun from the glove compartment of the car. I hadn't brought it in before because I had not needed it on previous visits, but now it was necessary. I also had bought a gas mask on the way over just in case the sweetness was toxic. I made sure to take some extra ammo and headed back toward the house, determined to get Benjy out of that place.

Margaret cried out, demanding to know where I was going, but I told her to stay outside and went through the open doorway. As I got closer to the cellar door, the sweetness flared up again, but nowhere near as bad as it had been, and going outside for fresh air had definitely helped.

I put the gas mask on, turned on the flashlight again, and ran down the stairs. There were fresh markings on the water heater now, a message for me to "*Leave Now*," but I ignored that. Benjy was in the corner where I'd left him; I was able to find him quickly enough with the flashlight's glare, and I ran to him. He was moving slightly, enough to let me know he was alive, but still clearly in some semi-conscious state.

"Let's get out here," I said, unsure if he could hear me. This time I did get him up and over my shoulder, and then there was a loud chittering.

There were two of them now, emerging from the dark hole in the wall, crawling quickly along the ceiling, big green blurs above me. I raised my gun and fired, the recoil shaking me enough to drop Benjy. They were fast, but I managed to get one of them, and it fell to the cellar floor, its legs frantically fluttering as it tried to right itself. At that moment, it made me think of Gregor Samsa in Kafka's classic story,

"The Metamorphosis." I pointed and fired again and again until its legs stopped moving.

I then looked up again, searching for the other one, and upon seeing rapid movement, fired the gun in its direction. This one fell right on top of me, lashing at me with its legs, snapping at me with its vile human jaws. I made sure to push Benjy away from me with my leg as I struggled to load the clip with more bullets. The thing bit the calf of my other leg, and I almost dropped the gun, but held on tight, and aimed.

It tried to scurry away, but I had injured it, and now unloaded the fresh clip into it, until this one, too, stopped moving. The bright green turned dull again.

I stood there, staring at the dark hole, waiting for more of them to emerge. Aiming the flashlight with one hand, and my gun with the other, in the semi-darkness.

When no more came, I grabbed Benjy's arm and lifted him again onto my shoulder, and moved toward the stairs.

Back in the car, I called Cook right away to tell him Bellerium's kid was safe. Margaret got in the back seat with Benjy, but the boy was barely responsive.

I turned to look at the house, and it was then that I noticed noise and movement from within, getting closer, and then there were a pack of those vile insects, running through the front door out onto the lawn. I had already started the car and instructed Margaret to roll up her windows as we screeched away. The insects seemed on the verge of catching the car at one point, but then I took a sharp left and left them behind.

* * *

I followed instructions on the phone as I drove, and went to an arranged spot. Bellerium was already there with some of his guys, and he hugged the boy close to him.

Benjy made a strange gasping sound and then opened his mouth to vomit. There were moving things in his regurgitation, and I turned away, intent not to look too closely. I heard the sounds of shouting and boots slamming down on the pavement, trying to crush something.

And then it was quiet again.

Bellerium thanked me profusely and said that payment would be wired to my account. But he had to take Benjy to the hospital now.

Before he carried his son to his car, he told several of his guys to go to the Doger house to tie up the loose ends.

* * *

When we got back to the motel room, I turned on the television. The local news was on with a breaking story. On the screen, I saw the Doger house, consumed in flames, as firemen struggled to contain it.

The stone wall that had been nearby was no longer there.

Margaret was still in a state of shock and stood in the middle of the room, staring at the screen, just like I was doing.

"Can you take me home?" she asked.

"Sure."

Despite all that had happened that afternoon, we barely knew each other, and she wanted to go back to somewhere familiar. I could understand that.

And I knew that, after I dropped her off, I would be checking out myself. There was no reason to stay in Rust Bottle anymore.

I knew I would never feel clean again until I left that place for good.

Necropolis

IT WAS A TUESDAY afternoon, and Fred Harrison could not help noticing how little traffic there was on the way home. Every once in a while a car passed him, but when he looked in his rearview mirror, there were only three cars lagging behind. The nearest car in front of him was almost a mile away. There was no congestion. No chance of a traffic jam. He felt an odd sensation overcome him; he felt his hands shake as he held onto the steering wheel. Bumper to bumper traffic during the rush hours, going to the office in the morning and driving home at night, had strangely provided him with a sense of security after all these years.

With congestion, there was normality.

He was a few miles from his turn-off, and straight freeway stretched out in front of him for as far ahead as he could see. It was then that he noticed the man standing in the breakdown lane. He didn't have his thumb out. He was just standing there, waiting.

Fred did not consider stopping for the man. He made it a habit never to pick up hitchhikers. But he did slow down a bit, not for any real reason. It was just something he did when he neared a pedestrian on the freeway.

The man standing in the breakdown lane gave no warning before he leapt out in front of Fred's car. Even though he had slowed down, Fred was still going fast, and he couldn't put his brakes on in time to avoid hitting the man. One of the cars behind him almost struck him as he put the brake pedal to the floor. But it was too late. The man had already bounced off his hood, over the roof of the car.

Fred panicked and put his foot on the gas. He kept driving. He looked in the rearview mirror and saw one of the other cars behind him run over the body a second time.

The further away he got, the more he convinced himself there was nothing else he could do.

* * *

Fred pulled his cellphone out of his jacket pocket and considered calling the police with his story. Surely one of the cars behind him had caught sight of his license plate and had reported him already. But he was so nervous that he couldn't think straight. The adrenaline was playing a drum solo in his brain. He headed home instead. Being with his wife and kids would help him come to grips with what had happened, give him a chance to think this through. This was something he needed help to cope with.

Besides, if he was going to jail, he wanted to see his family one last time.

He took his exit, and it wasn't long before he was parking his car in the driveway. He opened the door and practically ran to the house.

Once he got inside, he locked the door behind him and stood in the living room, listening to the sound of his own breathing. It was labored, pounding in his ears, playing a duet with the adrenaline.

He shouted out his wife Trisha's name to block out the noise.

No answer. He remembered that this was Tuesday and that this was the day his wife went out shopping with her sister. If the babysitter wasn't here with the kids, then they were probably over at Trish's mother's house. And he was all alone after all.

He ran to the kitchen and peered out the big bay window. The back yard was empty. Two bicycles lay on the grass. One red, the other green.

He was going to fix himself a drink, but then decided it was best not to, especially if he was going to be meeting up with the cops anytime soon. It wouldn't do to have liquor on his breath when he told them his story.

He didn't need suspicion of drunken driving added to his list of offenses. It was bad enough that he had killed a man, even if the guy threw himself in front of his car. And that he had fled the scene.

He took the stairs to the second floor, intent on taking a hot bath until Trisha and the kids got back home. He had to do something to calm his mind, to stop his thoughts from going a mile a minute, and a good hot bath usually did him wonders.

On the way to his bedroom, he passed the room his two sons shared. The door was closed. He was tempted to open it, but he had too much else on his mind. And besides, if they were home, they would have come to see him by now. There was nothing strange about the door being closed anyway. Trisha often closed it when it was empty. Although he was never really sure why.

He walked through the bedroom he shared with Trisha, to the adjacent bathroom. But he never got a chance to take a bath. The tub was already occupied.

Trisha was stretched out in the water, one arm hanging over the side of the tub. Her wrist was smeared with blood. A razor lay on the floor beside her. The water was reddish pink.

He stared at her, his mind a blank, unable to make himself move, and then, suddenly, the door to his sons' room came to mind, and he unfroze enough to go back there. He ran out in the hallway again and opened the door to their room.

The two boys were in their beds. George, the older, and Tim. Between them, on the night stand they shared that held the lamp, was a pill bottle. Fred went to it and picked it up. It was a prescription for sleeping pills, in Trisha's name. It was empty.

He did not touch his children. He backed out of their room, and stood in the hallway. He tried to close his eyes, but they refused to obey him.

Fred Harrison ran downstairs and out onto his front lawn. At this time of day, there were always children playing outside, people walking their dogs, cars passing by.

This particular Tuesday afternoon, nothing.

* * *

Unable to go over to the neighbor's house because of the fear of what he might find there, Fred went back inside his own house.

First, he turned on the radio, but he couldn't find any stations. All he heard was static. Eventually, he came upon one station playing Muzak.

He sat in the reclining chair in his living room. The television was on, but there was nothing on any of the channels. Only snow. The remote wouldn't work. *The cable must be out.* He sat there watching a big, white, hissing square.

He listened to the Muzak. He was waiting for a disc jockey's voice to come on. He knew that chances were the songs were pre-recorded.

At that moment, he was listening to a song that he knew he had heard before, but which, in its altered Muzak form, he couldn't name. In his head, he pictured his wife in the bathtub. His sons in their beds.

A voice abruptly cut off the song. It was the first human voice Fred Harrison had heard in more than an hour's time.

"I don't know if anybody's out there," the voice said. It sounded scared. "There's something weird going on, and I don't have any answers. Everyone in this building is dead except for me. I've been searching for someone else alive, but I can't find anyone. They all killed themselves. I tried calling the police, and no one answers their phones. I'm looking out the window, and there is no one walking around outside.

"I'm not sure what's happening, but if anyone is out there, won't you please get in touch with me somehow?

"Please?"

The Muzak came on again, and then after the song finished, there was just static. Fred couldn't bring himself to get up and try to find another station. He knew it was hopeless, and he just didn't have the energy to try again.

His eyes were fixed on the television and the glowing snow that crackled in front of him.

If you listened closely enough, the static sounded almost like music.

* * *

Fred got back into his car and drove around the neighborhood. No one was on the streets. Nobody stirred in the windows of the houses. He still couldn't believe what his thoughts were telling him, until he started to see corpses on some of the front lawns. Even pets had been killed. Dogs and cats with smashed heads lay next to their masters, limp leashes like umbilical cords between them.

The car radio was on, spouting more static. He couldn't help remembering how desperate the disc jockey's voice had sounded before he signed off.

* * *

When the gas ran out, Fred pulled the car over into the breakdown lane and got out. He was back on the highway again. He had no fear of oncoming cars—there weren't any more.

At first, all of this had been a tremendous shock to his system, but driving for a few hours had drained away some of the impact. He did not understand things any better now, but it did seem inevitable. Something that had been building up in the world for a long time.

He did not know why he felt that way.

He had no idea where he had driven to. What state he was in now.

As he started walking along the breakdown lane, Fred Harrison looked skyward. There were no planes. Nothing.

He stopped and took the revolver from his jacket pocket. The gun he had bought to protect his home from intruders. He had made sure to bring it with him when he left the house.

He placed the gun against his temple, thinking of Trisha, a limp doll in a tub full of water, her wrists circled in red. The boys, sleeping peacefully in their beds, their faces devoid of fear.

He dropped the gun, unable to go through with it. Too confused and scared to add himself to the numbers of the dead. He walked a few more steps and then sat down on the asphalt, tears streaming down his face. His hands hugging himself tightly. He closed his eyes, trying to get his thoughts together. Trying to stay sane.

When he opened his eyes again, he saw the gun, not five feet away from him on the ground.

It kept calling him, and the more it did, the more seductive it sounded.

Giving in to the inevitable, Fred started crawling toward it.

City Slayer

"**IS** THIS WHAT YOU were looking for?" Emmy said, in aisle five of Walgreens.

Abercrombie slid up behind her and took the package from her hand. It read, in big red letters, *EMERGENCY RAIN PONCHO*, and showed a picture of a man wearing one. It was made of clear plastic.

"Yeah, that's it," he said.

"Pretty weird thing to be looking for," she said. "It hasn't rained here in a while. Besides, why not just get an umbrella?"

"I told you it was something silly," he said. "You're the one who insisted on coming with me to do errands."

"Between this and the votive candles, you're a strange guy."

"Don't tell me you're having second thoughts?"

"No," she giggled, "I wouldn't do that."

Of course not, he thought. No matter what they thought of his rituals beforehand, they were always intrigued enough to stick around. That was one thing he could count on.

At the counter, he grabbed a handful of candy bars and added them to his purchase. Emmy was looking stick-thin and could use a little meat on those bones.

He turned and looked at her, in that midriff-baring shirt, and her blonde hair tied up in a pink ribbon. He imagined he could see her bones beneath her translucent flesh. And then he saw her skeleton rip apart in a sudden hot wind.

Abercrombie blinked his eyes and he was back in the Walgreens, and Emmy was giggling again. "Did you forget your wallet?"

"Huh?"

"The woman asked you three times. Do you need me to pay for it?"

"No," he said, and reached in his back pocket. He smiled at the woman behind the counter. "Sorry about that. It's been a weird day."

"No problem," the woman said, snapping her gum. She looked about thirty, and she clearly found him to be as attractive as Emmy did. His looks always made things easier.

He paid her, and they went out into the arid day.

"Not a cloud in the sky," Emmy said, looking up and shielding her eyes. She unhooked her sunglasses from her top and put them back on.

"I know," he said. "I just like to be prepared."

* * *

Back at the hotel room, she couldn't get out of her clothes fast enough. She was naked and rocking on the edge of the bed as he set up the candles on the coffee table.

"It looks like you're getting ready for church," she said with a giggle.

"It's my little offering to Saint Ranier of Admah."

"Who?"

"He's kind of like my patron saint," he told her. "I pledged myself to him when I was younger."

"Pledged yourself?" she asked, finding this getting weirder still. "You mean like you're some kind of monk or priest or something?"

"Kind of, I guess," he said, "but not really."

"Where's Admah?"

"I think it used to be in the Middle East somewhere. It was next to Sodom and Gomorrah. Remember that story from the Bible, where God destroyed those two cities because they were full of sinners? Well, he destroyed more than just those two cities. There were five in all. The other ones were Admah, Zoboim, and Bela."

He lit the candles, which gleamed behind purpled glass.

"That's better," he said, standing up.

"I didn't realize you were so religious," she said. "When we first met, you couldn't get me in bed fast enough. Now it turns out you're some kind of holy man."

"I've never taken a vow of chastity," he told her. "And I've never believed in the concept of 'sins of the flesh.' So you've got absolutely nothing to worry about."

He went to his duffel bag and unzipped it. He pulled out a statue just over a foot tall. He put it on the table in the center of the candles.

"Who's that?"

"I told you," he said. "Saint Ranier."

She couldn't really see it in detail, but it looked like a man bound in ropes. Parts of him didn't seem right. He looked misshapen.

Abercrombie had a portable kneeling bench that he'd unpacked. He knelt down on it now and crossed himself.

"Come here, stupid. I'm all ready for you," she said behind him.

He crossed himself again, stood up, and turned off the lights so that the candles were the only illumination in the room. It was kind of romantic and spooky at the same time. Shadows danced on the statue.

He watched it for a few minutes and then turned to look at her face in the flickering glow.

"Time to fuck," he said.

* * *

He knew she was lying about her age. When he had met her, she had told him she was nineteen, but he suspected she was really sixteen or seventeen. In another time, in a different part of his life, he might have been concerned about that, but considering what was coming, it really didn't seem all that important now.

She was sleeping beneath the thin sheet, tangled up in it and snoring softly. The air conditioning provided a steady drone—a backup singer to her snore's lead.

He wondered if anyone was concerned where she was, or if she was really as carefree as she pretended to be.

He'd met her in a bar, of course. Once he came into a new town, it didn't take long to find someone to gravitate into his orbit. Despite her make-up, or rather because of it, he'd wondered if she belonged in such a place, but the bartender seemed to know her and kept refilling her bright blue drinks. In fact, everyone in the bar seemed to know her. She was clearly a regular there.

She'd seemed a little tipsy by the time she noticed him and started hanging around beside him. He just drank his shots of whiskey and glasses of beer and was silent for the most part. He didn't need pick-up lines or any of that crap. He just turned up the wattage a bit on his magnetic personality. That was one of the gifts Saint Ranier gave him in return for his devotion.

One of many gifts.

He thought about that as he went to the table he had converted into an altar, knelt down before it again, and crossed himself.

He stared down at the porcelain statue he had had specially made years before, between the burned-out candles.

There was a storm coming. He could hear it rumbling. He could feel it coming closer. But it was in his soul. And it would take another day to get here, so he might as well have some fun until then.

But first, he spent some time in prayer.

* * *

The second night he was in town, Emmy found that she couldn't move, and wondered if he had slipped her some kind of drug.

Abercrombie was over by the coffee table, praying to his saint again. The votive candles had been replaced with new ones.

She tried to talk to him, but it hurt to open her mouth.

He crossed himself and stood up. He had a knife in his hands.

"It's almost time," he told her.

Then he went over to her and pressed the knife hard against her belly, and sliced. He reached inside her and started to pull out organs. She could feel the pressure of them being ripped from her insides, but she didn't feel any pain. She wondered if she was going into shock, but she could still hear him. Still see him, even though he was a little blurred now.

He hummed a song as he pulled out her intestines and wrapped them around her, lifting her upper body up to tie her arms with them. She knew she was bleeding profusely, because when he lifted her up, she saw that the sheets were stained red.

"Now you're like him," he said. And she stared at the statue on the table, which was also bound up by its innards, just like her.

It was the first time she realized that.

"Why am I still alive?" she wondered.

He put his mouth close to her ear.

"I can keep you alive as long as I want to," he whispered. "But don't worry, I won't make this last too long."

He propped pillows up behind her and pressed her back into them.

"Now watch," he told her.

He stood before her, naked and holding the knife still wet with her blood. He held it up, and then everything got very bright, and she saw him in other places, killing other people.

Hundreds, *thousands* of people.

Like Santa Claus, he went to all of their houses over the course of one night, defying any rules she knew about reality. But instead of presents, he brought only death:

An old woman who woke in her bed to find him hovering above her. He put his hand over her mouth and slit her throat.

A middle-aged man whose wife had recently left him, restless in his bed because he wasn't used to sleeping alone. Abercrombie appeared to him and stabbed him seven times in his chest.

Two young boys sharing a bed in a two-room apartment, hearing a noise and thinking that their mother had returned early from the late shift where she worked as a nurse, but it wasn't her. It was a strange man with long hair and a knife, come to put them back to sleep permanently.

He killed them all, one after another. And yet, in some way she could not understand, he was also there in the hotel room with her, saying, "Now watch this."

And then they were all dead, and he knelt before her, and she thought he would slit his own throat then, as some kind of violent coda to his crimes, but he didn't. Instead he got to his feet and went to her and slit away the intestines that bound her before he forced her eyelids closed with his fingers and cut her deeply from ear to ear.

And then his work was done for the night. The storm had passed.

He took a shower and packed his things and went outside, and began to walk toward the town limits. A long-haired man in a windbreaker and a wearing a backpack. Many of the buildings he passed were on fire, and there was a strong stench of brimstone in the air, but he was used to it.

Once he reached the sign that read, *You are now leaving Crystal Hills,* he put down his backpack, opened it, and put on the rain poncho he'd bought with Emmy.

There was a twister above the town now, swirling with screams and blood.

He could feel blood pelting down on him as he restrapped the backpack and continued to walk away from the town.

He did not look back.

* * *

Everyone in Crystal Hills was dead. And anyone who ever knew of the place, or had relatives or friends there, forgot that the place had even existed, no matter where they were, as if it had never been a real place at all.

And somewhere Saint Ranier smiled.

* * *

"Aren't you Leon Coles?" the female voice said from behind him as he was looking through the stack of old vinyl records.

He turned around. Always good to look them over first before he responded, he'd learned that much over the years. They were a twenty-something couple, a girl and her boyfriend, and the guy looked as excited as she did. The girl had a nice shape, but her face was kind of plain. The boy was actually a little prettier than her, despite some acne scars.

"Guilty as charged," Leon said, taking them in, the gears in his mind already in motion.

"I loved Honey Load," the girl said. "'Sexy Earth Mother' is one my favorite songs ever."

"I liked Cooze Patrol a lot too," the boy said, trying to show off that he knew about Leon's previous band, the underground one that had the cult audience before he got big. "Imagine seeing a real rock star here!"

"Yeah, imagine that," Leon said, making sure his cowboy hat was on tight to hide his baldness. It wouldn't do to ruin the illusion. Back when Honey Load was at the top of the charts, he'd had a lion's mane of blond hair.

But his face hadn't aged much. He thanked skin creams and good genetics for that.

"What brings you here, to the middle of nowhere?" the girl asked, squeezing the boy's hand and looking at him with a big smile.

"Just passing through," Leon said. "I'm something of a wanderer these days. Trying to take this whole country in, one mile at a time."

"Where are you staying?" the girl blurted out, and the boy instantly went red. Leon could tell they both wanted to know, but only the girl had had the guts to say it.

He was going to repeat that he was just passing through, that he wasn't staying anywhere in this minor city in the bosom of the great Midwest, but the two of them intrigued him. Especially the part about Cooze Patrol. Nobody talked about them anymore.

"Well, I'm not sure yet," he said. "Just got into town."

"We live right near here," the boy said suddenly. "I've got some of your old albums. Can I go get them? Have you autograph them?"

Leon flashed that cocksman's smile. "You live nearby? Why don't we just take a stroll over there. I've got nothing going on at the moment."

"Really?" the girl said. Then, "The place is a mess."

Which told him two things. The boy didn't live with his parents. And the two of them were living together. Two things that he was really glad to hear.

"Don't worry about the place," Leon said. "I've seen worse. Hell, I probably *caused* worse. We trashed a lot of hotel rooms in our day."

The couple laughed on cue, and then the excitement level seemed to ratchet up a bit.

"Sure," the boy said. "Let's go."

* * *

"God, you look good," the woman said, sitting two seats away from him at the singles bar. He knew that if she hadn't been drinking, she probably wouldn't have had the nerve to say something first, and as it was she seemed embarrassed as soon as the words left her mouth.

Abercrombie smiled, and that seemed to renew her confidence.

"I'm sorry," she said. "I guess I drank a little more than I'm used to."

"No problem," he told her. "You're kind of cute like this."

The puffiness around her eyes said she had been crying, and that put up a red flag. He was looking for someone he could connect with fast. Someone vulnerable. And she seemed to fit the bill.

"I never do this kind of thing," she explained. "It's been ages since I've been in a bar like this."

"You don't like to drink?"

"No," she said. "It's not that. I just don't normally hang out in places where people pick each other up. It's not my thing."

"And why is that?"

"Well, because up until recently, I was married."

He pegged her age to be around forty. She was pretty, and must have been a real looker in earlier times, but there were lines around her eyes and creases in her neck. Not that that changed anything.

If anything, that made her more attractive to him.

The song playing on the jukebox, some old hit by the band Foreigner that he couldn't name, stopped, and they were able to talk at a more normal volume.

"My name is Abigail, by the way," she said.

"Abercrombie."

"What, like *Abercrombie and Fitch?*"

"Yeah, I guess so."

"What kind of name is that? Is that your first name or your last name?"

He got the bartender's attention and signaled for another round of drinks.

"Tell me about your ex," he said.

"Do I have to?" She started to sound sad again. "I'm really trying to forget him."

"How long were you married?"

"Too long. Twelve years. It took me that long to realize I was living with a man I didn't even know."

"He cheated on you?"

"It's that obvious, huh?"

"So you're here, looking for a distraction from all the bullshit?"

"Well, I'm certainly not looking for another husband." She laughed after she said it.

"I'm staying up the block, at the Filbert," he told her. "You interested in taking a walk? It's a nice night for it."

She smiled. It made her face look younger. "Okay."

The new drinks came, and he told her to drink up. Not long afterward they were walking arm in arm down the street toward his hotel. The main reason he was holding her arm was because she could barely walk, the state she was in.

When they got back to his place, she asked if she could lie down for a minute. The room was starting to spin. He said sure.

A few minutes later, she was sleeping.

Abercrombie watched her for a while and then stripped down to his underwear and crawled into bed beside her. She was still in her clothes. He considered taking them off, but he preferred to look like a gentleman. It would do wonders to win her over.

* * *

"Yeah," Leon said as he squeezed her throat. He was just about to come, and he could see the eyes roll up in her head. It was a bad sign, and he wanted to let go, but it was a strong orgasm and he let it overwhelm him. When he was done, he was surprised he hadn't killed her. Somehow she was still breathing.

One of these days he was really going to fuck up and kill someone.

The guy was on the floor, naked and unconscious. Now there were two of them out cold.

He went and used the shower, then got dressed. He left a few hundred-dollar bills on the bed. The girl was starting to stir a bit, looking groggy. The boy was sitting up and holding his head.

Leon didn't wait until they were ready to talk. He just let himself out, went down the block to his car, and drove as far away as he could get.

* * *

"So what brings you here anyway?" Abigail asked as they stood out on the hotel room's balcony, watching the beach below.

"I've got business to take care of," Abercrombie told her. "Nothing too exciting."

"What do you do?"

He kissed the back of her neck. She giggled.

"So what do you see in an old lady like me anyway?"

"I'm not as young as I look," he told her.

When she had woken fully dressed on the bed, with him beside her, she had quickly showered and woke him up with some of the best sex he'd had in a long time. Chivalry wasn't dead, and he'd been rewarded.

Now he lifted her and carried her back to bed.

"It's a beautiful day," she told him. "It really is."

"So, do you have to be somewhere soon?"

"No," she said. "I just lost my job. I worked in the office at a box factory. They closed down and had to let everyone go last week."

"Sorry to hear it," he told her.

"I know. I must sound like a real loser. No husband, no job. The only upside is that I don't have to go anywhere," she said. "I'm all yours."

With his fingers, he traced the curve of her arms, then he outlined the shape of her breasts. Every time he came to a new town, he liked to find someone to kill time with. Abigail was nicer than most. He could almost imagine himself staying here. Starting a new life. Leaving all the death behind.

* * *

"No way," Leon said into his cell phone. "There is absolutely no way I'd agree to that."

"It's good money," his agent, Barry, said.

"It's petty thievery," Leon said. "I won't put the band together for that. I won't even consider talking to him until he starts the negotiations off at one million."

"You're not fucking serious."

"Fucking A, I am. You're my agent, Barry. You're supposed to be looking out for me."

"I thought this was a good deal, man. The band has been out of the public eye for a long time."

"Listen, we still sell lots of CDs or MP3s or whatever the kids are listening to these days, and we're still a bankable name. We're still worth something, Barry. The other guys might be willing to play for peanuts, but I've got final veto power. And I say we pass on this."

"Okay, if you say so."

"I say so. If they're serious, they'll come around and offer us some real money."

"This '80s nostalgia thing will only go on for so long," Barry said. "You've got to jump aboard the train while it's still on the tracks."

"Bullshit," Leon said. "You know I don't need the gig. I'm set. If I'm gonna put the spandex back on, there better damn well be a decent paycheck in it for me."

"Okay, okay. I get it."

"Call me back when they make a real offer."

Leon closed his phone and threw it under the passenger seat. The amount they had offered was an insult. He was just shocked that Barry didn't see it that way.

Maybe it was time to change agents.

The big green highway sign up ahead read *KINGSTON: EXIT 18.*

"Finally," he said, and took the turnoff.

* * *

She had dozed off, and when she woke up again, Abercrombie had taken his portable prayer bench out of his bag and had lit a bunch of candles. He was kneeling before an odd-looking statue that was standing on the couch cushion, obviously in prayer. She wanted to ask him about it but didn't want to disturb him.

So he's a religious man, she thought. *Maybe that's not so bad. Maybe a little church-going stability is what I need in my life right now.*

He crossed himself and stood up. He turned and noticed her watching him.

"You're awake."

"Yep. I didn't realize you were such a pious man."

"Not quite," Abercrombie said.

"Who's that?" she said, pointing to the statue. "A saint?"

"Saint Ranier," he said. "You probably haven't heard of him."

"What's he the saint of?" she asked.

"I beg your pardon?"

"Well, like Saint Jude is the saint of lost causes. I know that one. What's Saint Ranier the saint of?"

"I guess he's for lost causes too," Abercrombie said. "I never really thought about it before."

"Tell me about him."

Abercrombie smiled. It wasn't often someone was really interested in his beliefs, and it was nice to have someone to talk to.

"Well, he was kind of a nomad. His people were originally from Admah."

"Admah?"

"Remember the story of Sodom and Gomorrah? The two cities that God destroyed back then? Admah was another one."

187

"I didn't know that."

"It's not generally known in secular circles, but Saint Ranier was descended from people who somehow escaped death when Admah was destroyed. They became nomadic and wandered around for centuries, cursed to never find another home to replace the one that was taken from them. Ranier himself was famous for healing people along his travels, to make money. But he didn't want this gift and was persecuted as a witch for performing his miracles. He cursed God to take his abilities away, but was disemboweled and mutilated for his troubles."

"Sounds awful."

"They removed his organs, one by one, and showed them to him. Because he had the gift of healing, he tried to heal himself, but they just kept mutilating him more and more. All his powers could do was keep him alive, in agony, as he was tortured. When his final organ was removed, he closed his eyes and died."

"Terrible."

"Yeah, it *was* kind of terrible. But a lot of the saints were persecuted for their beliefs. A lot of them were martyrs for their cause. The difference with Ranier is that he never wanted his gifts. He never wanted to be a martyr."

"So what drew you to him?"

"He has a lot of wisdom to give to us," Abercrombie said.

She was starting to think that maybe this guy wasn't as stable as he appeared to be. Who prays to a saint like this? But he had been so nice so far that she didn't want to offend him. She nodded her head.

"I don't expect you to understand," he told her. "You probably think I sound like one of those nuts who are shouting about Jesus in the street."

"No, of course not."

They were both getting uncomfortable.

"It's a nice day," he said. "Let's go for a walk on the beach. We've been inside so long. It would be nice to get out and clear our heads."

"Sure."

* * *

"You can scream all you want, Fella, but it won't change my mind," Leon was shouting into his cell phone. "You ought to know by now that you're not going to intimidate me into doing what you want."

There was a knock at the hotel door. He walked over and opened it.

A young guy, maybe nineteen, wearing jeans and a Cooze Patrol t-shirt, was standing in the doorway.

"How did you get up here? I don't have time for fans right now."

"Mr. Oswald sent me," the kid said.

"That's different; get inside."

The kid walked in, and Leon closed the door.

"I don't give a fuck what the rest of the band wants," Leon said, getting back to his conversation. "You know full well that I'm the deciding vote in this equation. So what you guys want means fuck-all to me."

The kid sat on the foot of the bed and swung his legs back and forth.

"I'm crazy? You really should choose your words better, asshole. That's not exactly how you get me on your side."

He shut his phone off and stared at the kid with hate-filled eyes.

The boy gulped.

"It's not you," Leon said. "It's this goddamn band of mine."

"Cooze Patrol?"

"You should know better than that, unless you just wore that t-shirt to impress me. Three of those guys are dead from overdoses. No way I'm getting *that* band back together. No, I'm talking about Honey Load. They wanna get the old gang back together and play for peanuts. Well, I stopped being an elephant a long time ago."

"Gee," the kid said, "that would be cool if you guys got back together."

"Yeah, sure."

"They won't pay you what you're worth, huh?"

"You can say that again," Leon said. "But don't worry your pretty little head about shit that doesn't matter. Enough business talk."

The kid smiled. "You know, when Mr. Oswald told me what was up, I told him I'd come here for free. I've been a fan of yours forever."

"Sure you have," Leon said. This fanboy shit was starting to get on his nerves. "There's a wig in the bathroom. Put it on. And get out of those clothes."

"Sure thing."

Leon watched him go inside the bathroom and close the door.

He threw his phone across the room.

"Fucking peanuts," he said, and started doing jumping jacks. He hadn't gotten down to the gym earlier in the day like he had wanted to. And that pissed him off too. He hated it when he got off his routine. That's what sucked about being on the road. Reuniting the band—going on tour—would be a hundred times worse.

The kid came out of the bathroom, naked and wearing a long blond wig. It looked just like the way Leon's hair used to look, back in the day. When he was the biggest fucking stud on the planet.

Now he kept his cowboy hat on all the time to hide the receding hairline.

"Looking good," Leon said, finally able to get his mind off the bullshit. "You know, on second thought, go put the t-shirt back on."

"Really?"

"Yeah, sure. Might as well play the fan up to the hilt. It might be fun."

"I'm really a fan, you know."

"All the better."

The kid went into the bathroom, then came out fitting the shirt over his head.

"Now get on the bed," Leon said. "On all fours. I'm gonna buck you like a bronco."

* * *

For some reason, they held hands as they walked along the shoreline.

It had happened so organically, without thought, that when Abercrombie noticed it, it made him feel butterflies in his stomach. This kind of thing never happened, and he wasn't sure what it meant.

She pretended not to notice, but he could see her smile from the corner of his eye when she turned her head.

The comforting sound of the waves coming in provided a relaxing soundtrack to the moment.

"So what are you going to do now?" she asked him. "You said you had some business, and then you're leaving?"

"Something like that," he said. "My job demands I travel all the time."

"I'm not sure I'd like that," she said. "Unless I had someone to travel with."

He took her hint. "Yeah, it does get lonely sometimes, I guess. But I deal with it."

"I know there's nothing keeping me here," she said, being more blatant about it.

"That's too bad."

"Seriously, these past couple of days have been wonderful. Can't we make it last a while longer?"

"You're asking me to take you with me?"

"I guess so," she said, suddenly not sure of herself. "But I don't want to presume."

"I'd be lying if I didn't say I was thinking about that myself," he said. "I mean, we do seem to have good chemistry together."

"And we're certainly compatible in bed," she told him.

"I'd agree with that."

"So what about it?" she said. "You want a traveling companion?"

"Let me think about it. This is something new for me. I usually enjoy flying solo."

"No reason why that can't change," she said.

"I guess not."

They were both smiling.

"Let's go in," she said. "The water's nice and warm today."

"Yeah," he said, "let's."

They walked into the surf and wallowed up to their waists.

"Not too many people around today," he said.

"I wish there weren't any," she said. "I can think of some things I'd like to do on the beach."

"There won't be as many people after sundown. So you might get your wish."

"Cool."

* * *

Leon was looking for his cell phone. It was somewhere over by the window, he thought. But then he found it under the bed. It must have ricocheted.

The kid was in the bathroom, taking a shower.

He turned it on and saw he had five messages already. So he shut it off again and put it on the nightstand. There was a thick sheen of sweat covering him like a second skin and he couldn't wait to use the shower himself.

Finally, the kid came out and grinned sheepishly.

"I thought you'd never get out of there," Leon said.

The boy was dressed now and stood there in front of him.

"Well," Leon said, "what are you supposed to be? A fucking statue?"

The kid just stood there, not knowing what to say.

"Oh, I get ya. I thought you said you'd do this for free."

The kid didn't say anything. Leon had noticed the bruises he'd left on the boy's abdomen and figured it was better to just get this over with.

He found his pants on the floor, picked them up, and got his wallet. He counted out what he owed and added a little extra.

The kid smiled and made his way for the door.

"Aren't you forgetting something?"

The boy turned, momentarily confused.

"The fucking wig," Leon said. "Leave it here."

The kid took off the wig and put it on top of the desk by the door on his way out.

* * *

"So is that it?" Abercrombie asked.

They were sitting in the rental car outside of a dull gray house. Abercrombie always rented cars from locally owned outfits instead of the big national chains. It just seemed to make more sense.

"Yeah, that's his house."

Abercrombie had shut off the engine. They were across the street, in the shadow of a big oak tree.

"You going inside or something?"

"Naw."

"Then why have me take you here?"

"I was just curious," Abercrombie said.

"Curious where my ex-husband lived."

"Yeah," he said, "I wanted to see where someone stupid enough to dump you spent his days."

"I have to admit, I was a little leery about giving you directions," she said. "I had no idea what was on your mind. I definitely didn't want anything violent to happen."

"Violent?" Abercrombie said. "Why would it? I don't know him. And what you two had has nothing to do with me."

"Then, I have to ask again: why come here?"

"Curiosity," he said, "pure and simple."

The garage door opened and a middle-aged guy with a Bengals sweatshirt hauled a couple of trash cans down the driveway and left them near his mailbox.

He didn't even look up once. Didn't even notice them. Not that they would necessarily be easy to spot, hidden under the tree with the engine off.

The guy had a pot belly but had strong arms. Strong legs too. He obviously worked out.

Not that it mattered much.

They could hear a woman's voice coming from the house now. There was the silhouette of someone in the lit living room window, behind the shade. They couldn't hear what she was saying. "So that's the other woman, huh?"

"I guess so," Abigail said. "Unless he's moved on to someone else by now."

The guy went inside the garage and closed the door again. The woman moved away from the window.

Abercrombie waited a few minutes before he turned the key and started the car again.

"We going back now?" she asked.

"Yeah."

"That's it?"

"That's it. Like I said, I was just curious. Weren't you?"

"Not really," she said. "This all seems like a big waste of time to me."

"Yeah," Abercrombie said. "Just another way to kill time."

"I could think of a lot better ways to do that."

"Maybe we can stop on the way back, get something to eat. You got any preferences?"

"I could really go for a pizza," she said.

"Done. And then when we get back to the hotel, I'll take you up on that offer you made earlier."

"Which one is that?"

"Sex on the beach," he said. "That's a drink too, isn't it? I never had one of those. Maybe we should hit the bar first."

* * *

"Why didn't you call first?" Gloria asked when she saw Leon standing outside the front door. "You can't just pop up like this unannounced. I've got rights."

"You've got whatever rights I give you," he said. "You've got my son. Isn't that enough?"

He pushed past her. The television was on, some inane action movie, and his son, Ricky, was stretched out on the couch, wearing those baggy pants he always wore. He had an earring in one ear now. Something new.

"Hi, sport," Leon said, sitting beside him on the couch. "What you watchin'?"

The boy just stared glassy-eyed at the screen.

"I'm not going away until you talk to me," he said.

"Hi, Dad," the fourteen-year-old boy on the couch beside him said.

"Hello to you too."

"We don't want you here," Gloria said, standing beside the television. "Neither of us."

"It's been a long time since I saw my son," Leon said. "I don't come out this way very often. And if you had your way, I'd *never* see him."

"Which is just the way we'd like it."

"The kid can speak for himself," Leon said. "He doesn't need his bitch of a mother to talk for him. Do you, sport?"

He saw his son's lower lip trembling a bit. He must be remembering things from a long time ago, when Leon lived with them.

"Don't you ever want to come visit your dad anymore?" Leon said. "I'm a big fucking rock star. Most kids would be dying to come stay with their dad if they were in your shoes. I never understood you, sport."

"Exactly," Gloria said. Her hair was mousy brown now, but Leon remembered a time when she was a bottle blonde who gave one mean blow job. A groupie who was at almost every show, always trying to get backstage and get a piece of him. Well, she had a piece of him now. Ricky. And she wasn't really good at sharing.

"You never understood *either of us*, which is why we're glad you left."

He looked her up and down, remembering when she was young and hot and he actually looked forward to fucking her. She would do absolutely anything in bed, and it used to be fun. He wondered if she was still fun anymore. Did she swing from the chandeliers with her new husband? That semi-retarded grease monkey she lived with now.

"Yeah, yeah, I get it. I'm the fucking Ebola virus. You're glad to be rid of me."

"A perfect analogy," she said, and he was surprised she knew words that big.

"I just stopped by to see my son," he said. "And find out when he's coming for a visit."

"How about never?" Gloria said, wiping stray hairs out of her eyes. She still kept her hair nice and long at least.

"I told you, I want the boy to speak for himself," Leon said. "He can speak, can't he? Or did you take his tongue, the same way you took his balls?"

"I can speak," Ricky said, still staring at the television.

"Well, it's about time, sport. I was starting to think you'd gone mute on us."

"I don't want to visit you, Daddy," he said. The way he said "Daddy" made him sound like a little kid again. The five-year-old who used to cry whenever Leon hit his mother. The same wuss he always was. Time hadn't succeeded in making a man out of him yet.

"You don't want to visit me?" Leon said. "I find that hard to believe, sport. Don't I spoil the hell out of you?"

"Andy's coming home soon," Gloria said. "His shift is just about up."

"How is old Andy?" Leon asked. "I haven't seen him in forever. Maybe I'll stick around and say hi."

"Please, Leon, just go away."

"What kind of visit is this? You both aren't very hospitable."

"Please go, Daddy," Ricky said, never once taking his eye off the television, even during the commercials.

"Yeah, I'll go. I certainly don't want to hang around someplace where I'm not wanted."

"You're *not* wanted," Gloria said. "You haven't been wanted around here for a long time."

"I hear ya," Leon said, and chuckled. "Look at the mouth on you. I remember when I used to like that mouth. When it knew its job. Sucking my dick."

"You *are* the Ebola virus," she told him, using his metaphor against him. "Everything you touch turns to shit around you. We don't want you here."

"You have a tendency to repeat yourself," Leon said. "It gets tiresome. It's a wonder Andy-Boy puts up with it. But then again, I bet he puts up with a lot of things I wouldn't."

Leon got up from the couch and started walking toward the door. He pushed past Gloria, just barely brushing her with his arm, but she jumped back as if she'd been burned by a cigarette.

He turned in the doorway and looked at his son one more time.

"You into hip-hop now, with those baggy pants?"

The boy didn't answer.

Leon laughed and went to the front door. He didn't look back as he let himself out. He considered sticking around in his car and waiting for Andy. It might be fun to fuck with another member of this sweet little family, but he decided he just wanted to get away from this place. It wasn't worth his time or energy.

He started the Lexus and his tires screeched on his way down the street.

* * *

The tide washed up over them, and it was just like that scene in the old movie *From Here to Eternity*, except it was dark, and they could barely see each other in the light of the moon.

"That was wonderful," Abigail said.

He stretched out on his back and let the water wash over him.

"Did I ever tell you how young you make me feel?" she said. "How you make everything shitty good again?"

He made a noncommittal noise.

"The water is so warm," she said.

"Shh," he told her, "just be quiet and enjoy the moment."

She would have taken offense, but he said it so softly, so gently, that she didn't consider it an insult.

She rested in the crook of his arm, staring up at the moon. The water was just high enough to wash over them but not cover them.

"The moon sure is beautiful tonight," she said.

"Yeah."

"So you never told me," she said, "what's your first name?"

"It doesn't matter," he said.

"Sure it does. If we're going to be traveling together. Why keep it a secret? Is it something embarrassing?"

He didn't say anything, and then he sighed. "Yeah, it's embarrassing."

"Come on," she said, "confide in me. I'll tell you a secret if you tell me."

"Why is it so important to you?"

"It just is. Come on, let's trade secrets."

"Okay, okay. You first."

"When I was about 30, I had a brief affair with my sister-in-law. She was five years younger and really cute. I never did anything with a woman before. Not really. And it was kind of sad to let it go. But it was just too much trouble to keep it a secret."

"Uh huh."

"Okay, so tell me. What's your real name? It can't just be Abercrombie. What's your first name?"

He looked at the moon and imagined it exploding in the sky.

"Abner," he said.

* * *

When he got back to the hotel, Leon found Fella Faze—the lead guitarist for Honey Load—waiting for him in the lobby. They had talked a lot on the phone lately, but they had not seen each other in person in years. Fella sure was looking old, and his hairline was in worse shape than his.

"Hi, Leon," Fella said. He'd been pacing back and forth and looked relieved to stop. "They told me you were out. So I thought I'd wait for you."

"You came all the way here to see me?"

"I came all the way here to talk some sense into you."

"Then you wasted your time."

"Give me a chance," Fella said. "I came all this way, like you said."

"Yeah, yeah. I always have to give everyone else a chance. Nobody gives me a fucking chance."

"What was that?"

"Nothing," he said. "Nothing to do with you. I just tried to go see my son."

"Ricky? How is the kid these days?"

"I wouldn't know. The little fucker won't talk to me."

"Come on, man. You really look like you could use a drink, and the bar is just over there."

"Yeah, okay."

* * *

Abercrombie knelt before the candles and the statue of Ranier and he prayed, just like he did every night. She watched him from beneath the sheets. It was almost kind of fascinating, watching him pray to that ugly sculpture.

That's the one thing about him I'll never understand, she thought.

He crossed himself and got up. Then he reached for her on the bed.

She thought he was going to take her into his arms, but instead, he rolled her over and punched her in a special part of her back.

"What!"

He rolled her back over, so that she was looking up at him.

"I can't move," she said.

"It's time to get down to business," he said.

He looked sad as he stared into her eyes for a few minutes.

"Why?"

He went over to his backpack and pulled out a long knife in a sheath. He took it out with a great sense of ceremony and held it before her.

"You're going to kill me," she said, amazed that her head could still move, that she could speak. Even though the rest of her body was paralyzed.

He wouldn't answer. Instead, he knelt down and raised the long knife high over his head. She couldn't help but stare up at the shiny blade.

And then, it was like she was inside his head, and they left the hotel room.

* * *

"Why can't you see it from our point of view?" Fella said, throwing back another shot of tequila. They had a row of shot glasses lined up in front of them. He then took a gulp from his beer.

"I just don't need the money enough to beg for it," Leon said. "Can't you see that what they're offering is an insult?"

"I don't see it that way," Fella said. "It's been rough since the band broke up. I thought we'd just all go on to other bands, keep playing, but it didn't happen that way. Everyone kept saying how great a guitarist I was, but once we split apart, nobody seemed to want anything to do with me."

"Those fucking Seattle bands," Leon said. "That grunge shit ruined things for everybody."

"Yeah, well, that's over, and we're getting a second chance here. I'm sick of taking jobs I hate. Do you know I'm a plumber now? I unplug people's fucking toilets, man. It pays good, I'm not really knocking it, but it's nothing like being in a band again. I'm sick of practicing in my garage for nothing. I know you went on to do your solo stuff. I know that if you say the word, you could have people playing with you in a New York minute. But we don't all have those options."

"It ain't my fault, man."

"But don't you feel that you owe us anything?" Fella said. "I mean, Honey Load is what made you a star, man. A bona fide rock star."

"What about Cooze Patrol?" Leon said. "You'd be surprised how many fans that band still has. Hell, I'm surprised."

"They gave you underground cred," Fella said. "But they didn't make you a star. They didn't get you on MTV, back in the days when that channel actually played videos twenty-four hours a day. Cooze Patrol didn't turn you into a rock god. We did that."

"You didn't do shit for me," Leon said. "We did it together."

"Exactly, man. I didn't mean to imply otherwise."

"Let me think on it, Fella."

"So you're considering it? I'm telling you, if the reunion tour goes well, it could lead to bigger money. It could lead to bigger venues. All they need is a taste of us again and they'll be hooked, and we can start bringing in the long green again."

"Maybe you're right," Leon said. "I don't know anymore."

"All I ask is that you consider it, man. You can't just dismiss it without really giving it some real thought."

"Yeah," Leon said. "I'll think about it. Let me sleep on it, and I'll call you in the morning."

"Do you mean that?"

"Yeah," Leon said. He didn't know if he was really having a change of mind or if he was just getting drunk, but at that moment he really meant it. "Yeah, I'm serious, man. I'll consider it."

"Terrific," Fella said. "You don't know how grateful I am, man."

"Don't celebrate yet," Leon said. "But I promise to give this a fair assessment before I decide once and for all."

"That's all I can ask," Fella said. "Well, I gotta go now."

"You don't have a room here?"

"You shitting me? I can't afford this place. I'm staying at a motel about twenty minutes from here."

"So, you sticking around until you get my decision?"

"What choice do I have? It'll be a ten-hour drive back to Michigan. I'll stay here as long as I can, but please don't take forever."

They shook hands. Like business partners. There was a time when they had actually been friends. Leon remembered a time when they were both fucking groupies on the same bed. They were thick as thieves.

"Thanks, man. I'll look forward to your call. You've got my cell number, right?"

"Of course I do," Leon said.

"G'night."

Leon watched him go. He thought it was funny the guy hadn't even offered to pay for the drinks, hadn't even offered to pay for his share.

Leon drained the last shot glass and then threw a fifty down on the bar and took the elevator back up to his room.

* * *

She saw Abercrombie in front of her, raising the knife, but she also saw him in a thousand other places. Cutting throats, stabbing out people's eyes. Occasionally, someone she knew, mostly people she'd never known. They all went by in a jumble of images, but she knew somehow they were real. That he was killing all these people in blinks of an eye. And then it slowed down for a moment, and the blur of scenarios stopped and became just one.

It was her ex-husband Danny's house. He and his whore, his bitch, Melissa, were asleep in their bed, and Abercrombie turned on the light. They woke, disoriented, and he immediately stabbed Danny twice, leaving him on the floor, bloody but conscious. The man she used to love stared up as Abercrombie put his hand over Melissa's mouth and stabbed her hard between the breasts. Over and over again.

Then he moved toward Danny, who was cowering on the floor, raising an arm to protect himself, and Abercrombie stabbed the arm until it lowered, and then he stabbed Danny over and over in the head until he stopped moving too.

The images sped up again then, as hundreds of other people met similar fates. Only he didn't linger over them like he had Danny. He did it all fast, and vicious. Like he had a time limit.

It all seemed so inconceivable to her. This had to be a dream. There was no way anyone could kill so many people so quickly. At the same time, she could still see the blade raised up by his hands as he knelt before the bed.

She closed her eyes, but it didn't help. The flashes of people dying played on the inside of her eyelids, like a movie in fast-motion.

When they stopped, she opened her eyes, and he was standing above her.

He was crying.

"I'm sorry," he said, and he reached down. She couldn't move her head enough to see, but it looked like his hand went right down *inside* her. But she couldn't feel anything. He held something up in front of her face. It was red and wet.

She turned her head and saw a whole row of wet, bloody things on the bed beside her, and she knew they were all from inside her. He yanked out a long rope of intestines and then leaned over. One hand reached forward and closed her eyes for her again.

And then he slit her throat, deeply, letting the final bits of life leak out of her.

He wrapped himself up in her intestines, still crying, and began shouting at the ceiling until he realized it was useless. He rose and went to take a shower. Then he got dressed and left the building. There were bloody bodies all over the lobby.

He walked through them and went outside, just in time to hear the tornado winds ripping through the town, swirling blood and flesh up into the sky.

Abercrombie had remembered to don his rain poncho so that he didn't get too messy as he walked toward the town limits.

* * *

Leon woke with a hangover and went into the bathroom to soak his head under the shower. He stood there a long time, not moving, just letting the spray drench his hair, his temples. He let the heat temporarily stop the throbbing in his skull.

Then he went back out to the bed. His cell phone was still on the nightstand. And he noticed the bed was empty. He hadn't slept alone in a long time. But now that he thought about it, it felt weird. He'd obviously tossed and turned a lot. The blanket was on the floor. The sheets were tangled up.

But the air conditioning felt good on his naked skin.

"I guess I better call Fella," he said, not really sure why he gave a fuck. Maybe it was something about seeing the guy in person. To see how age had deteriorated that once-handsome face, and Leon knew that it had done the same to him. He'd been so adamant against plastic surgery, but now he wondered if maybe it might not be a bad idea.

Age was the enemy.

That bastard knows me too well, Leon thought. *He knew if he came here, spoke to me face to face, that it would bring back the memories.*

We can't escape our pasts. Even if we wanted to.

He pushed the button for his address book and then scrolled down to Fella's name. He pushed the button again and the phone rang.

Fella picked it up on the second ring. Like he had woken early and was waiting for the call all morning.

"Leon, is that you?"

"Yeah."

"Did you think things over? Did you consider what we talked about?"

"Yeah, I guess so."

"So what's your decision?"

"I still think it's a bad deal," Leon said. "I still think they're fucking us."

"So your answer is no?"

"No," he said, "I've changed my mind."

"You have?" The happiness in Fella's voice was so alien to him. He hadn't heard that emotion directed at him in a long time. "You really have?"

"Yeah," Leon said, and as soon as he said the word he felt like a sucker. He knew he was selling himself short, selling them all short. But something about Fella's plea had made him realize how much he missed being up on a stage singing. It had been a long time, even since his last solo project, and even though Fella thought he could get another band with a snap of his fingers, Leon wasn't so sure about that anymore. It had been too long since he felt relevant, just one in a long line of disappointments, and it was starting to make him mean. "I'll do it."

"I'll tell the guys," Fella said. "I'm going to head back right now."

"Okay," Leon said. "I'll call Barry and fill him in on the details."

"You're not fucking with me, are you?" Fella asked. "You're not going to wait till I get back to Detroit and then call me and tell me you changed your mind again, are you? You're not doing this just to fuck with my head?"

"No, Fella," Leon said, "I'm not fucking with you."

"You don't know how happy you've made me, man. It will be amazing to work with you again, to work with the band again. I really can't wait to start rehearsals."

"Me too," Leon said, as it really started to filter into his skull. It had been a long time since they had made music, and it was something he really did want to go back to. "I guess I just didn't realize it until now."

"That's terrific news, man. I just don't know what else to say. I'm ecstatic."

"Well, you better start heading back. At least I didn't make you wait too long, huh?"

"Thanks for that. I would have stayed by the phone all day if I had to."

"Rats," Leon said. "On second thought, I should have waited. Made you sweat a little."

Fella laughed and then they finished the call and Leon put his phone down.

What a strange turn of events, he thought. *I guess I better call Barry and give him the update.*

* * *

Abercrombie washed the blood off himself in a lake. The water was a little cool, but he had to make himself presentable if there was any chance he would be able to hitch a ride. At least the rain poncho had taken the brunt, and he just tossed that away. They were cheap enough to replace.

So where to next?

He climbed out of the water and dried himself with one of the towels he'd stolen from the hotel room. Not that anyone there would be needing it now. He was going to need another backpack soon. This one was full to bulging, and he'd had a real hard time trying to get the bloodstains out. If anyone asked at this point, he'd just say it was paint.

As he got dressed, he could feel Saint Ranier hovering over him somewhere nearby, just out of sight. He knew that the saint was happy with him, and he suddenly felt a flash of euphoria wash over him.

He went back out onto the stretch of highway and watched for oncoming cars. Whenever one would approach, he'd stick his thumb out, but most of them just passed him by.

Finally one stopped, and he slid inside.

"Where you going, young man?" the old guy behind the wheel asked. "Not often you see someone out here all by themselves."

"My car broke down a ways back," Abercrombie said. "Thanks a lot for the ride."

"I didn't see no abandoned cars back there," the man said. "But I'm not one to ask questions. You didn't answer *my* question, though."

"Wherever you're going is fine with me," Abercrombie said. "I'm happy to get as far away from here as I can."

"What about your car?"

Abercrombie laughed. "You got me. I got in a fight with my girlfriend—my ex-girlfriend—and she dropped me off in the middle of the highway."

"You don't need to be embarrassed around me," the man said. "I've had my share of ornery women. I know what it's like. My name is Bill. Bill Cody. Just like that son of a bitch Buffalo Bill Cody. Except he's dead and I'm alive. And I don't own any buffalo."

Abercrombie shook his hand. "Bob," he said. "Bob Abercrombie."

"Nice to meet you, Bob. I'm driving quite a ways. You sure you want to stick around for the whole ride?"

"Yes, sir," Abercrombie said, "I'm sure. I've got nothing else to do."

* * *

Leon ironed out the details with Barry and then shut off his phone. It had been a long day and he was talked out. What he really needed was a distraction from all this business bullshit.

I need to get the fuck out of here, Leon thought. *I'm going stir crazy in this place.*

He put on some clothes and took the elevator down to the lobby. The manager, Mr. Oswald, was in today and seemed very happy to see him.

"Mr. Coles, so nice to see you, I hope you're having a pleasant stay."

"Terrific, can't ask for more."

"Well, if there's anything else you need, don't hesitate to ask."

"You know me better than that," Leon said, and then headed toward the lobby.

As he approached the glass doors, another man came inside. He was tall, with long blond hair, and the only luggage he had was a backpack strapped behind him. Leon hadn't seen a guy this attractive in a long time, and he did a double-take. The guy didn't seem to notice.

I've got to figure out a way to meet him, Leon thought. *But first, I'm going to go get a big, juicy steak.*

* * *

When Abercrombie got into his hotel room, he didn't even bother to turn on the light. He just slipped off the backpack and crawled into bed. It had been an exhausting trip out here, and he just wanted to sleep the rest of the day away.

It was a good thing he remembered to take some money during his last killing spree. It wouldn't do to kill so many people without grabbing a little cash along the way. You never knew when it would come in handy, and it wasn't like anyone was going to miss it. He never got too greedy, but there was no reason why he couldn't live in at least a small level of luxury during his travels. He was doing a saint's work, after all.

I have to remember to get candles tomorrow, he thought.

He felt a rumble of hunger in his stomach and realized it had been a while since he last ate, but sleep was the more dominant force right now, and he lay back on the sheets and let it crash down on him like a tidal wave, not even bothering to take off his clothes.

* * *

"Hey, you mind if I sit here?" Leon asked, walking up to the bar.

"No, I don't mind," Abercrombie said, taking a long pull from his beer glass.

"So what brings you here? Business or pleasure?"

"Excuse me?"

Leon hated this small talk bullshit. He'd hoped the guy would just recognize him. It made things a lot easier. But no such luck. Maybe he wasn't a metal fan.

"People usually stay in a hotel because either they're on a business trip, or they're on vacation. Which are you?"

"Oh, business, I guess."

"So what kind of business you in?"

The guy stared straight ahead. It was clear he didn't want to talk about it. But Leon had asked, and the guy was thinking up an answer.

"Insurance," Abercrombie said eventually. "Disaster insurance."

"Plane crashes, that kind of stuff?"

"Yeah."

"I don't remember hearing about a plane crash around here recently."

"We do a lot more than just cover plane crashes," Abercrombie said.

"Oh."

This was going to be a lot harder than he thought.

"So you got plans for tonight?"

Abercrombie looked at him, puzzled. "What?"

"I just thought, if you're new in town, you might have nothing to do. I was gonna go check out some music. Thought you'd like to come along."

"Oh."

"You're not going to ask?"

"Huh?"

Leon sighed. "You're not going ask me what I'm doing here?"

Abercrombie just wished this guy would leave him alone. "Okay, I'll bite. What are you doing here?"

"I'm in a rock band. Ever hear of Honey Load?"

"Yeah, I think so."

"We're getting back together."

"Is that so?" Abercrombie said, not sounding all that excited.

"Yeah," Leon said. "It's been a long time coming. I'm the singer. My name is Leon."

"Good to meet you. I'm Abercrombie."

"Like *Abercrombie and Fitch?*"

Abercrombie ignored the question.

"So what about it?"

"What about what?'

"You interested in seeing some live music, or would you rather just sit here and drink the night away?"

"Are those my only two choices?"

Leon smiled. "Yeah."

"What the fuck?" Abercrombie said. "Where's the music at?"

"Not very far from here. There's a band I want you to see."

"Me? Why me?"

"You ask a lot of questions," Leon said.

* * *

They were a cover band called Sweet Leg Action. A band that pretended to be Honey Load at their peak. The lead singer looked to be in his 20s and had long blond hair, much like Leon did back in the '80s. Here, he kept a baseball cap on.

Leon handed Abercrombie a beer. The kid didn't look all that different from the guy onstage. He was young, blond, and muscular-looking. He reminded Leon a lot of himself.

"You like the music?"

"It's okay, I guess. I was never really into hair bands. I was more of a punk, I guess."

"Punk, huh?"

"Yeah."

"All that anger. That doom and gloom. What you guys need is to get laid more often and you wouldn't be so pissed off all the time."

"You think so?"

"Yeah, listen to this stuff. It's music about happiness. About getting drunk and getting laid. None of that 'I hate the world' bullshit."

"So is that what it's all about? Getting drunk and getting laid?"

"Yeah, kinda."

"Thanks for clearing that up."

Leon laughed and pointed to the stage. "You see that guy up there. He's pretending to be me."

"Really? Where's his baseball cap?"

Leon smiled again. "You're a real ball-buster, huh?"

"Sometimes."

"That kid up there, he must be half my age, and he wishes he was me. What I wouldn't do to be *him*."

"Well, not really him, right? You'd want to be yourself at that age."

"Yeah, you're right."

They were shouting to hear each other over the music.

"Wanna go closer to the stage?" Leon asked. "It's no use trying to have a conversation in here."

"What?" Abercrombie said and then smiled.

Leon rolled his eyes, and the two walked closer to the stage.

After a couple of songs, Leon suddenly jumped up on the stage. Nobody tried to stop him. When the singer saw who he was, he looked dumbstruck and handed Leon the microphone.

Everyone in the audience seemed to catch on at once, and they all cheered.

"Y'know," Leon said into the mic, "I've heard a lot about you guys. You're supposed to be a really good cover band. And you are."

"Thanks," the singer said, slightly off-mic.

"But no matter how good you are, you're never going to be as good as the real thing."

Leon then broke out into song, singing "Sweet Leg Action."

The band instantly caught up with him and played along.

The singer just stepped aside and watched in awe.

Leon kept looking down into the audience, at Abercrombie in particular.

Abercrombie wanted so badly to just leave. He hated this kind of music, and this Leon guy was making him uncomfortable.

But for some reason he stayed put and watched Leon finish the song.

When he was done, Leon jumped off the stage. Everyone in the room was cheering and trying to touch him. He slapped a lot of hands and dodged a lot of girls trying to shove their tits in his face.

Leon grabbed Abercrombie by the arm. "Let's get out of here."

Abercrombie pulled his arm away. He felt like decking this guy, but didn't.

"Okay," he said.

* * *

An hour later, they were back in Leon's hotel room, naked and grunting.

Sometimes, Leon pretended that the guy was the lead singer of Sweet Leg Action, but most of the time he focused on Abercrombie himself. He was young and handsome, and there was not much reason to fantasize about anyone else.

At one point, Leon had his hands tight around Abercrombie's throat. The other man did not resist, even though it was clear he'd have hand marks on his neck in the morning.

When they were done, Leon rolled over on his side, covered in sweat.

"You never did anything like this before, did you?"

Abercrombie didn't say a word.

"Talkative type, aren't you?"

"You seem like you're more than happy to do the talking for both of us."

"There's that sarcasm again. You love to be the smart-ass, huh?"

Abercrombie grunted.

"Well, I like it. And I like you too. Even though you pretend to be such a hard-ass bastard."

Abercrombie stared down at the mattress.

"You can't tell me you didn't have a good time just now."

"It's late," Abercrombie said. "Can't you just roll over and go to sleep."

"Sleep? What the fuck are you talking about? The night's still young!"

Fifteen minutes later, they were both asleep.

* * *

Later, they'd moved to Abercrombie's room.

"So what's the statue all about? You some kind of priest?"

"It's just a saint," Abercrombie said.

"Which saint?"

"Saint Ranier. You probably never heard of him."

"No, I didn't. And I had no idea I was fucking a priest last night."

"I'm not a priest."

"Then why all the candles and prayer stuff?"

"You wouldn't understand."

"Try me."

"Look, I need some time alone. Can you just leave for a while?"

"What, you want some time to pray?"

"Yeah."

"Gotta confess your sins from last night?"

"No."

"Why can't I watch?"

In the past, when he'd brought girls up to his room, Abercrombie had never had a problem praying in front of them. But for some reason, with Leon here, he felt weird.

"Come on. Can't you just give me some time to myself?"

"I don't want to go," Leon said. "I want to watch you pray. I bet it's cute."

Cute sounded like such a strange word coming out of Leon's mouth. Like he had said it just to twist the knife a little more.

Hell, that's *exactly* what he was doing.

"Whatever," Abercrombie said.

He lit some candles, knelt down on his portable prayer bench, and prayed to Saint Ranier.

Leon sat on the edge of the bed and watched, not saying a word.

Abercrombie prayed in complete silence.

Leon stared at the strange statue. Some deformed-looking guy wrapped up in ropes. It sure looked like a strange saint to be praying to.

* * *

"So tell me more about Ranier," Leon said.

"I told you all about Admah, about Sodom and Gomorrah."

"You told me his people were from there, that he wandered around healing people. That they strangled him with his own intestines. But you left something out."

"What?"

"Why the hell do you pray to such a guy?"

"Because he's powerful," Abercrombie said. "Because he works through me."

"How?"

"In order to explain that," Abercrombie said, "I need to explain what happened after he died."

"Cool," Leon said. "That's the kind of stuff I'm interested in. So tell me already."

"Okay," Abercrombie said. "After they took out all of his insides, after he finally died of his wounds, Ranier went to the afterlife. But he cursed God for what had been done to him, and he refused to enter heaven. But he refused to enter hell either. He just hovered in limbo, whole and separate and able to survey what had happened to him. For some reason, he was stronger in death than he'd ever been in life.

"And he found something out in the afterlife: that he had a penchant for acquiring the powers of others. He began with the two angels who had destroyed Sodom and Gomorrah, and his family's place of origin, Admah. He sought them out and stole the powers they had. He drained them and left empty husks. And then he went seeking other powers. Other divine gifts that never would have been given to him by God directly. So he simply took them, using angels like you or I would drain bottles of alcohol. Drinking every ounce of power they had. Until he was pretty damn powerful himself.

"Among his underground followers, he has a strange nickname, The Reversible Bondage Saint, because he was bound in his own intestines by his tormentors, and his organs were removed one by one and shown to him. Sometimes he appears to the living, either in his normal form, or in the form of his mutilated self. Reversible."

Leon stared at him. "So he appeared to you."

"Yes, he called upon me to serve him. And I accepted."

"So what do you do for this guy?"

"Whatever he demands."

"And you mentioned underground followers. Does this mean there are others like you?"

Abercrombie nodded. "But I've never met any of them. Not face to face. I've talked to a few of them on the Internet. The ones I know of, they live overseas. One's in South America. There aren't many of us"

"You do realize that you sound like a nut, right?"

"Yeah, I realize that."

"I like you, but I sure don't need a religious nut in my life right now."

"I didn't realize I was in your life."

Leon laughed. Then he leaned over and kissed Abercrombie for a long time.

* * *

When Abercrombie woke up the next morning, he found himself in bed alone. A whole day had disappeared in a blur. It wouldn't do to lose track of time like this.

This was easily the weirdest morning of his life. He'd never been so aggressively pursued by another guy before, and he'd never given in so completely before.

What the fuck was going on?

He got up from the bed and rubbed his stomach. It was probably a good idea to go down to the gym and work out for most of the morning. He had been ignoring his exercise regimen lately.

He figured he would just have to shower again later anyway, so he threw on some clothes and headed downstairs.

As he got in the elevator, he could feel Saint Ranier hovering nearby, just outside of his field of vision. Moving in a strange, spidery way, demanding his attention. His awareness.

It would be time again for Ranier to feed.

Abercrombie did his best to ignore it. This thing he did, moving from town to town, had devoured his entire life without his even being aware of it. He hadn't stopped to think about that in a long time. He found himself thinking about it now.

Did he still want to be the avenging angel of Saint Ranier? Did he really want to live his life in service to a being who slew whole cities, reducing them to ashes?

Abercrombie felt a wave of guilt rush over him. It was the first time he had ever really felt an emotion about what he had been doing, and it almost brought him down to his knees.

No, he heard the voice in his head. *Do not feel guilty. You did nothing wrong. You did it for **me**.*

The elevator seemed to move in slow-motion. It didn't stop at any of the other floors. Nobody else got on. Abercrombie expected it to take him all the way down into the bowels of the earth. Into the very heart of hell itself.

"I can't do this anymore," he said.

The elevator stopped. The doors opened.

Abercrombie didn't feel Ranier's presence anymore as he got out and walked to the gymnasium.

* * *

Leon got off the phone with his agent, Barry, and popped the champagne.

"Gimme your glass," he said. "We've got some celebrating to do."

Abercrombie's ribs were bruised and aching as he moved forward on the bed. He thrust his glass forward. Room service had delivered the cart minutes before: two glasses and champagne in an ice bucket.

"There's more where this came from," Leon said, filling both glasses.

"So I'm guessing the comeback tour is a done deal?"

"Yeah, and I guess I'm feeling better about it now," Leon said. "But do me a favor and don't call it a *comeback* tour, okay? I don't need to come back from anything."

"Of course not."

"Oh, and thanks for putting that statue away," Leon said. "It was starting to give me the creeps."

Abercrombie nodded and drank from his glass.

"How long you been toting that thing around with you anyway?"

"A long time."

"Why bother?" Leon asked. "What the hell has some dead saint ever done for you? Sounds silly to me, you know."

Abercrombie didn't say anything.

"You say he's got the power of angels. That he can destroy cities. You know that's all bullshit, right? You know it's just a story?"

"I guess so."

"We're good for each other," Leon said. "We ground each other."

He refilled their glasses.

"So are you coming with me tomorrow?"

"I've been thinking about it."

"Well, don't think any more. Just do it. I got plane tickets for both of us, and I won't have time to debate it tomorrow. I've got to sign those contracts before someone changes their mind."

"I'm surprised you're not the one to change your mind."

"I didn't say I wasn't," Leon said. "I want to get it over with before I decide I don't want to do it."

Leon called down to room service and ordered another bottle of their best.

"So you're coming?"

"Yeah, I'll go with you."

"I like you," Leon said. "You're hot as hell, and you can take a punch."

They both started laughing at that.

* * *

Abercrombie woke up in the middle of the night. He was crouched on the floor, with a knife in his hand. He had no idea how he had gotten there. A thin layer of light came in from outside the window, seeping through the outline of the blinds, and he could see the statue of Saint Ranier on the countertop in the kitchenette. Over near the mini-bar.

He put the knife down on the floor and stood up. He went into the bathroom and splashed cold water on his face.

Abercrombie turned on the light and looked in the mirror. He was crying blood.

I've got to get out of here, he thought. *Just for a little while. Until this moment passes. Maybe I can go downstairs and work out. Work this out of my system.*

He shut off the water and went out to the bedroom. Leon was asleep on his stomach, snoring. The sheet barely covered his naked butt.

He thought about how those fists had pummeled him the night before. How those fingers had choked him almost into unconsciousness. And he knew there was no way he could kill Leon. No way he could do Ranier's bidding anymore.

This city would be spared.

Abercrombie put on some shorts and a t-shirt and grabbed a towel. He left the room and went down to the gym, which was open twenty-four hours a day.

He got into the elevator, and the doors closed.

I'm going to do this, he thought.

And then the elevator car suddenly dropped, as if its cables had been cut, and went plummeting down ten floors like a rocket, knocking Abercrombie to his knees. To his stomach. He screamed as he realized there was a good chance he was going to die when it finally hit bottom.

* * *

Once you pledged yourself to me, the bond was complete. Never to be broken.

The words formed in his brain without a voice. Abercrombie opened his eyes and looked up. The elevator doors were open. He was one level below the lobby, where the gym was located. He had no idea how long he had been there. How long the elevator doors had been open.

He didn't know what time it was, but as far as he could tell, nobody else was up and about. At least not on this floor.

He lifted himself up off the elevator floor and walked through the open doorway. And then he stopped in the middle of the hallway, as if suddenly frozen on the spot.

He couldn't move forward.

It is a bond of blood, the words came again. *It is a bond of souls.*

Abercrombie lifted his hands. All he could think about was ripping his own eyes out. But he didn't go through with it.

* * *

"You destroyed it," Abercrombie said. He was back in his hotel room. Leon was sitting up on the bed.

"It had to be done. You were starting to obsess over that thing. When I woke up it was sitting there, watching me. I saw you pack it away. What made you take it out again?"

"I didn't."

The statue was in pieces, scattered throughout the room.

"Listen to yourself. You trying to tell me you did this in your sleep?"

"I'm not sure."

"And your eyes. You're bleeding around your eyes. What did you do to yourself?"

"I'm okay."

"Is it because I asked you to come with me?" Leon said. "Are you freaking out on me?"

"No," Abercrombie said, then thought about it. "I don't *think* so."

"Look, it's either me or that crazy religious shit you've been obsessed with. You can't have both. I'm offering you a hand up to reality again. Don't you see that?"

"Yeah."

"Then why won't you take my hand? Why won't you let me help you?"

"I'm just stubborn, I guess."

Leon jumped out of bed then and grabbed both sides of his head.

"Stop it," Leon said. "Just let go of it."

His fingers were tangled in Abercrombie's hair. Their faces were close, and they were staring in each other's eyes.

"You think I'm insane."

"I think you need help," Leon said. "And I can get it for you. I can get you anything you want."

"Thank you," Abercrombie said, and meant it.

"Now come back to bed," Leon said. "In a few hours the sun will be up and we'll have to get ready to leave. Let's sleep a while longer."

"Okay."

Leon pulled him by the head, by the hair, back over to the bed, and Abercrombie let him. He did not offer any resistance.

They were on the bed now, side by side. And Leon put an arm around Abercrombie's shoulders, pulling him close.

* * *

Leon woke up and saw something glowing in the room. It looked like a man who had been turned inside out. He moved quickly around the room, but his movements weren't normal. They seemed more like a spider than human.

The man didn't look like a spider, he just moved like one.

He kept moving from one end of the room to the other. Then he was standing right over Leon's head. There was a gaping wound in his skull, and his brain was exposed.

The man extended a bloody hand and touched Leon's forehead.

"I'm dreaming," Leon said, and closed his eyes.

Pledge yourself to me, words said without a voice, inside his head. *You are strong. I need you.*

"No," Leon said.

Abercrombie is no good to me anymore. I must have you.

Leon mouthed the word *no* again, keeping his eyes closed.

He felt a burning sensation on his forehead. And then he drifted back to sleep.

* * *

He woke up again. The room was filled with burning candles.

"It's half an hour before daybreak."

"What?"

"There's still time," Abercrombie said. "Time to fix things."

Leon sat up and was racked with terrible pain. Someone had sliced him open, from just below his throat down to his groin. He felt groggy. Why hadn't he woken up before this?

"What the hell did you do to me?"

"Don't worry," Abercrombie said. "You won't die. Not yet."

"The pain."

"It would be a lot worse," Abercrombie said, "but I'm trying to control it. You can still think. Still speak."

Leon leaned back against his pillow and looked around him on the bed. His organs surrounded him. He saw his liver. Two kidneys. Other organs that weren't so easily recognizable.

He saw his heart, still beating on the sheet.

Abercrombie raised the knife toward the ceiling and prayed.

"What did you do to me? What kind of fucked up ritual did you drag me into?"

"Don't worry," Abercrombie said. "I can keep you alive."

"Why would I want to be alive like this?" Leon tried to scream then, but his voice wouldn't cooperate.

And then the room began to spin, and Leon saw a series of images. Abercrombie was killing a whole series of people, one after another, all in the same moment.

An old woman who had an oxygen mask on her face, shedding tears as she was finally delivered from her pain.

A baby in its crib, not given the chance to grow. To live its life.

A gymnast who had just been informed she had been accepted for the next Olympics.

A woman dealing with insomnia and postpartum depression. Hating the images in her head, and now free of them forever.

And it went on and on. Everyone around them dying. The hotel was at the very center of the city, the beating heart, and death spread out in all directions.

Abercrombie killed every last person within the city's limits, without mercy.

He was the hand of Saint Ranier. The slayer of cities.

Abercrombie was in all places at once, and then he was just in the hotel room. His work done, he lowered his hands, dropping the knife to the carpet.

"I can save you," he said to Leon, and ran to the bed. He started putting back his severed organs one after another.

"I can keep you alive," he said. "And I can heal you. Like this never happened."

"How?"

"You and I will be the only survivors. I know how to do it now. I know how to save you."

Leon closed his eyes. The pain had been replaced with numbness, and he was sure that this was all a dream. That there wasn't a deep incision down the front of his body. That he wasn't wrapped up in his own intestines.

He opened his eyes again, just in time to feel life draining away.

His eyes turned glassy.

* * *

"You promised me," Abercrombie said, as he threw Leon's heart across the room. It splattered against the nearest wall. "You told me I could save him when it was done."

But he couldn't feel the saint's presence in the room anymore. No more spidery movements just outside his field of vision.

He was the only one left alive. And it was time to clean up and get out of this place, before it all came crumbling down.

Time to move on to the next place. A bigger city this time. A bigger population of souls.

* * *

Fella Faze dialed Leon's cell number again. The other guys were starting to get antsy, and Leon's agent, Barry, was pacing the room.

"I couldn't reach him," Barry said. "What makes you think *you* can?"

"I don't know," Fella said. "It just keeps ringing."

"He's fucked us," Ricky the bassist said. "I knew it was too good to be true. I knew he wouldn't show up for the signing of the contract."

"No," Fella said, "he'll be here. His plane must have been delayed or something."

"He's three hours late," Barry said. "The chauffeur I hired said the flight came in, and Leon wasn't on it."

"He must have missed his flight," Fella said. "He'll be on the next one."

"He fucked us," Ricky said. "Why can't you just accept the truth?"

"He wouldn't do that," Fella said. Leon had seemed so genuine the last time he'd seen him. Fella believed he'd had a change of heart. He could usually tell these things. He was one of the few people on the planet who could read Leon's intentions. Not even Barry could do that, after decades of being his agent.

"You're deluding yourself," Ricky said. "Not only would he do it, he *did* it. He purposely got us all here, just so he could leave us hanging."

"Maybe he's still at the hotel," Barry said. "Why don't you call there instead? See if they can ring his room. Maybe he got drunk or sick or something."

"Yeah," Fella said, "that's possible. Let me call the front desk and ring his room."

Then there was a long silence.

"What's wrong?"

"What was the name of the place where he was staying?" Fella asked. "For the life of me, I can't remember."

"The name of the hotel or the city?"

"Either one."

"I can't remember either," Barry said. "But I'm sure I wrote it down somewhere."

"You were just there two days ago," Ricky said to Fella. "Don't you remember?"

"Shit," Fella said. "My mind's drawing a blank."

They all stood in the room, not saying anything, until more time went by and they each decided to go home.

And the Sky Was Full of Angels

WHEN HIS TIME IN the war had come to an end, Cyril went back to a home he did not recognize. It wasn't that the town had changed that much, but that *he* had. He had been away much longer than he thought, and was still disoriented. He had sustained some pretty serious injuries, and wasn't sure if he would ever heal enough to be the self he was when he left.

Mama and his brother Donny were waiting at the train station when he got off. The same train station he had left from three years prior. It was like the station was frozen in time, but Mama looked older, and Donny was a few inches taller. The way they looked at him made it obvious he had changed a lot since they had last seen each other, but then again, he knew that already.

Clearly, from their reactions, he had not changed for the better.

Mama hugged him and Donny took his duffle bag, and they walked out to the parking lot and the pickup truck, which looked a little more beaten-up than before. There were patches of rust, and a smattering of dents and scratches. They asked him to get inside the cab between them, but Cyril hopped in the back and stretched out in the truck bed. No one asked him twice. Instead, Donny started the engine and they drove away from the lot.

Cyril watched the train that had taken him there speed away to its next destination. He wished he was still inside, moving forward forever, but never stopping.

* * *

His father didn't bother to get up when they got home. He was sitting on the couch and remained there as they went inside, looking Cyril up and down, but making no effort to stand. Cyril had heard that his father hurt his side in a fall a few months back, so it was understandable that he wouldn't want to get up.

"Your son's home," Momma said. "Don't you have anything to say to him?"

His father kept staring—it was almost a glare—and then he reached out his arms and Cyril went over and hugged him.

"So how was the war?" his father asked.

"How do you think it was?"

"Well, you're back in one piece. Could be worse."

Momma asked him if he wanted something to eat, but he had eaten on the train. He said he just wanted a lie down and Momma told Donny to take him upstairs. So the two of them went up the staircase and Donny showed him to his old room, which was exactly the way he had left it, except now his duffle bag was on the bed where Donny had put it.

"I guess you don't need any help taking a nap," Donny said. "I'm sure you know how to do that."

Cyril nodded and forced a laugh, and clapped his brother on the shoulder and told him it was good to see him again. But Cyril didn't go so far as to say it was good to be home. Because he didn't really believe that. He hadn't wanted to come back here, but he had nowhere else to go.

* * *

There was whistling in the middle of the night that woke him, and he got up and went over to the window. There was a missile shooting up into the sky from where a nearby military base was, but he never remembered it launching missiles before. Cyril could almost read the lettering on its side. He wondered where it was going. There were a lot of possible destinations, but it was probably just a test. He just had never seen one so close to a civilian population before.

He could hear the whistling in his head long after it was gone. In fact, it got louder in his mind after it was out of sight, because it was taking on the whistling of a hundred other missiles he had seen, combining into one long screech that threatened to make him go deaf.

He waited it out, and like everything else, the sound eventually went away.

He tried to go back to sleep, but it was useless.

* * *

"How long have you been home?" Chan asked. "It's so good to see you!"

When Cyril had seen her in the back of the deli, sitting at a table with a friend, he was sure she would pretend not to notice him, but she got up from her seat and rushed over to him.

"You have to come sit with us," she said, leading him and the bag he was carrying back to her table. "You know Anna," she said. Cyril looked over at Chan's friend and nodded.

"I just got back," he said. "Yesterday. I felt so exhausted that I took a nap and slept like 24 hours."

"You must have been very tired."

It still hurt to see her. Even after all he had been through, the memory was still fresh in his mind of her breaking up with him. It was the incident that made him decide to join the military. Back then, she had seemed so cruel the way she had told him she found someone else and that she was leaving him. He was just a kid and it felt like his world was ending.

"So how's Harry?" he asked.

"I wouldn't know," she said. "We broke up a long time ago. Maybe six months after you went away. He graduated and went abroad. We haven't talked in over a year. Good riddance, I say."

While he was glad to know his rival was out of the picture, he couldn't help feeling a sense of loss. He could have tried to get her back after they split, but he was an ocean away, tempting death to finish him off. He had missed the opportunity.

"I missed you, Cyril," she said. "I didn't know if you were ever coming back. If you'd *want* to come back, after the way I treated you."

"Did you treat me badly?" he asked. "I don't remember."

Her smile said that she would be happy if he'd forgotten. Too bad he couldn't.

"So are you with someone else now?" he said, just blurting it out. The girls laughed at the awkwardness of the question.

"No, not right now," Chan said. "Do you want to get together sometime?"

"Sure."

He ate, noticing that the girls were done and just stayed around to talk to him. He told them a few stories from the war. Nothing too graphic or scary. Weird customs he had come across, and a few close calls. Then Chan and Anna got up and Chan asked for his phone. She punched her number in. "Call me."

He watched them go. He finished his lunch and then walked around town, going in some stores, killing time until Donny came back to give him a ride home.

* * *

"Cyril?"

"It's no use. It didn't work."

"Cyril, can you hear me?"

"No, no, don't wake him. Here, let me give him another sedative."

"But I want to know how he's feeling."

"It doesn't matter now. This one was a failure."

"Maybe we can salvage it somehow."

"No time. We were told to just move on to the next one if something doesn't work. We've got a schedule to stick to."

"But all that time hooking it up. All that expense."

"They'll just write it off as a loss. There's insurance for these things. It really doesn't matter."

"I heard a grunt. Cyril? Can you hear me?"

"He can't hear anything. He's not really conscious."

* * *

"So, how long are you planning on staying here, freeloading on your parents?"

Cyril turned his attention from the television to his father.

"Cyril can stay here as long as he wants," Momma said.

"No, he needs to get a job. He needs to pay rent if he stays here."

"Dad, he just got back home," Donny said.

"Well?" his father asked. "Do you have plans for the future?"

"I won't be here too long," Cyril said. "I just wanted to get my bearings. I'll be out of your hair soon."

"Make sure of it. I can't afford to be feeding all kinds of extra mouths."

Cyril had money put aside; it just accumulated while he was in the army. He didn't spend much, just put it in the bank. He was sure it was enough to hold him over until he got a regular job. But he wasn't going to give it to his father. He was going to find a place of his own in town.

"I heard you were talking to that Andrews girl," his mother said. "Did you see her in town?"

"Yes, it was unexpected."

"Stay away from her," his father said. "You know how much grief you got the last time. Her folks don't want anything to do with people like us."

"All I did was talk to her," Cyril said. "It was nothing."

"Don't even do that."

* * *

He had let his buddy Andy talk him into going to a party at the beach. A lot of his old friends were there. People he had gone to high school with. There was a bonfire crackling on the sand.

Chan was there, with her friends. She watched him from the other side of the fire, and then came over to him when she noticed him looking back.

"Good to see you again," she said.

"Yeah, it's good to see you too."

"I'm going to get some wings," she told him.

"What?"

"Wings," she said. "My father arranged it all. It will happen this weekend. I'm so excited."

"That must cost a fortune."

"Well, my daddy's got it," she said. "What else is he going to spend it on? I've wanted wings my whole life."

"They've made a lot of progress," he said. "I saw a doctor talking about it on television. He said they perfected it now. You can get all kinds of amazing things these days."

"They call them accessories," she said. "I already picked out what they'll look like and everything."

"You do seem pretty excited."

"I am. I really am. This is the most exciting thing I've done in years. And there won't be time when I get a real job and settle down and have kids and all. Not to do something like this."

He nodded.

"While you were gone, I kind of went through a long depression," she said.

"Oh."

"Not because of you. Not anything you did. I just took it really bad when Harry and I broke up. And I guess I felt some guilt about how I treated you too. Things got pretty awful there for a while. I wasn't eating or anything. Finally, we found a medication that helped. I don't get so sad anymore."

"I'm really sorry to hear it."

"I'm sorry for the way I treated you," she said. "Sometimes I think about how we ended things, how *I* ended things. I feel really bad about how I did that. You didn't deserve it."

"I got over it," he said.

"You almost got killed getting over it," she said. "I know you joined the army because of me."

"No, I just needed to get away, to see the world outside of this stupid town. I would have left anyway."

"If we had stayed together," she said. "I'm sure you would have stayed here."

"I don't know."

"Did you think about me while you were over there?" she asked.

"Sure. Lots of times. You're not someone who's easy to forget."

She looked like there were tears welling up in her eyes. She had always been an emotional girl. He found it attractive. "I'm sorry, Cyril. Honest I am."

"I believe you."

"And I'm so glad you didn't die in the war. I'm glad you came back, even if you hate it here."

"I'm glad I'm not dead too," he said, and laughed, trying to lighten the mood.

Andy came over to where they were talking. "Cyril, let's go. There are other parties to go to."

He didn't want to go, but Chan said goodbye to him and went back to her friends, and there was no reason to stay.

* * *

He woke up with pains in his chest, and a strange heat in his spine. Cyril sat up in bed and tried to get past it, tried to wait it out, but the pain wouldn't leave, so he called for his mother, and she got upset and went for his father, who of course had to take charge of the situation. His father demanded he get it checked out and helped Cyril go out to the truck, and they took him to see the family doctor.

Dr. Hammond admitted him to the hospital in town and they did some tests. When the last test was over, the doctor called Cyril into his office. He was feeling better by then. There were X-rays hanging on the lighted part of the wall.

"I have to admit, I've never seen anything like this before. It's awful strange," Dr. Hammond said.

He showed Cyril where there was a black box inside his chest.

"Can't make heads or tails of it. Looks like it's hardwired directly into your nervous system. I don't think I could remove it, even if I wanted to. It would be much too dangerous."

Looking at the X-rays, Cyril realized he had made a mistake calling out, that he should have suffered in silence, no matter how long it took. There was no reason to involve anyone else in this.

"So, you said that you were badly injured in the war. That you were in a coma?"

"Yes," Cyril said. "For five months, they said. There were times when I went in and out of consciousness, but what I remember about it doesn't make a lot of sense."

"Well, someone obviously put this thing inside of you," the doctor said. "I don't have a clue what it is, or what it does, and I'd be terrified to touch it. Like I said, it's connected to *everything*."

"Let's just drop it, Doc," Cyril said. "I'm okay now, and it's obviously something they put in me when they saved my life. A military thing."

He looked at the X-rays again. He knew that they put something inside him; he could feel it. And he knew that he should not have let his father bring him here. But he admitted to himself that he had really wanted to *see* it for himself. Seeing it made it suddenly seem more real.

"I could ask some colleagues of mine about it, if you want."

"No," Cyril said. "Don't bother. I'm pretty sure I remember now, something about a new kind of pacemaker. My memory's just blurry sometimes."

"Well, you've been through a lot," Dr. Hammond said. "I guess that's what it could be. And you seem to be okay now. Aside from this, you appear to be in pretty good shape, considering all that's happened. But I can at least give you some medication, in case the pain comes back."

"No, I don't need any drugs," he said. "You haven't told my parents about this, have you?"

"It's not like the old days when you were just a kid. You're a grown man now, Cyril," Dr. Hammond said. "I've only told you. It's not my place to tell anyone else."

"Well, please don't," he said. "Let's just forget about this for now."

Then and there he promised himself that he would never make another sound if it happened again.

* * *

They had begun texting each other throughout the week. He started it, since she had put her number in his phone. He reached out to her, not expecting to hear a reply. She told him to meet her at the beach where the party had been. It had gotten colder, and they were alone.

"I'm glad you came," she said. "I'm going for my wings tomorrow. I'm not sure how long I'll be away."

They kissed on the secluded beach, as the tide came in. It happened so naturally.

"Remember when I said I was so sad when Harry broke up with me?" she asked.

"Yes."

"That wasn't true. I never really loved Harry. And I broke it off with him. My parents wanted me to marry him so badly, but I couldn't go through with it."

"Then why the depression?" he asked.

"I always regretted breaking up with you," she said. "My parents kept pressuring me. Telling me it could never work out. They threatened to cut me off financially."

"They pressured my parents as well. They won't talk about it, but I think they threatened them somehow. In a way, I was glad when you found Harry. You deserved better."

"But I didn't really. Don't you get it? I always wanted you. But everyone conspired against us."

He didn't know what to say to that. But she did not wait for his reply. Instead, she kissed him again. It was like all those years they lost hadn't happened. It didn't take long for her to begin removing his clothes, then her own. He did not resist, and they made love on the sand.

When they were done, she said, "You're the last person I'll ever have sex with without wings," she said. "Tomorrow I'm leaving, but I'll be back as soon as I can. And we'll go far away from here."

"I'll plan on it," he said.

She kissed him again and slipped away into the night.

* * *

"You're always moping around the house," his father said, watching him from the couch. "I thought you were going to find a job sometime soon."

Cyril was waiting for Chan to get back, and was worrying about her. She had told him she probably wouldn't contact him for most of her convalescence, but that didn't make him worry any less. She was having major surgery, after all.

And he certainly couldn't call her family to see how she was doing.

In the meantime, he was just biding his time. Why find a place now, when they were going to leave town once Chan healed up?

"I thought you said you were going to find your own place," his father said.

"Why do you want me out of here so much? I'm paying rent now."

"Barely. You're just taking a long time getting back on your feet," his father said. "And I'm afraid you'll stay here forever. I have a lot of friends whose kids came back home after a divorce or whatever, and then they never leave."

"You don't have to worry about that," he said. "I'll be out of here soon enough."

"Not soon enough for me. Donny's going away to college in the fall. I thought we were done raising kids."

Cyril's mother entered the room then and looked from Cyril to his father. "Are you two fighting again?"

"Of course not," his father said.

"Why do you have such a problem with me?" Cyril said. "You've been hostile ever since I got back."

"Hostile? I have no idea what you're talking about."

"Of course you do. You used to talk about your time in the army all the time. I thought you'd be proud of me for going too."

"Sounds like you spent most of the time in the hospital instead of the battlefield."

"That's not true," Cyril said. "I got injured, sure, and it was pretty bad. But I saw a lot of fighting before that happened."

"Your son was a hero," his mother said, intervening. "He got hurt saving his friends."

"Some hero," his father said. "I like soldiers who don't spend most of the time in a hospital bed."

"You didn't even try to contact me to see if I was okay."

"We didn't find out what had happened until much later."

"I knew they'd take care of you," his father said. "They have the best doctors money can buy. Hardly anybody dies in war anymore."

"Mama, I thought you'd at least write."

"He wouldn't let me," she said, her eyes welling up with tears. She excused herself and left the room.

"Now look what you've done," his father said. "She'll be blubbering for hours now."

"I'll never understand you," Cyril said.

"Of course you won't. That's why we never bonded, you and I. Ever since you were a teenager, it's like I had a space alien living in the house. Your brother Donny is so normal. I don't know what happened to you. I raised you both the same way."

Cyril thought about things Donny had confided in him over the years. He was tempted to bring them up, to throw them in his father's face, but he couldn't bring himself to do it. His brother had trusted him, had said those things in confidence.

"I'm going to my room," Cyril said.

"Of course you are. That's what freeloaders do."

Upstairs, Cyril texted Chan again, but didn't hear anything back.

* * *

"So you're really leaving town again when she comes back?" Andy asked. They were sitting on the beach, passing a joint back and forth.

"Yeah, and I can't wait to get out of here. My father's driving me insane."

"He's always been a real hard-ass," Andy said. "For as long as I've known you."

"He hasn't changed."

"You mean your running away to join the army didn't win him over?"

"Not even close."

"My father used to be a prick too. I'm glad he took off on us. All he did was argue with my mom all the time."

Cyril nodded his head and took the joint back, took a long drag. There wasn't much left of it.

"She's getting wings," Andy said.

"Yup," Cyril said.

"I bet they look amazing," Andy said.

* * *

It was 28 days when he finally heard back from her. He had almost given up on things, thinking she had changed her mind, so the text message surprised him.

Meet me @the beach at midnight

She probably wanted to make a big deal about the unveiling of her wings, and he didn't blame her. As he responded, telling her he'd be there, he couldn't help getting goosebumps. This was going to make the long wait worthwhile.

* * *

Back on the day he left the military hospital, no one said a word to him. Doctor Fresno, who had always been hovering somewhere nearby, who always seemed so interested in his case, was nowhere to be seen that day. Cyril asked about him and a nurse told him it was his day off.

After the explosion that took him out, Cyril drifted in and out of consciousness for a very long time. And the voice he heard when he came to was almost always Dr. Fresno's. As he got dressed that last day, he looked at himself in the mirror, and was amazed how *whole* he looked. How normal. If they had replaced anything, he couldn't tell. He could feel some differences, some strange aches and pains, but it was nothing he could put his finger on. He was physically heavier, although he didn't look it. In fact, he had lost weight during the months in bed, living on a liquid diet for most of it. The lean face looking back at him was the thinnest he had ever been. But when the nurse had him get on the scale earlier in the day, he was amazed at how much he weighed.

It made him wonder what that thing was that was inside him. The X-rays that Dr. Hammond had shown him confirmed that it was some kind of a black box. Beyond that, he knew nothing. He knew he wouldn't get any answers, and had no desire to pursue it.

He remembered looking at his medical chart the day he left the military. It was written in a handwriting he couldn't read. But there was a word that was clear at the bottom. *Failure.* It was circled several times, with enough force to almost tear the back of the page. When the nurse saw him looking at it, she quickly took it away, and she claimed to know nothing when he asked her questions.

Dr. Fresno had never answered questions. He always changed the subject.

Cyril didn't like Dr. Fresno. One of the few reasons he wanted to go home was to get away from the man.

Looking in the mirror that day, at his thin, nude body, he couldn't help but wonder why they didn't send him back to the battlefield after he healed up. Why they discharged him instead and sent him home. It didn't make sense. He could have gotten back in shape, and they needed men on the battlefield. The war was getting bad again.

And then he'd remember that word. Failure. *Circled.*

* * *

It was a little before dusk when Cyril got the beach. Chan was there with some of her friends. When she saw him, she ran over.

"You came."

"Of course I did."

"I was worried."

"It's good to see you back," he said.

"I thought about you all the time. I'm sorry I didn't text you more. Most of the time, they wouldn't let me have my phone. My father kept saying I had to rest."

"So you have the wings now?" He looked her over. "I don't see anything."

She was wearing shorts and a bikini top, and she turned around so he could see her back, and there were the tiniest of scars on her shoulder blades, but that was it.

"You'll see," she said. "They're beautiful."

Looking at her back, he couldn't figure out how anything could be there, but he decided to wait and see.

"Who are your friends?" he asked.

"Girls I met in the hospital," she said. "We became friends. There wasn't much else to do there. They agreed to come here today. We're going to put on a show for you."

"Just for me?" he asked, looking up and down the beach.

"Yeah."

It was starting to get dark and she said that it was almost time, so she ran back to her friends and he squatted down and sat on the sand and waited. He couldn't take his eyes off her, even though he could just see her outlined in the moonlight as it got darker.

And then the wings sprouted from her back. It happened so quickly, so unexpectedly, that it almost knocked him off balance. They sort of telescoped out of her. They didn't look like birds' wings with feathers, they looked like they were made of glass, fiberglass maybe, and they glowed bright white. Like the light people say they see sometimes, when they have a near-death experience. A beautiful white light. A *heavenly* light.

The other girls started to release their wings too, and they were other colors. All glowing brightly like neon lights.

And then they each started to fly.

Their wings flapped like birds' wings and they were up in the sky, holding hands, like a chorus line of angels.

* * *

He stared up at them, amazed. They were so beautiful.

And this is the girl I'm running away with, he thought. *I'm really going to get a second chance with her.*

The girls let go of each other's hands and made a series of geometric shapes in the sky, like some kind of airborne Busby Berkeley movie with glowing, multi-colored lights.

Cyril started to feel dizzy, and he thought it was the lights, but there was a rumbling in his stomach, and a high-pitched keening in his ears that was getting louder. He felt like he was going to throw up. He tried to fall over on his side, but instead his legs were forcing him to stand, and he felt like he was overheating. He tore at the fabric of his shirt, ripping it away.

It felt like his chest and his spine were on fire.

In his mind, he could hear Dr. Fresno's voice saying something unintelligible, except for one word that sounded like *drones.*

And like the wings that had magically sprouted from Chan's shoulders—the wonderful products of miraculous technology that had given her beautiful, functioning wings—something emerged from his chest. Something that looked like a cannon, or some kind of gun.

And the keening in his ears got louder still, blocking out all other sounds, and he heard something like radio chatter and static.

The gun thing aimed up at the sky, and fired something like looked like lightning. One of the girls screamed and then was silent, falling back to earth, with her wings weakly beating, trying to save her, until she crashed into the ocean below.

There was a whirring and more chatter and another of the girls was hit and falling, and then another, and then Chan.

The angels were gone from the sky, and the thing in his chest felt like it was revolving frantically, and then it went back inside of him, and he felt a sharp ache inside.

Cyril looked out over the water, in the light of the moon, trying to see if anyone made it up to the surface, and then a wing must have emerged, because he saw a faint green light. He forced himself forward, despite the pain, and ran into the water, and broke into a swim, forcing himself toward where they fell. It was so awkward at first, because he was much heavier than he realized and started to sink, but then he adjusted himself. He had always been a strong swimmer.

Another wing broke the surface, and then another, and he swam toward them. He saw one that was glowing white, but not as brightly as before.

He found himself in the middle of a ring of floating bodies and broken, dimly lit wings, none of them moving.

Cyril stared up at the moon, and the keening began again.

Publication History

These stories first appeared in the following places:

"Something Blue" first appeared in *Shroud Magazine* in 2009.

"Little Black Dress" was first published on *Gothic.net* in October 2001.

"Second Chances" was first published on *Gothic.net* in December 2002.

"Holiday House" was first published in *Epitaphs: The Journal of the New England Horror Writers* in 2011.

"Animal Biographies" was first published in *Lullaby Hearse* in 2004.

"Beyond the Haze" was first published on *Horrorfind.com* in 2002.

"Crocodiles" was first published on *www.llsoares.com* in 2007.

"The Click of an Unhinged Jaw" is new to this collection.

"Sometimes the Good Witch Sings to Me" first appeared in *Cover of Darkness* in 2007.

"Rotten" was first published *Aoife's Kiss* in 2005.

"Venus" was first published in *The Best of the Horror Society* in 2013.

"Still Life, With Soul Juice" was first published in *RAW: Brutality as Art* in 2009.

"A Full Canteen" was first published as "The Gulch" in *Welcome to Hell: An Anthology of Western Weirdness* in 2012.

"The Sweetness and the Psychic" first appeared in the collection *Wicked Weird* in 2019.

"Necropolis" is new to this collection

"City Slayer" first appeared as "Slayer" in the anthology *Living After Midnight: Hard and Heavy Stories* in 2011.

"And the Sky Was Full of Angels" was first published in *Zippered Flesh 3: Yet More Tales of Body Enhancement Gone Bad!* in 2017.

About the Author

AFTER ANSWERING THE SPHINX'S riddle incorrectly, L.L. Soares was sentenced to walk the earth forever. So, in the meantime, he tells stories. His books include the novel, *Life Rage*, for which he won the Bram Stoker Award for First Novel. His oeuvre also includes the novels *Rock 'n' Roll*, *Hard*, *Buried in Blue Clay*, and his most recent novel, *Teach Them How to Bleed*. He has written a novella, *Green Tsunami*, with Laura Cooney, and shared a short story collection, *In Sickness*, with her as well. His short fiction has appeared in dozens of magazines and anthologies, including *Gothic.net*, *Cemetery Dance*, the

Zippered Flesh anthologies, and *Wicked Weird*. For more than a decade, he co-wrote the movie review column *Cinema Knife Fight*. He lives in the Boston area with his wife and their iguana, Osiris, named after the Egyptian God of the Dead. To keep up on his adventures, please go to www.llsoares.com.

www.ingramcontent.com/pod-product-compliance
Lightning Source LLC
Chambersburg PA
CBHW020400030726
47496CB00007B/2224